JACK IS BACK

IN

CORPORATE CARNIVAL

P.G. BHASKAR

HarperCollins *Publishers* India
a joint venture with
THE INDIA TODAY GROUP
New Delhi

First published in India in 2012 by
HarperCollins *Publishers* India
a joint venture with
The India Today Group

ISBN: 978-93-5029-351-5

2 4 6 8 10 9 7 5 3 1

HarperCollins *Publishers*
A-53, Sector 57, NOIDA, Uttar Pradesh – 201301, India
77-85 Fulham Palace Road, London W6 8JB, United Kingdom
Hazelton Lanes, 55 Avenue Road, Suite 2900, Toronto, Ontario M5R 3L2
and 1995 Markham Road, Scarborough, Ontario M1B 5M8, Canada
25 Ryde Road, Pymble, Sydney, NSW 2073, Australia
31 View Road, Glenfield, Auckland 10, New Zealand
10 East 53rd Street, New York NY 10022, USA

Typeset in 10/13 Charter BT
Jojy Philip New Delhi 110 015

Printed and bound at
Thomson Press (India) Ltd.

CORPORATE CARNIVAL

P.G. Bhaskar is a twenty-first century banker and in that capacity needs everyone's empathy. A chartered accountant, he left India for Dubai in 1992 and, what with one thing and the other, stayed put, watching the city grow. He now lives there with his wife and teenage son.

Bhaskar is one of the modern world's thinkers and philosophers. He thinks deeply about several things, including but not limited to, the ups and downs of Indian cricket, why Pluto stopped being a planet, who chose February to have fewer days than other months, and his frequently missing handkerchiefs. He has come to no conclusion on these issues, or indeed on any issue. Nevertheless, he continues to ponder. In the meantime, he has decided to write books, despite being warned that nobody below the age of seventy-two reads nowadays.

Praise for *Jack Patel's Dubai Dreams*

'Jack Patel might sound like the proverbial banker but his rather quirky sense of being and tongue-in-cheek humour gives you a new perspective on a man whose dreams don't seem too far from reality.'
The Hindu

'P.G. Bhaskar's lines are packed with wit that ring with sincerity and spontaneity, eliciting some hearty laughs. He has an amazing ability to strike a chord despite the scene.'
The New Indian Express

'A witty book, full of inventive one-liners, humorous asides and smart observations'
The National, Abu Dhabi

'*Jack Patel's Dubai Dreams* is a delightful, funny read. Written with the financial crisis as a background, one might expect a heavy, sad tome, but it surprises us with its dealing of some sad times with its light-hearted treatment.'
New Global Indian

'Read it for the humour, for the quirkiness and to understand the wisdom of depositing Rs 5000 in a recurring account every month!'
tabla

'An ideal way to while away a lazy afternoon'
dawn.com

For my mum Amma,
the gentlest, most soft-spoken person I have ever met, and for my sister Sheela, a rebel, an entrepreneur, a go-getter and do-gooder. They both left me in June 2012, but will hopefully read this book in heaven, if my publishers can make it available there.

Heaps of love,
Chinni

1

Déjà vu Dubai

I hate it when the Indian cricket team loses. It might not have been a big deal in the sixties and seventies when, I am told, we lost most of the time. But now that we have tasted success quite often, it is a bitter cup to swallow when we go down, especially if we do so without a fight. I had been looking forward to this match. But belying my every expectation, the men in blue were succumbing to pressure as one batsman after another walked back to the pavilion. But maybe all was not lost. Dhoni was still at the crease and there was another batsman to follow. The next over or two was critical.

'Does my bum look big in this?' Mina asked.

'No,' I said quickly. On the verge of celebrating my first wedding anniversary, I was a veteran of twelve months at disposing of such questions. Maybe India could still make it, I thought. I mean, they don't refer to cricket as a game of glorious uncertainties for nothing. Miracles *do* happen.

Oh, damn! This just wasn't Dhoni's day. Now there wasn't a chance in hell, unless, of course, Zaheer Khan managed to hit a few out of the park. I remembered him displaying some heroics with the bat before, some four years back, maybe five. Go, Zak, go!

'Jai, you're not even looking at it!'

Yes! *Yesss!* Edged down to the third man fence. Hah! Like the commentators say every time, it doesn't matter how they come, as long as they do.

'Jai!' This time Mina's voice was sharper and louder. 'I *said* you're not even looking at it.'

'Honey, we have known each other almost three years. I know exactly what it looks like.'

There was a pause.

'I'm talking about the *dress*, Jai.' The voice was softer now but I could sense the iron fist behind the velvet glove. I turned around quickly.

'It looks perfect, Minoo. That's a terrific figure your dress is wearing.'

She melted at once. Clever me. A little tact, a honeyed word, it's all that's required on these occasions. Now if only these blokes could somehow get under the ball and heave. How come yorkers seem so much more effective when Indian batsmen are at the crease? This is so irritating. Hit the ball, mister. Oh, man, he's gone! Bugger it!

'I wish you would stop watching this silly cricket. Such a colossal waste of everyone's time. There! They've lost. See? I told you. A whole evening down the drain.'

Less than an hour later, we were at Kitch's and Galiya's apartment in Bur Dubai.

This was our second innings in Dubai. Over a year ago, we left Dubai, licked to a splinter by a worldwide economic crisis that engulfed Myers York, one of America's largest investment houses, and brought our little world crumbling down. We returned from India a year later to a new Dubai. Its sands had shifted under the fierce impact of the financial Armageddon that followed the collapse of Lehman Brothers. The resurrected emirate had assumed a new shape, a new avatar that was in sync with the new reality; sober but not bitter, aware but not drowning in regret, reflective but with its vision and optimism intact.

This time round, Kitch and I were living quite some distance away from one another. Kitch and Galiya didn't want to leave the perennially lit up and bustling areas that formed the heart of Dubai. Mina, on the other hand, couldn't bear to move into an apartment. She had only lived in an apartment in the brief period that she spent in London, and hadn't enjoyed it one bit. For Mina, a house isn't complete unless there is a garden attached to it.

She is never really happy unless she is somewhere in the backyard talking life into a plant or taking life out of a pest. As a compromise for getting her to return to Dubai, we had bought this house, not far away from where Kapoor lived. Kapoor was a family friend, an elderly, rather swash-buckling gentleman who had greatly helped me with my previous assignment here.

Kitch and Galiya had moved into their apartment only a couple of weeks ago and this was our first 'formal' visit after they had settled in. We rang their doorbell, which involved pushing Minnie Mouse's nose, upon which a series of nursery rhymes started playing inside the house. The bell amused Mina but, frankly, I found it rather embarrassing. When God blesses a couple with a child, I think he tends to take away their balance. To think that an old pal, a hard-nosed, regular guy like Kitch would attach a soft-nosed Minnie Mouse to his door… But then, in some ways, Kitch had changed since the wedding and more so after the baby. Among other things, he was now clean-shaven. A year's persistence by his wife and his rather prominent moustache had – like the Berlin Wall – fallen and with it, I suspect, many of his whims. As we walked in to the tune of 'Humpty Dumpty', Mina grabbed little Olga from Galiya and folded her into a hug. Kitch got up morosely from the couch in front of the TV.

The presentation ceremony had just ended. We exchanged a silent look of commiseration.

'That's it,' he greeted me gloomily. 'We're well and truly out of the tournament.'

'Now there's nothing for us to do but sit and mope,' I said.

'And,' he added, 'hope that Pakistan gets thrashed by Australia.'

'What!' I exclaimed in mock surprise. 'You mean you don't want the trophy to remain in the subcontinent?'

'Screw the subcontinent,' he cursed, promptly attracting a wifely glare. 'If India doesn't win, I don't care if the damn cup goes to the other end of the universe.'

Kitch and Galiya lived a few minutes away from where they lived earlier. This was a bigger apartment, with three bedrooms. They showed us around the place. Their spacious living room was done up in black and white. White marble tiles, a big black couch with white cushions and smaller white ones with black cushions, a black dining table and black chairs with white seats. The master bedroom was in beige and brown. It had a double bed, as well as Olga's crib. They all slept in the same room, though Olga had her own room, done up in pink and yellow, liberally dotted with pictures of Minnie Mouse, Barbie and a few other characters I didn't recognize. In the master bedroom, just above their bed, was a framed picture of Kitch and Galiya on their honeymoon in Cambodia; Kitch was wearing a white t-shirt with the letters 'L' and 'O' printed on it, his arm around Galiya's shoulder; she was in a black one that said 'V' and 'E'. When I stepped into the room, Kitch blushed and mumbled something about Galiya insisting on putting that picture up there. Just goes to show, I thought, that you should think a million times before getting your photograph taken. A few quick ones here and there, a snap taken during an inebriated, youthful moment and there you are, potentially faced with a lifetime of shame and sorrow and, thanks to Facebook and YouTube, an audience that can quickly run into thousands. On the opposite wall was another huge picture of the two lovebirds holding a glass each in front of a bar called 'Angkor What?', a corrupted version of Cambodia's famous tourist attraction.

We sat down to dinner. What a year in Chennai can do to a girl! Galiya – of French and Kazakh descent – served us idlis (made, of course, from the ready-made dough now available at Dubai supermarkets) and homemade vada, or vadai as Kitch calls it.

'Do you know,' Galiya told us, 'at one of our restaurants in Chennai, we actually stopped making vadais, because we realized that between

Kitch, me, the cooks and the waiters, we were devouring about forty a day. I kept calculating how much weight we were putting on.'

'And I kept calculating how much money we were losing. But the customers got upset; after all, you can't have a Chennai eatery without vadai, so we put it back on the menu, but at almost double the price.'

Over a year ago, Kitch, Galiya and I had all been part of Myers York. Kitch and Galiya got married while we were working there. When we lost our jobs, the two of them went to Chennai, where they opened three restaurants. I married Mina – whose Kenya-based family members were my clients – amidst a lot of turmoil in the world markets and upheaval in our personal lives. We ended up buying and running a farm in Brahmadesam, Tamil Nadu, racing against time to pluck acid lime fruit before they became too ripe, trying to predict the weather so we could water the crops just right, convincing a van driver that his van was not a truck and that it was perfectly okay for him to take our produce to the city in the middle of a local truck drivers' strike.

We enjoyed it for the most part. But Kitch and I couldn't resist another shot at the private banking business. I think it had something to do with the way we left Dubai, amidst ruin and disaster, without so much as a friendly wave in the direction of our clients who had faced so much shock, and with such little warning. I also had a nagging feeling that I had left a task incomplete. I felt like a footballer who, having gone past the defenders and the goalkeeper, finds the ball being blown away by a gust of wind. As much as I tried to convince myself that it was the markets that did everyone in, I was plagued by guilt. Besides, looking after the farm was quite a struggle. There was a lot to do and we were a good way away from making real money.

Kitch and Galiya too, while they were enjoying their restaurant business, were still in the red. They lived with Kitch's parents. While Galiya said she loved the comfort and atmosphere of a large family – she herself having come from a split home – I think she missed being able to tuck into kedgeree and goulash at will. Kitch's family were strict vegetarians and even something as simple as having an omelette had to be planned well in advance and away from home. Besides, the weather in Chennai, as Galiya put it, fluctuated between bad, terrible and downright awful. I could empathize with her there. Chennai – or Madras, as I still tend to think of the city – is hot and sticky and it can drain you of your energy like a vacuum cleaner, leaving you weak, limp and almost soggy. Galiya was also unused to being 'fully' dressed as she had to be in the presence of Bala uncle and Dharini aunty, Kitch's parents. Gone were those twelve inches of bare midriff which were so prominent two years ago. There was another reason as well for their move back here. Kitch's younger brother had just got a job in Dubai and, given the lad's somewhat chequered and notorious background, his parents felt a lot more comfortable with big brother Kitch lurking in the background, keeping watch.

The clincher for both Kitch and me was when Peggy, our boss at Myers, told us that the two of us could form a team within the private banking unit and work with her at Abbott-Adriaan Bank, a British-Dutch combine of two banks that had come together last year in a bid to become stronger. It was now one of the largest institutions this side of the Atlantic. The offer appealed to Kitch and me at once.

Peggy was a workaholic, but she never treated work like a chore. I had never seen her weighed down by anything, even though she had to bear the brunt of the market collapse in 2008: repeated phone calls from angry and fearful customers, lawsuits, central bank investigations, compliance issues and god knows what else. When Peggy came to Kitch's for dinner on the evening of our first day back, she was her usual smiling self.

'Gee, what a wonderful feeling it is, being together again! Awesome! So guys, how do you like our new workplace? I hope you aren't comparing the training with what you got at Myers?'

'There's no comparison at all, Peggy,' I said. 'It's like apples and... umm... eggplant.'

Kitch chipped in, '*This* training is almost entirely compliance related. Rules, procedures, policies, guidelines, documentation... I'm going crazy.'

'I'm sorry, guys. I know it's not the same but, hey, these days it's the brand that matters. This is a solid, conservative blue chip name with one hell of a pedigree. That's what clients want now. Business has changed, honey, we have to face that. It's a cautious, risk-averse world that we have inherited from the crisis, still very nervous about sudden noises and prone to panic. What's that dark sauce, Galiya dear? Do I pour it on this thingy?'

'Yes. I call it VK. I can never remember its full name and wouldn't be able to say it even if I did. But I'm completely in love with it; I even use it as gravy for some meat dishes. But today is vegetarian night, because of Mina and Kitch. I hope you don't mind, Peggy.'

'Aw, shoo!' Peggy said, brushing it aside. 'I love all this. Mina, honey, I didn't know you were vegetarian, too?'

'Oh, I've been one for a few years,' Mina said. 'But I eat anything that's veg. Unlike him.' She pointed at Kitch. 'He is fussy even with his vegetarian food;

it has to be the right colour, texture and taste to suit his requirements. No mushroom, no zucchini, no eggplant and several other things.'

'Mmmm,' said Peggy, closing her eyes and taking in the aroma. 'This stuff is incredible! Oh, wowie! But y'know what? I can feel smoke coming out of my ears already. Someone hold me if I pass out. Kitch! What is this liquid dynamite called? Is it one of the words we were taught at your wedding... one of those z-h words that only Tamil Brahmins and Jack here can pronounce?'

We all laughed.

'Actually, it is!' Kitch replied. 'It's called vathakozhambu. It's supposed to be eaten with rice, but short of adding it to tea and coffee, Galiya uses it in everything.'

'That and Ranbir Kapoor are the two Indian things she has fallen most in love with,' Mina said.

'Kitch is only the bronze winner, *after* those two,' I added. I considered showing off by pronouncing the 'V' word, but refrained. It seemed like a tough one, even for me who pronounced 'zh' TamBram style.

'And what are those little black things in here? It ain't pepper, is it?'

'No, that's called manathankali,' Kitch replied. 'I'm not sure if there's an English word for it. I think it is some kind of berry which is dried, deep-fried and then added to this.'

'I'm surprised you even get these things in Dubai. But I guess the number of foreigners who live here makes it possible. Richard Weatherford, the compliance guy, was telling me he gets everything *he* wants, from mushy peas and fish-and-chips to chicken tikka and vindaloo.'

'Peggy, that fellow is so stuck-up, it's like he belongs to the nineteenth century. Do you know, when he answers his phone, he doesn't just say "This is Richard" or "Dick"; he says "Richard Weatherford, Head of Compliance". Every time, Peggy! With an emphasis on the word *Head*. So pompous! Jack and I call him Dickhead!'

The girls giggled. Galiya, who was halfway through a Breezer, ended up spitting a portion of it on the brand new carpet, and she and Mina spent the next few minutes trying to remove the stain.

'You are such a rogue, y'know,' Peggy told Kitch, dabbing some vathakozhambu on Kitch's face. 'You shouldn't be let loose.' The gravy formed a dark smear across his upperlip. 'Ah!' she exclaimed. 'That's more like the Kitch I used to know. What made you shave off your moustache? I thought you loved the thing.'

'He loves sex more,' I said, provoking another round of laughter.

'It was just the *kissing* part!' Galiya protested. 'How can anyone kiss with hair in the way?'

Peggy laughed. 'You have to focus on the lower lip and let him go for your upper lip, that's how! I had the same problem with Rich.' Rich was Peggy's former boyfriend, the chap she used to see while we were at Myers.

'By the way, Peggy,' said Kitch, continuing to whine, 'they are really buggering us out here at the training centre. I don't think they plan to give us much room to operate. We have been saddled with some 600 pages of compliance requirements to write a test on tomorrow.'

'Well, mind you do a good job, fellas. You don't want to hear any sarcasm from old man Rutherford. And anytime you find yourself thinking this is painful, just put yourself back eighteen months and ask yourself where you'd rather be. 2008 Myers, or here in 2010.'

'Please don't even talk about it, Peggy,' I begged. 'If there's one thing worse than losing your own money, it's losing the money of someone who trusted you with it. We'll sweep Dickhead off his feet, don't worry.'

'Y'know, the weird thing about this bank is that they don't seem to have decided who's going to be the boss, the Adriaan Dutch team or the Abbott Brit team,' Peggy said thoughtfully. 'I can sense a cold war in a thinly veiled slugfest, as both teams tussle for power. As a bank, the numbers add up great, the synergy seems good and that's pushed the stock price up, but there are plenty of issues to sort out. Everyone thought it would be a friendly merger. I did too, but it doesn't quite look like it. But the good thing is that as of now, we are on the side of the Brits and we seem to be winning.'

Living several miles away from 'town' in Dubai took some getting used to.

It was magical waking up to the musical chirping of the birds. It was what Mina had been used to all her life, but for me it was an altogether new experience. Mina would wake up at the stroke of dawn and get busy with her lemon, ginger and honey health drink followed by deep breathing and yoga. I, on the other hand, would open an eye when Mina got up, experience the early morning magic for a few seconds, and then promptly go back to sleep. By the time Mina had breathed deeply a few hundred times, stood on her head, tied herself in knots and rolled her eyeballs, I would be ready to stagger out of bed, with one single thought for starting the day on the right note: hot coffee with milk and lots of sugar.

Coming back to the magical chirping, there were all these birds whose existence in Dubai I had never suspected. I must confess, though, that on days when one hoped for a lazy morning in bed, the chirping seemed more like a cacophony. There was a nice patch of greenery behind the house where Mina and I enjoyed a cup of something sometimes. It was a luxury of space for the three of us – our dog 'The Boss', Mina and I – in this four-bedroomed 'villa'. On the flip side, it was undoubtedly a bit of a pain to have to learn new routes, especially since the office was in town, closer to where Kitch lived. Also, at night, the house felt a little spooky, what with trees swaying unexpectedly outside or a tiny bird flying past the window, the light effects causing a large shadow to flash across the bedroom wall.

This was the first time I had ever lived in an independent house and it took some getting used to. Like most cities with a large immigrant population, Dubai is a city of dreams. People stream in with optimism in their hearts, aiming to work hard, live comfortably and save well. The ultimate materialistic executive dream for most youngsters remains a villa and a spanking new four-wheel drive, that widely accepted king of the road that brooks no nonsense from either man or machine, on or off the asphalt.

Apart from Mina and myself, our newly acquired villa had its fair share of guests from the reptile world, mostly ants and flies. And if you happened to be a fly on the wall of our house last week, you would have spotted me standing, initially on a dining chair and then on the dining table. A minute later, you would have seen me make a miraculously long leap to the sofa, emitting simultaneously a terrified yell. Mina would have been darting around, concentration writ large on her face, a long-handled brush in her hand, trying to persuade a small lizard to leave the room, urging me to remain calm and not behave like a baby. My next move, prompted by a sudden about-turn by the creature, was to attempt to fly to another sofa and the upshot of the whole thing was that I landed on its edge and crashed to the floor with another piercing scream that scared the lizard back to the garden. I have no issues with tigers, lions, elephants or bears. And I love dogs. But for some reason I have always been petrified of lizards.

That one forgettable incident apart, both our families settled down fairly quickly within a month of reaching Dubai. We were well and truly ensconced in domestic bliss and comfort, aided undoubtedly by the very welcome amount of 50,000 dollars, the sign-on bonus Peggy had negotiated for us.

It was office life that was creating problems. We were finding it difficult to get used to the new working methods at Abbott-Adriaan (popularly known as AbAd). Unlike Myers, which was a brokerage house with a simple, flat hierarchy, this company seemed to have a complicated matrix structure, a three-dimensional one at that. There was the private banking outfit which Peggy had been asked to form and lead, but there was also an 'NRI' team and a 'Premier Banking' team, both of which had several clients who would have qualified for private banking. Some clients had separate accounts with each team. Some had only one account but both teams claimed it as theirs. There was also a team known as 'Investment Services' which overlapped these two teams and now ours as well. The management hierarchy chart had lines all over the place – clear lines, dotted lines, straight lines and curved lines.

The structure apart, the bank had a bureaucracy that was all-powerful. There was an internal audit department that focussed on routine procedures and processes. There were compliance people whose job was to interpret regulatory requirements and ensure adherence. Post crisis, most banks had swung like a pendulum to one extreme where controls ruled the roost, Abbott-Adriaan probably more than most. The staff in the compliance and audit departments strutted about with an arrogance that one normally associated only with immigration officials from the developed world before the crisis. One would have expected the guys in finance to remain firmly in the background, but no. Out here, they too behaved like they owned the place, spoke rudely, interpreted petty internal rules differently at different times, and generally made life difficult for employees. And they seemed to gain perverse pleasure from doing so. Business trips had to be sanctioned not just by the business head but by finance, who had to approve the estimated cost, *and* by compliance, whose job was to ensure that marketing guidelines were followed for all countries where we did business.

When I made a business trip to Kuwait, I stayed at a hotel other than the one that had been officially approved, because I could not get a booking at the approved hotel. The finance chaps pinned their ears back and refused to reimburse me. After a lot of back and forth, Peggy had to talk to the local head, Chris 'Fergs' Ferguson, to get them to do it. When Kitch spent two days each in Nigeria and Zambia during a business trip, they questioned his laundry bill because their policy stipulated 'minimum three days' stay' to be eligible for claiming laundry expenses. They claimed he had not 'stayed' in a place for three days. Again, they had to give in because it was, after all, a single trip, but it resulted in some friction and wasted a lot of time. Compliance approval was required even to open an account. Three of my new accounts were still pending with them two weeks after submission. Phone calls made to them were stonewalled by the compliance secretary, a stuck-up Irish woman whose breasts and nose both pointed upward, defying all known laws of gravity. 'Miss Up-titty', we named her.

Sometimes it seemed like the office was packed with heads. Every other guy was head of something or the other. There was a head of corporate bank, retail bank, compliance, finance, internal audit, credit, private bank, NRI, premier bank, investment services, loan recoveries, technology and several others. Within each of these, there were sub heads and unit heads. Separately and laterally there were regional heads, sector heads and country heads. Being a head was everyone's goal. There were so many heads that you wondered where the other body parts were. It was a Ravana of a bank. But who did all the work if everyone was a head? Despite all this, business remained steady, predominantly, I suspect, because of the brand name, general risk aversion and the fact that retail accounts continued to grow.

In the middle of all this, Peggy told us that the chairman of the group, Sir Sidney Wilkinson, was visiting Dubai and would formally inaugurate the private banking business during a client 'do', part of a series of visits organized by the group as a public relations exercise. They called it the 'Back to Growth' campaign. It was supposed to announce and demonstrate to the world that AbAd had come out of the recession strongly and was poised for growth in a world that was recovering. The CEO of the Middle-East region wanted ten of our 'top clients' to be at the venue to meet the chairman. He would not take no for an answer and Peggy herself was quite upset about the way the matter was thrust upon her without even a discussion. We hadn't even opened that many accounts yet. 'This place is all about politics,' Peggy grumbled, 'politics and perception. Everything else takes a backseat, especially business.'

2

In Search of Business

Business didn't take a backseat for long, however. Just a few days later, I was on a flight to Uganda thinking about the giant sniffing dogs I had seen at the airport the last time I went there. In my previous role at Myers York, I could attribute a good portion of my success and my subsequent troubles to my clients from East Africa, many of whom had been introduced to me by an old friend and well-wisher, Yashpal Kapoor. My experiences there – particularly in Kenya and Tanzania – had been richly varied and exciting, if not always pleasant. The clients I met there ranged from a whisky-swigging, womanizing, safari-suited potato chips manufacturer in Nairobi to a buck-toothed, miserly shop owner in Dar-es-salaam whose wife took an unexpected fancy to me.

It was in Kenya that I first met Mina and her family. I had some wonderful times there. But when I recall some of the things that happened during the financial crisis, I can still feel a chill going down my spine. It is not funny to have a client who also happens to be your prospective father-in-law raging at you, accusing you of being a thief and driving you out of his premises in full view of curious onlookers!

This time around, Mr Kapoor insisted on my meeting a very wealthy, elderly gentleman whom he knew in Uganda. He had apparently lived in Europe for several decades, but had decided to settle down on an island just off Uganda. The son of an Indian father and Spanish mother, he had been born and brought up in Africa and moved to Europe after getting married.

I had tried to get Kapoor appointed as a consultant by my new employers, but they wouldn't consider it. 'I'm afraid it doesn't quite fit into our scheme of things,' the British HR lady told me with a shrug. It was what people at this bank often said whenever they had to consider anything new or different. But Kapoor insisted on helping me, nonetheless. 'If I can help with something, I will do it, Jai,' he told me. 'Money is not everything. You can't take it with you, can you?'

At the Uganda airport, the dogs were still very much present, but they seemed much smaller now than they did when I first saw them. Perhaps because I had got used to being with 'The Boss', who, in the space of just over a year, had grown quite huge. Outside the terminal, a lady from the hotel was waiting with my name on a board. She asked me to wait for the other guests to arrive, so she could put all of us in one vehicle. I waited quietly in a corner for about twenty minutes before approaching the lady again.

'How long do I have to wait, ma'am?' I asked.

She looked at me blankly. 'Are you staying at our hotel, sir?' she enquired.

I reeled. 'You asked me to wait!' I told her, peeved. 'I have been waiting for almost half an hour.'

'Oh! Oh, my god! But, but...' She was completely flustered, looked repeatedly at her list and darted about here and there. 'I'm really sorry,' she said, coming back to me after a few minutes. I thought that other Indian was you. He looked exactly like you.' I had closely observed everyone coming out and could swear there had been no one even remotely resembling me. It occurred to me then that just as most Chinese, Japanese or African people look pretty much alike to Indians, it was possible that most Indians appeared alike to others. It was a humbling thought. I mean, to be just one among some 700 million brown men in the world...

At the hotel, I met Kapoor along with his elderly friend whose name, rather amusingly, was

Prospero Pindoria. An appropriate name for a private banking client, I thought. He looked pleasant and amiable, fair-skinned and rather European in appearance. He had a bald, dome-shaped head with just a few wisps of grey hair at the sides, eyes puckered at the edges into a series of crows' feet wrinkles, and a mild smile on a slightly vacant face. He and Kapoor were seated in the crowded coffee shop, occupied mostly by African businessmen and executives, with a handful of Indian and white men for variety.

As Prospero placed his order in a high-pitched voice, Kapoor whispered to me in Hindi, 'You need to be patient with him, Jai. Don't give up.' I wondered why. Maybe the old man would talk a lot. He looked the rambling type.

My new acquaintance beamed at me. 'Nice of you to come!' he said in a loud and shrill voice, making me feel very conspicuous.

'It was good of you to give me time,' I replied suavely, recovering fast.

He looked at his watch. 'The time is a quarter to eight,' he shouted.

I was taken aback. 'I said it was very good of you to give me time,' I repeated, a little louder.

'A quarter to eight!' he hollered. 'Eight forty-five.'

I dumped a sachet of sugar into my coffee and took a grumpy sip. I had figured out what Kapoor had meant by his bit of advice. I could sense several pairs of eyes focussing on us. Prospero's voice had a tremor in it, like the bleating of an excited sheep, and it cut through the general drone with the effectiveness of a gunshot. It had the added advantage of both continuity and comedy, thereby attracting even more attention.

'Kapoor told me the name of your bank,' he announced, 'but I have forgotten.'

Several curious ears turned in my direction to find out the name of my bank.

'Er… AbAd,' I mumbled.

'What was that?' he shouted, tilting his head. 'Can you talk louder? My hearing is a little weak.'

'AbAd. Abbott-Adriaan.'

'Abbott! I know Abbott!' he said enthusiastically. 'It is the Queen's bank. The Queen has an account there. Did you know it is the Queen's bank?'

I shook my head meekly.

'You don't know your own bank!' he admonished me, while eighteen eager listeners stopped their sluicing and browsing and revelled in this free entertainment show.

'Yes,' he shouted after a brief lapse into deep thought. 'Yes, I'm quite sure. Abbott is the Queen's bank. Queen Elizabeth,' he added, to make it amply clear, 'or maybe Queen Victoria. I am not very sure. My memory is a little weak.'

I looked at Kapoor helplessly. 'Jai is a family

friend,' Kapoor told Prospero, leaning into his ear in a bid to keep his voice as low as possible. 'He is looking for clients like you in Switzerland...'

'Switzerland! I was in Switzerland last month!' Prospero informed me, Kapoor and the other occupants of the coffee shop. 'Holiday! I go there every March. It is not too cold and not too warm. Just the right weather.'

'... or Singapore,' Kapoor concluded.

'Very clean city! I was in Singapore in 1995. Or maybe '96 or '97. They have very strict fines there for littering.'

There was a pause. Prospero seemed to have gone into hibernation. The audience went back to what it had gathered there to do.

Suddenly Prospero returned to this world. 'You must come to my house,' he shrieked. 'You will like it.' His face broke into a smile.

'Prospero lives on an island. They have a lovely colony of houses there,' Kapoor told me, trying to uses his hands to maximum effect to make it clear to Prospero what he was talking about.

It worked. Prospero nodded his head vigorously. 'Twenty blocks with three houses in each row. I am at number T1,' he shouted. 'T for tea,' he added and then, deciding that he rather liked the simple comedy involved in this, repeated it. 'T for tea,' he screamed and lifted the teacup and pointed it in every direction, first towards Kapoor, then me and then the guests at the tables nearby. 'T for tea!' he chuckled.

This was followed by another long silence. 'I need to put my feet up on the chair. My legs are a little weak,' Prospero announced, and then allowed me to help him.

Over the next few minutes, waiters brought two more tables into the coffee shop and several chairs. The place seemed to be the city's most popular destination that evening. Meanwhile, the crowd was regaled with information about Prospero's vacations. Among other things, he told us that he went to Pamplona in Spain every year to take part in the 'running of the bulls' event.

'I live the rest of the year for that one day,' he trilled, suddenly eloquent. 'It is about life and death. Life and death, hand in hand. Take it from me, young man, you are most alive when death is staring you in the face. Pamplona is the one place I would not give up for all the wealth in the world.'

It is easy to make lofty statements, I thought cynically, when you have 60 million dollars stashed away. The topic changed to Prospero's issues with his prostate. He went into its details and I went into my shell. There was no way I could crack this prospect. That, combined with my inability – under the circumstances – to make meaningful conversation, was enough to make me feel very despondent indeed. I picked up a toothpick and made a hole in a sachet of sugar. Then I made holes in all the sachets. I pushed the toothpick through the sachets one by one and then rotated the toothpick to see if I could get all the sachets to swing around it. I ate the cookie that came with the coffee. I took the toothpick and stirred the remaining froth at the bottom of my coffee cup, waiting for the meeting to end. Moodily, I ate another cookie. Prospero was still talking loudly in the background but I had lost all interest in him. This was obviously going to be a wasted trip.

Prospero stood up abruptly.

His face wore a pained expression and he was staring at the table like a soul in torment. He seemed to be wrestling with something; an inner turmoil, some deep emotional turbulence. He fixed his eye firmly on me, gimlet like, and bore into me. Then, pointing at me accusingly, he screamed, '*You!* You took my cookie!'

I stared at him, dumbstruck.

'I had saved my favourite carrot coconut cookie for the end and you took it, young man. *You ate it!*'

I stood up and looked at him in shock. I had frozen completely. The city of Kampala rubbed its hands in glee. I opened my mouth to protest but no sound came out. The only sound I heard was the scraping of chairs against the wooden floor as some of the other guests shifted their chairs to get a better view of the proceedings. I closed my mouth. Something had obviously happened to my larynx or vocal chords or whatever it is that enables one to talk.

'You *stole* it!'

I shook my head and wrung my hands helplessly.

'Gone! All gone! And under my very nose!'

'I say, no! I mean, really! I… I didn't…'

'Don't lie to me, young man! It was here. On my plate. You stole it!'

'I didn't know, I… I must have taken it without thinking. Sorry!'

'I always save that cookie for the end. And you… you…!' He spluttered and ended up choking.

Kapoor, who seemed to have congealed somewhere in the background – like the policeman in old Hindi films while the hero is fighting the villain – suddenly came to life and simultaneously to my rescue. In increasing decibel levels, he shouted, 'We will get another one, Prospero. We will get another one. *Another* one!' A frenzy of activity suddenly produced two waiters with three carrot coconut cookies between them.

By now the seated crowd had been joined by some standees. They heaved a collective sigh of regret. Obviously they had been hoping for nothing short of a police complaint followed by a formal arrest.

Prospero sat down and gobbled down two of the cookies. The third he wrapped in a tissue and put it in his jacket pocket. 'I am taking one home,' he told the city at large. 'I cannot eat too many because my stomach is a little weak.'

Two hours later, Kapoor came to my room. He was apologetic. 'Jai, I am sorry about this. I haven't met Prospero for quite some time and he really seems to have aged in the last three or four years. His mind is not what it used to be. But I have some good news. He tells me he has a younger brother in South Africa, called Pedro Pindoria. The two of them are heirs to the family fortune. Why don't you meet him? He is worth as much as Prospero.'

'I wouldn't meet him if he was the last client on earth,' I replied. I was in a nasty mood. I was upset with Kapoor for lugging me all the way to Uganda to meet this rich, fuddy-duddy nutcase and I meant to show it.

'Jai bhai, this business is all about long-term relationships. You must have some more patience.'

'I cannot have more patience,' I replied coldly. 'My patience is a little weak.'

3

'Tsunami' Andy Hits Dubai Shores

As a somewhat belated first wedding anniversary present, Mina and I took Peggy, Kitch, Galiya and Rachel out for a celebratory drink to the Buddha bar at the Dubai Marina, followed by dinner at Asha's, a restaurant that is apparently owned by the legendary Indian playback singer of that name. Rachel had been our colleague at Myers York. After spending a little over a year in Australia, she and her newly acquired, scholarly looking fiancé – a specialist in alternative energy – had decided to give the UAE a try. She had put on a little weight, especially, as Kitch was quick to notice, on her legs and hips, prompting him to dub her 'thunder thighs'.

I was delighted to see her again. It was good to have her adding to the sunshine around here rather than remain 'thunder down under'. I hoped I would get to see a bit of her, though her fiance's project on alternative energy seemed likely to be based out of Abu Dhabi. The conversation initially centred around the forthcoming investment 'circus' as Peggy labelled it – the Sir Sidney do.

We decided to be practical about the whole thing. If a show was what was required, we would put up a jolly good one. We had just three clients: Saxena, Harsh and one of Kitch's. But so what? We could 'create' some good clients and get them to meet the chairman. All we needed were a few guys with enough knowledge of English to reply to the old man when asked a question. And of course, they needed to be in possession of a good suit and be able to last an hour without chewing tobacco or spitting.

The chairman was also meeting a very big Arab client, someone who had over a hundred million dirhams lying in his current account for a year. CEO Fergs had called for Kitch and me to brief us on the programme. When we went into his room, he was talking to his secretary, Susan Inglesfield. He seemed worried.

'But has Mr Al Fadhar confirmed the meeting at eleven?' he asked her.

'Umm... he said "Insha Allah", Mr Fergusson.'

Fergs looked up in annoyance. 'I need to send the the itinerary to Sir Sid. I need a proper confirmation for eleven sharp, Susan. Please call him again and make sure there's no room for doubt.'

Susan dialled the number from Fergs's desk. 'Mr Al Fadhar, this is Susan Inglesfield again. Mr Fergusson would like to be absolutely certain about your meeting with our chairman at 11 a.m. on the 22nd. I see. Er... may I take that as a yes, Mr Al Fadhar?' She cupped her palm over the receiver. 'He keeps saying the same thing!' she said to Fergs. 'Insha Allah!'

'What's that supposed to mean?' Fergs asked in a terse whisper.

'It means "God willing",' Susan whispered back.

'I know that!' the CEO moaned, wringing his hands. 'But I can't go back to the chairman with that! Susan, please make sure *he* is willing. We need to be sure.'

'Er... umm... our CEO would just like to make sure you are definitely available for the meeting, Mr Al Fadhar.'

She replaced the receiver and looked at her boss.

'Well, what did he say? Did he confirm? Did he say yes?' Fergs looked like he was on the verge of a nervous breakdown.

'He said, if Allah was willing to let the meeting happen at that time, how could he, a mere servant of Allah, not make himself available?'

It was the first time I saw a CEO clutch his head and whimper helplessly.

The thing that was worrying me, however, was not so much the chairman's visit as the steady stream of negative news pouring in from Europe. Even as we signed up with AbAd, there was talk of Greece being in a spot of bother. Now Spain was in pain, so was Portugal and we received depressing bits of information almost daily. When we took the decision to join two months ago, the idea of working for a big European bank that seemed to have escaped the worst of the 2008 crisis had been a major plus. Now the question everyone was asking was this: after America, was it Europe's turn next? There was talk of contagion and a barrage of media reports about the indebtedness of European countries, even some of the larger ones like Italy.

There was another issue that was troubling me. At Myers, the entire system was focussed around opening accounts and doing business. Out here, it seemed that different forces were working in conflicting ways, each with a point to prove. It was like a game of football with several teams, multiple goal posts and no referee.

'It's great being together again, Peggy,' I told her later, 'but honestly I'm beginning to have doubts about whether this is the right place for us. Europe suddenly seems far less solid than it did three months back and this place is more about ego than ethos, more about scoring brownie points than doing business.'

'Frankly, Jack, I couldn't agree more. But let's give it a year, please, sweetheart. I think there's some change on the way. Hopefully, if we build a good team, we will be able to create an impact. While the rest of them focus on fudging figures, maybe we can work some real numbers.'

The following week was busy. Mina and I flew down to Chennai for a family get-together to celebrate my father's sixtieth birthday. There were about forty of us tucked away at the Fisherman's Cove resort an hour away from the city. We read out speeches and anecdotes about my father, much to his embarrassment, staged a small skit based on incidents in his and my mum's life, gifted him various things (none of which he would ever use) sang songs, played volleyball, swam and generally pigged out.

My sister Kitty told us that she and her football fanatic husband Shree were planning a ten-day holiday in South Africa during the FIFA World Cup which was to be held there later in the year. They had already spoken to our uncle Kaushik who was the Director of UniFoods Africa, the African division of the Dutch foodstuff giant in Johannesburg. I decided I might join them there. Not to watch football, but to meet the chap Kapoor had recommended.

After a few days of merrymaking, Mina went

to Brahmadesam to check on the farm, while I had to escort Kitch's brother Anand to Dubai.

Anand was to take up a job with one of Kitch's father's friends. His family was anxious to get him settled into a good job as soon as possible. He was just a couple of years out of college and some of his 'achievements' had already unnerved the family. While at school, he was the scourge of his teachers. Kitch told me his parents were once called to the headmaster's room in the presence of a seething couple, parents of a girl whom young Anand, all of twelve with wide-eyed innocence, had invited to 'come and sit on my lap'. Two years later, with the first flush of adolescence yet to abate, he was suspended from school for writing a love letter to his teacher.

When I first heard this story, I thought, here was a man after my own heart. I too had lost my innocent heart to a teacher in high school, though I had never dreamed of putting my thoughts down and presenting it to 'ma'am'. Kitch's father had to use all the force of his networking and his skills of persuasion to get Anand into another school, away from the woman of his dreams. In his first year at college, the young man, moved by the plight of the victims of the tsunami that hit the coast of Chennai, moved a few truckloads of homeless and hapless fisherfolk to his college. Those hundred-odd people loved their new mansion. They spread out in style, occupied every room in the college and refused to budge, thereby necessitating the cancellation of all classes for a week. When the distinguished principal came to plead and negotiate with them, he was firmly told by the fishermen that the college had been given to them by 'Anand sir' and that they would be damned if any bald-headed son of a whore tried to get them to move. A second suspension in three years was very much on the cards and would certainly have come through if the media had not picked up on the event and turned young Anand into a local hero. He was interviewed on a couple of television channels and was hailed by the regional press as a messiah of the downtrodden and emerged from the whole scene as the Great Young Indian Hope. The principal felt, under the circumstances, that any action against Anand would generate negative publicity for the college, apart from turning the youngster into a martyr and a celebrity, and decided to let him stay on.

He was a sweet chap to talk to; all humility and respect, very earnest, curious, straightforward – almost embarrassingly so – and always full of cheer. He certainly didn't look like someone who had brought his college to a standstill for a week.

We were to leave the next day. Anand was driving me to his house so I could meet his parents. He stopped some distance away from the house, outside a pharmacy. 'I say, Jai anna, can you do me a favour?' he asked, looking me straight in the eye. 'Can you buy me a Durex ten-pack?'

I stared at him dumbly, then at the steering, the rearview mirror and the accelerator in that order. Was he asking what I thought he was asking?

'You see, anna, all the pharmacies and groceries here know the whole family. It is a little embarrassing for me.'

'Okay,' I croaked, feeling decidedly uncomfortable.

What exactly does one do when the kid brother of one's best friend asks for something like this out of the blue? Besides, we were leaving the next day, so what on earth was he planning to do? But I walked into the pharmacy, feigning nonchalance. Between you and me, I don't even buy my own condoms. Mina does it for me. As I pointed and mumbled, the shopkeeper drew my attention to another one. 'New in the market, sir,' he said helpfully. 'Paan-flavoured. Madam may like it.'

I gulped down my surprise. I could understand paneer pizza and McAloo Tikki, but paan-flavoured condoms? What next?

Anand's parents seemed rather pleased with the way things had panned, though they were still a little apprehensive. 'Jai, you are like a son to us, just like Kitcha,' his mother told me. 'We are depending on you to take care of Anand and show him the right path.'

I felt like a modern-age Gautam Buddha. I wondered what I had done to be put on such a pedestal. I found out soon enough.

'We want him to work hard and achieve success. After two or three years, we would like him to get married to someone within the community, just like you have, so sensibly. Of course, we are very happy with Galiya. We could not have asked for a nicer girl as our daughter-in-law. But Jai, I don't want both our sons to get married to foreigners. We cannot keep having Stephen and Gloria or Abdul and Jaibunissa as our… what is it you say in Gujarati for sammandhi? Vevahi? What will we talk to them about? What relationship can we ever hope for? Whenever we are together, we will just have to sit and stare at the ceiling. We are not like Westerners. We want to remain in close touch with our sons all our lives. So their wives and their families are also important. We want our own people. We sacrificed this for Kitcha. Anand is a good boy, but maybe he is impulsive and a little… mischievous.'

I wondered how much they knew about the 'mischievous' part of his life. 'Kitch and I will do our best,' I assured her, making up my mind to leave the bulk of the responsibility to Kitch.

After Anand's recent request to me outside the pharmacy, my level of confidence in myself to 'take care of him' was not very high.

In the meantime, from somewhere nearby, a noise that could only have been made by a thousand half-crazed monkeys was reaching a crescendo.

'Aunty, what is that noise?' I asked. 'I have been wondering ever since I stepped inside the compound.'

'Oh, that's the municipality school behind our house. They provide free primary education, mainly to children from low-income families. We are used to the noise. In fact, we feel uneasy on weekends, without the children shouting. Go take a look from the balcony.'

I did, and watched open-mouthed. A few hundred children, all aged between five and ten, were running around in a frenzy in an area dotted with desks and chairs and covered overhead partly by an asbestos sheet and partly by a tree. Some of them were running around the place clockwise, some the other way. Some ran over desks, some under them, and some ran at random. A few kids were beating up some others and getting kicked at in return. Two of them were pulling each other's hair. Some were turning cartwheels. A few were swinging their school bags over their heads, some were banging their fists on the desks and a small group of diligent students were trying to dent their desks with the pointed end of their pencils. But all of them, irrespective of their choice of activity, were screaming. It was the one thing that united this diverse group of young thinkers. A few of them saw me, smiled and waved excitedly. I waved back.

'They like our family because of Anand. For the last four years, he has been buying sweets for them regularly. He distributes them every Monday. That gives them an incentive to attend school after the weekend. Anand has made us promise to continue this practice when he goes to Dubai. With his Dubai salary, he wants to make it twice a week.'

My respect for the young man went up several notches. This was obviously a guy with his heart in the right place.

On the flight to Dubai, Anand dug his elbow into my ribs and, nodding towards a light-eyed airhostess, said, 'That one looks hot!' A few minutes later, pointing at the lady sitting in front, he whispered, 'Y'know, I get really turned on by black bras!'

He seemed completely at ease with me. I was the one who was getting unnerved. I started reading a book. Maybe then he would stop sharing his most intimate thoughts with me.

'Jai anna!' he whispered. 'Have you ever been with any black and white women?'

I looked up, startled. 'Black and white women? What do you mean?'

'You know, black women... white women? Have you been with them? Not *now*,' he added hastily, noticing the shocked expression on my face. 'I meant before Mina, before marriage.'

'Mina is the only woman I have ever *been* with, as you put it,' I replied coldly. It's best to nip these things in the bud.

'Really? Kitch told me you used to be on the wild side, if you know what I mean.'

'Kitch,' I declared, 'is an ass.' I went back to my book, looking at the words with what they call unseeing eyes. I made up my mind to give Kitch a good talking to.

As we neared Dubai, he asked, 'Anna! What are the babes here like? I was told that Dubai is full of beautiful women.'

'Listen, mate!' I told him, sounding like a grandfather. 'The UAE is an Islamic state. Even if you forget everything else, please remember this one thing. Maybe you should have a nice cold shower when you get home, Anand. You resemble strongly a bull in heat.'

He grinned. 'You can call me Andy,' he said. 'Everybody does.'

Probably, I thought, because it rhymes with 'Randy'.

4

Pickin' up Steam

Kitch popped a moody peanut into his mouth and took a sip of coffee. Kitch makes his own coffee from this stainless steel double-compartment thing where he puts the blend of coffee and chicory on top and fills it up with hot water. The customized poison gathers, drop by drop, in the lower section. He was sitting at his desk, his tie neatly rolled into a ball and placed on the table. Kitch hates wearing ties and keeps removing his from to time. He claims he feels like he's being strangled, just knowing it's around his neck. Halfway to suicide, he calls it.

'What's happening, dude?' I asked.

'Shit is happening,' he replied. 'I don't know which is worse, machan, Myers York with the recession, liquidity crisis and margin calls – or this place filled with bureaucrats with bloated egos.'

'We have jumped from the frying pan straight into hell,' I agreed.

'Hell is right, Jai. There are demons, evil spirits and monsters all around here.'

'Especially green-eyed monsters.' I was referring to the storm that had been whipped up over my acquisition of Sunny's account.

Satwinder 'Sunny' Singh Bali, a Myers client and a well-wisher of mine, had recently moved from Kuwait to Dubai. It took me a whole month to get his account opened, after satisfying everyone concerned that neither Sunny nor his wife was into drugs, money-laundering, arms-dealing or terrorism; that Sunny was a legitimate businessman and further, that the 'Sunny Singh' that they had discovered on their electronic name-checker was a thirty-two-year-old, one-eyed pickpocket in Ludhiana and therefore not the same as my forty-seven-year-old, highly successful, two-eyed, Dubai-based businessman. Three days later, Sunny Singh remitted 15 million dollars and all hell broke loose. Someone discovered a dormant 1,400 dollar account of Sunny Singh's in the erstwhile Abbott bank unit and claimed that the relationship belonged to him. A girl from the NRI team complained to the regional CEO that she had been 'marketing' Sunny Singh for the past two years and that a new private banking bully had stolen her account. Her boss sent a nasty email to Peggy with a copy to the head of retail business both in India and in Dubai, the regional CEO, the head of HR and several others. I thought it best to let Sunny know what had happened. He let out a forceful expletive, an anagram of DK Bose. 'Bloody nonsense! It is *my* hard-earned money and I will decide who handles it. I will go straight to your chairman and tell him that only Jack Patel should handle my account. Nobody can make losses like him.' He saw the look of alarm on my face and guffawed. 'Take it easy, yaar, I'm joking. Aaja, lassi peele, drink some lassi and chill kar, bhai.'

As it turned out, a flurry of phone calls were made to Sunny Singh by various employees of the bank, each trying to claim him for his own. He patiently told each one that he could stuff himself. Two weeks later, this issue died a natural death, but the battle lines were now clearly drawn. There had been problems earlier between the retail banking, premier banking, investment services and NRI teams. Now, albeit temporarily, they were united. They had a common enemy: those 'arrogant sons of bitches', the new private banking team. It was not just about this account. There was talk in the pantry and around the corridors about the 'big fat sign-on bonuses' that Kitch and I were supposed to have received (the estimates of which far exceeded the actual) and the fact that the salaries of some of the new recruits – including us – were a little higher than the others in the bank were used to.

We detested the finance head, a guy called Ramanathan who pronounced his name 'Ram-

Naythan' to make it sound Western and introduced himself to everyone as Naythan). Notwithstanding the fact that I myself am called Jack by some of my colleagues, I have always had a little sneer reserved for Indians who go out of their way to Westernize their names. Besides, Nathan's nose was so high up in the air that he seemed to be perennially looking at the ceiling. You would often find him lumbering around the office with his secretary or a flunky in tow. He would mumble things which the other would scribble in a notepad. He was also known to be very close to the regional CEO.

On one such 'visit' through our office, I casually remarked, 'Ah! One of your usual trips around the bank.' It was an innocent, if somewhat uncalled for, off-the-cuff remark. In response, he glared at me with such fury I nearly fell backwards.

'It may interest you to know, young man,' he replied pompously, sounding more Brit than the Brits themselves, 'that Mr Fergusson values my observations. I think I know exactly what to tell him about you.' Then he turned on his heel and left, throwing another dirty look in my direction.

We couldn't stand the compliance people either, the whole lot of them from old 'Dickhead' down to their secretary. The audit guys were a little better in that they were not nasty or overbearingly stuffy, but they were every bit a pain in the butt; rigid, irritating and hard to please.

There also seemed to be no clear norms or guidelines about internal service quality or even internal pricing. Sometimes the treasury staff took us for a ride by adding on a profit margin even before quoting to us and then adding further for the customer rate. In the process, the client got a bad rate, we were saddled with excessive cost and treasury made a bumper profit that set them up for super bonuses, while doing precious little. Credit, operations, compliance took their own sweet time to deliver. Sometimes they responded to an email only after a week or two, that too with a silly query about something they could easily have deciphered from the given information.

Even Peggy found things frustrating. She had to attend so many meetings with the various heads that she had little time left to plan anything in her own head. It was the accepted practice at the office to stay late, often up to 7.30 or 8 p.m. There was nothing very constructive that was accomplished in the last two or three hours, but the norm was to hang around, usually chatting, cribbing and gossiping. It was also important, if possible, to get noticed staying late by senior people. All this was a far cry from the atmosphere we were used to at Myers. There was no point comparing the two, but we just couldn't help reminiscing about the freedom, the focus on work, the technology, the clarity of objectives, the abundance of product ideas, the research and the complete absence of daily irritants.

I was glad the World Cup was just round the corner, mainly so I could get away briefly from the negative atmosphere that prevailed in the office. After several emails to justify my trip, I got the required approval from finance. Then compliance sent me an email with a list of forty dos and donts, many of which I found impractical. Mina had been itching to go to Nairobi, where her parents and sister lived, so we decided to go a few days early and hit Kenya first.

It was with some trepidation that I approached Mina's house. There were many happy moments I associated the house with. It was there that I met Mina for the first time and it was under the trees of the garden behind that house that we shared our first kiss. But it also brought back a rather unpleasant memory: of the time her father had branded me a thief and shown me the door. It seemed a very long time ago, though it was less than two years ago. So much had happened in this time that it appeared distant and hazy, like a nightmare on the morning after. Yet, as with a nightmare, the memory suddenly sharpened and a nameless fear passed through me as I walked past the gate. Luckily for me, Mina's father was not at home, which helped ease the strain. Even better, Mira, Mina's elder sister, was there and as we all got chatting, the tension evaporated.

My apprehension was no less when I went to meet my erstwhile client, Dilip Kochar. In the midst of the liquidity crunch, the value of his portfolio, like that of many others, had crashed. At that time, in a fit of drunken fury, he had once called me, cursed me and referred to me as his 'enemy'.

'Oho!' he greeted me now, his left cheek bulging with tobacco. 'Bloody fellow! You are back! Welcome, welcome!'

He was dressed in a safari suit, his trademark attire. This one was white and it was accompanied by white shoes. Dilip Kochar was the manufacturer of the popular Moto Moto brand of chips. I noticed from the various packets on his table that he had added his own picture to the design on the wrapper, along with a tag line under the name that read: 'It's just too good, bwana!' I rather liked the tag line, though the picture of an elderly, bald, stern-looking man on a packet of chips was rather absurd.

After talking of this and that for a few minutes, the conversation spluttered to a halt. He looked at me. I looked at his safari suit and thought about how ugly it was.

'So, when will we open the account?' he asked.

My heart leapt. 'Will we... will we open the account?' I said joyfully.

'Of course, bloody fellow,' he told me. 'How else will we recover the past losses? Besides,' he added, getting slightly mixed up with his phrases, 'known devil is better than unknown devil.'

He signed the complicated account forms without murmur. In fact, he went a step further. He referred a friend of his in Mombasa, Kanti Shah, who, he said, was also looking for a good bank to shift his account to. I was delighted. There was no devil in Kochar today, as far as I was concerned, known or unknown. In fact, in his white safari suit, he seemed rather like an angel in disguise.

As I left, he shouted after me, 'Tell Kapoor I have stopped drinking now. I am just chewing tobacco.'

Mombasa was a coastal port in Kenya, less than an hour's flight from Nairobi. I had barely taken a sip of my apple juice when the pilot announced our descent and the red-dressed airhostess of Kenya Airways came back for the empty tetrapacks.

It was an evening flight and the view from the window was beautiful, the plane giving us alternate glimpses of greenery and water.

Mr Shah had recommended a hotel for me to stay in. It was close to his house, where I was to meet him the next morning.

It was an interesting hotel, built with substantial amounts of wood. The place seemed rather old, the walls filled with pictures of the British gentleman who had started the hotel decades ago, as if they were worried that someone would cast a doubt over its antiquity. If that didn't convince you, the bathroom certainly would have, since the wash basin had separate taps for hot and cold water. So if you were among the vast majority of people who like their water somewhere in between scalding hot and icy cold, you had to take a glass and mix water from the two taps.

That night, after carefully drawing the mosquito net on all sides and making sure there were no gaps, we went to bed, the two of us – I and a well-hidden mosquito. The latter, possibly frustrated at being trapped within a net and not being able to leave after having its fill of blood, gave vent to its frustration by feasting some more on the former. When I woke up in the morning after a fitful, painful night, I was a series of mosquito bites in human shape, not to mention the bruises I had acquired as a result of a couple of vicious slaps I had dealt myself in an attempt to eliminate the mosquito. But as advised by Norman Vincent Peale and other proponents of positive thinking, I tried to think positively about not getting malaria and proceeded towards my destination, scratching and fuming.

To reach Kanti Shah's house, I had to go past the Tiny Toddlers nursery school, which he owned. I saw two boards in front of the school, one beneath the other. The first read: 'Vision Statement – to uplift the children of Kenya'. The other one read: 'Mission Statement – to uplift the children of Kenya through quality education'.

The door to his house was half open. As I reached for the bell, a lady pulled open the door, smiling at me. 'Kanti is stuck up,' she told me. She was not accusing her husband of being a snob, just letting me know that he was delayed.

He came soon enough. A short, rotund man wearing a panama hat, he looked rather like Elmer Fudd, his round, childish, almost silly face punctuated by a broad, easy smile. He always did his morning rounds, he said, at both his schools, to meet the management team and those parents who insisted on meeting him.

'I am starting a third,' he told me. 'Can you suggest any good names? My existing two schools are called Tiny Toddlers which is a nursery school and Laughing Lilliputs which is a primary school. I want a similar name for the third one, which is for big boys. Both words should start with the same letter, like Delhi Daredevils, not like Mumbai Indians. But it should be a little more serious than the junior school names.'

'I get you. An alliteration,' I murmured. 'How about simply Big Boys? Both words start with B.'

'No, it will have girls also.'

'Hmm… What about Smart Scholars?'

He mulled over it, biting his lip.

'Or Shining Stars?' I persisted.

He brightened considerably. His eyes lit up, rather like the potential name of his third school. 'Shining Stars!' he exclaimed. 'I like that. Yes! I really like that.'

I looked suitably gratified.

'Do you have any children?' he asked suddenly.

'Er… no, not yet.'

'When you do, they are welcome to join the Shining Stars school, free of charge. Free! That is my reward to you for your suggestion.'

I thanked him. However remote the possibility of my children studying in Mombasa's Shining Stars school, I appreciated his spontaneous gesture.

'Jai bhai, I will open the account now with a small sum,' he told me with just a touch of guilt. 'For big money, you know, you have to approach government people. It's just like India and every other country. Anybody connected with the government will have cash to spare. That's how the system works. Day in and day out, the official machinery has to be greased. We are businessmen who have to work hard for our money. But don't worry, next year I will have more money.'

'Because of the new school?'

'That is one reason. But I am also planning to raise the fees sharply for the existing ones. I have created a good name, so now I can squeeze the parents. Every government says school fees should be reasonable. I say, let them put their money where their mouth is. I will be happy to retain the same fees if we get a subsidy. Talk is cheap, you know. But this is business like any other business. We also have a real estate business in India. Have you heard of Milk Builders? M-I-L-K?'

What a ridiculous name, I thought. I furrowed my forehead and shook my head.

'We are still somewhat new,' he said defensively. 'We have completed two projects in Rajkot and one in Baroda. We have taken up one project each in Baroda and Ahmedabad. My two sons are taking care of the whole thing.'

'Why "Milk"?' I asked.

He smiled a clever smile. 'My elder son is Mehul, my wife's name is Indu. My second son is Lalit and my name is Kanti. M-I-L-K,' he said, simpering. 'And that's not all. Milk contains protein to build the body, to make it big and strong. My company MILK has all the things needed to construct buildings, to make them big and strong.' By now he was bursting with pride.

I was appalled. Milk builders? Like protein for the body? How tacky can one get? But he was a prospect. And he seemed like a nice guy. I forced my facial features into an approving smile, hoping to convey admiration. It worked.

'Yes,' he said with a hideous smirk, 'I thought of it myself. And very soon we will be constructing a hundred-storey building in one of the major Indian cities.'

'A hundred floors!' I exclaimed. 'But will the infrastructure in our cities take such buildings? I mean, power, water, parking, roads… and what about the fire brigade? Can they reach such heights if needed?'

'Jai bhai, we are builders,' he said. 'The municipality gives specifications for construction. We will meet them, no problem. But if the fire brigade cannot reach the top floor, that is not my problem, it is their problem. I can do my work but I cannot think for others. If I start worrying about roads, fire brigade and everything else, I will not have time for construction.'

I got Kanti's account forms completed and then realized this was going to be my lucky day. Kanti put me onto a friend of his in Mombasa, who had recently sold his hardware business. Ramesh Doshi was a gentleman who looked every inch a Gujarati and spoke every bit like one too. 'My name Ramays,' he told me. 'You pleajh come home for the deener, Jai bhai, I want to make the wheel.'

'*Make* a wheel? Why?' I asked, not unreasonably.

'Becaujh to geeve thees thees thees things to the dhikra and thees thees thees things to the dhikri. After my dayth, you understand, geeving to the faymeely. Making the wheel. The Kantibhai said you wheel haylp me make the wheel. Wheel you?'

Now I understood. 'Oh, a will! Yes, of course I wheel, er... will.'

'I am saventy-ate,' he told me, changing the subject. 'Steel I am speaking the Englees. Bayter than my dhikra also. Good, na?'

'Very good,' I said, wondering how his dhikra, his son, would speak.

'I am speaking the good Englees becaujh my teacher raped me.'

My heart sank. I didn't want to hear a sad story from this sweet old man. This was one problem with meeting people in places like Kenya. Stories about crime were in abundance. They tended to depress me. And worse, when you met people in a group, they would try to outdo each other, with the result that within half an hour, your ears were filled with half a dozen appalling crime stories.

'Yays,' he continued. 'Every time I am speaking the wrong Englees, my teacher, he is raping me on my knuckles. With foot rule. Like thees. Tak! Tak! Tak! Tak!'

I heaved a sigh of relief.

5

Blackbeard the Pilot

Even before I reached the Mombasa airport, I got a call from Kochar. 'Jai, when are you coming back to Nairobi?'

'I'm heading for the airport now,' I told him. 'I will be in Nairobi in about two hours.'

'I will meet you at the airport. I am taking you straight to open a new account with 20 million dollars. I have already spoken to the people concerned, the pilots. It is legal pilot money. So you will have no problem. They are ready with the cash.'

For the entire flight, I thought sweet thoughts about Dilip Kochar. There had been a moment, a year or two ago, when I had felt like breaking something on his bald head, but I realized now that it was just my immaturity. The man was pure gold. Naturally, when his investments had halved overnight, he had lost his cool – but who wouldn't? And what was wrong with having his picture on the wrapper? It wasn't a bad idea at all. And if he looked a tad grim in the picture, so what? I needed to curb my tendency to make an issue of things and go by the facade rather than appreciate the real worth of something. Twenty million dollars was a nice bit of jam. It would take care of this month entirely. And if the client was a pilot – an employee with a clear source of income – it would be so much easier to convince compliance. But how could a pilot have so much money? Perhaps he had won a lottery. Kochar did say 'legal' money. Maybe it was a fund of sorts... The only snag was that he said they were ready with the money. There was no way I could open an account in less than two weeks, pilot or otherwise.

I saw Kochar almost before I saw the airport itself. He was literally on the runway. Apparently he had connections with the airport staff.

'C'mon, let's go,' he said as soon as he saw me. 'Need to be on time.'

'Dilip bhai, it is really nice of you to do all this for me. I got a positive response from Kanti Shah as well.'

'You had better take extra care of my account. It has recovered a good bit, but in two years we have made zero returns. In the next one year, let us see some growth. Otherwise I will come to Dubai and tell that beautiful boss of yours a few things. Your Peggy will think she has been caught in a storm.'

'Leave that to me, Dilip bhai, I will do my best for you. But tell me about this pilot. Which airline does he fly? How did he run into all this money?'

'What pilot?'

'The pilot you spoke to me about. The guy we are going to meet.'

'What are you talking about, young man? I think the prospect of such a big account has melted your brain a little. I never spoke about any pilot.'

'The 20 million dollars that's coming in. You said it was legal pilot money.'

'Not pilot, dumbhead, I said legal *pirate* money. Which pilot has 20 million?'

'P-pirate!'

'Yes, pirate. But it has been negotiated by a leading law firm, so there is no problem. It is fully legal. You must have seen it in the papers a few days back. The Somalians had initially asked for 30 million but the Europeans negotiated 20 through these lawyers.'

'B-but Dilip bhai! I can't open a pirate's account! They'll laugh at me! I'd be sacked if I even asked.'

'Arre, bakwas! Don't be a cartoon, yaar! It is perfectly legal. The law firm is handling the matter, so what is the problem? I'm telling you, it was in all the papers, everybody knows about it. It is fully official.'

'No! I can't open this account. I *won't* open this account!'

'Bloody fellow, don't behave like an idiot. If you don't open it, someone else will. Do you think you're the only banker in town? Hundreds of bankers are waiting to pounce on such deals. And don't worry, man, you will not actually be meeting the pirates, only the lawyers.'

'No! Please stop the car. I'm getting off. This is illegal.'

'Abbey gadhe, what illegal? When your bosses' ancestors took the Kohinoor diamond, was it legal? When they wiped out the wealth of all the countries they colonized, was it legal? *Ghanta!* This is a normal thing that keeps happening here every month. Where do you think all the ransom money has gone? Either into property or into banks. This is reality. If you want to do business, you have to turn a blind eye to such things.'

'A blind eye? Well, maybe I should wear an eye patch like the client! Stop the car *now*.'

'Damn it, are you man or mouse?'

'It doesn't matter!' I hollered. '*Stop the car*.'

'You're a wimp! You're a little girl!'

'I don't care. I'm getting down. Stop the car.'

'You… you scaredy cat! You son of a jelly!'

'Stop it *now*!'

He stopped and I jumped out.

'Jai, try to understand,' he said, gesticulating furiously. 'I have committed to them. I will have mud on my face if I don't take you there.'

'You said there were hundreds of other bankers!'

'Yes, there are!' he screamed. 'I should have just gone to one of the experienced mzungus. Some good white man dhoriya banker instead of a half-baked fellow like you who has probably not even tasted his mother's milk! You're a darpok ding-a-ling... a spineless spaghetti!'

He changed gears and glared at me one last time. 'You will never be a success. *Pakadke baithe raho!* Hold onto your thing and sit in a corner. Nincompoop! Chikne chutiye! *Khrwaaaagh, thhooo!*' he went, and spat out a ball of saliva and tobacco within an inch of me.

I turned on my heel and moved away. An angry screech of tyres made it clear that he was doing the same. My ears burned with what I had just heard. I couldn't see my cheeks but they seemed all red and heated up. I was pretty much in smoke. I stopped, breathing heavily. In front of me, all I could see were two boards. They had words written on them in letters of fire. The first one read: 'Vision Statement – to kick Dilip Kochar's ass'. The other read: 'Mission Statement – to kick Dilip Kochar's ass so damn hard that his spine sticks out through the back of his neck'.

I stood for a moment, contemplating the two boards. All around me people were walking briskly to their respective destinations. A few who had seen the final altercation between Kochar and me hung around waiting for my next move. A beggar was making persistent demands of my wealth. Hawkers milled around trying to interest me in peanuts, bananas, a picture of 'The Last Supper', scrolls with Arabic writing on them, dark glasses and folding umbrellas.

For a moment, I thought I would ask Mina to send a car to pick me up from here. I was about a kilometre away from her house. Under most circumstances, that is what I would have done. Thoughts of getting mugged were never far from my mind when I was in Nairobi. Then I decided otherwise. This was my wife's home. She was born here. Her family – the four of them – had lived here all their lives. They had gained a lot from this country. They had lost nothing except two fingers of my father-in-law, when he was shot at during an attempted burglary. Suddenly my thinking changed.

I was safe in this place. I may not be a son of the soil, but I was their damaad, their son-in-law. These Africans – small, big, black, brown, well-dressed or otherwise – were my brothers and sisters. They would not harm me. It took me half an hour, but I walked home.

Mina opened the door. 'Jai,' she said after just one look at me. 'Are you all right?'

'I am fine,' I replied. 'I'm not going to let that buffoon spoil my day.'

'Who? Dilip uncle?'

I stared at her. How on earth did she know?

'Someone from his office just brought a ton of chips with a note that says, "Jaibhai, please don't mind. Very sorry. Dilip".'

I looked at the hundreds of packets of Moto Moto chips, at the forbidding picture of Dilip Kochar on each one of them. I read the note and I looked at Mina's bemused face. Then I sat down and laughed my gut out.

6

Winning Over Sir Sid

Abbott-Adriaan Bank had decided on the world's first (and so far, only) Armani hotel as the venue for the chairman's visit. It was his first visit to the country. More than anything else, it was symbolic of the importance that AbAd attached to the region. In a sense, I could understand the rush to get the chairman to 'inaugurate' the bank's private banking business in the MESA (Middle East and South Asia) territory. They wanted to reinforce the perception that, at least as far as AbAd was concerned, things were getting back to normal and businesses were growing.

Visiting senior bankers were not a scarce commodity in Dubai. In the last few years, investors had seen more economists, fund managers and product specialists than camels and sandstorms. Indeed, after two major crashes in the last decade and several smaller ones, after several forecasts went wrong and several predictions turned out to be mere predilections, there was little or no appetite among investors to brave the traffic and listen to another 'expert'. Even the wining and dining wasn't worth it. Drunk driving in Dubai could lead one straight to prison, no questions asked. There wasn't even a facade of a tolerance limit; one whiff of suspicion and in you went to count iron bars with nothing to look forward to except the biryani that would be served on Friday. As for the dining that came along with the presentations, well, most investors who were worth anything were probably already suffering from diabetes, high blood pressure or high cholesterol, in some cases all three. It was probably keeping this in mind that the bank chose Armani, at the base of the world's tallest building, as its venue for the chairman's party, hoping, no doubt, that novelty would sell.

Clients had been allotted tables and were expected by half past seven. The chairman had a flight to catch at 1.30 a.m. and the plan was to wind up by 11 p.m. That night at nine, there were about twenty-four employees (three of them from private banking), eighteen spouses of employees (two of them from private banking) and fourteen clients (*ten* of them clients of private banking). Simply put, in that first one hour of the event, we turned into stars. CEO Fergusson must have realized the predicament he would have been in had it not been for our clients. As a result, he fawned on Peggy and the rest of us like he had never done before. He laughed with us, patted us on our backs and was at his suave best with our clients. He praised us to the skies and told the chairman that we were the jewels in the crown of AbAd Dubai, its main hope for a bright future. The CEO had 'mandated' fifty clients from the local premier bank, twenty-five from the NRI team, twenty-five from the investment services team and ten clients from us (the 'fledgling private bank' as he had referred to us in his email). Our ten had arrived in the first thirty minutes of the party. And while a few of the local bank's clients did stream in after 10 p.m, there was little doubt that, by then, impressions had already been well and truly set in Fergs's mind as well as the chairman's. The show had flopped. There could be no late recovery.

When Mr Fergusson spoke, he addressed an audience that consisted primarily of his own employees and their spouses. This was followed by a musical performance by a threesome: a svelte, dark-haired young lady on the violin, a middle-aged man on the saxophone and a youngish fellow with a sculpted body and ponytail on some kind of a drum which he placed between his legs. Towards the end of their performance, they increased the tempo and tried to get everyone involved. My sister Kitty (yes, she and her husband Shree were among our 'clients' that day), who can never keep still when there is music, had already been clapping and swaying, but now she left the table and started dancing. Sunny Singh promptly joined her, delighting the musicians with some impromptu bhangra steps.

The beats quickened and as the finale cruised towards a crescendo, Sunny kept pace, showing an incredible reserve of energy. With a terrific sense of timing that I had never suspected of him, he broke into a series of lightning-fast Punjabi moves, with his own booming vocal accompaniment that went 'Aha hadippa, Oho hadippa' and finally ended with 'Oye balle balle balle balle, brrrrrah!' Coinciding with the last notes, he did a little hop, skip and jump and landed, perfectly poised, in front of the chairman with both hands raised, index fingers pointing skyward, ending in a neat little bow.

There was a standing ovation from the limited audience and a special hug for him and Kitty from the chairman's wife. Dinner was followed by the chairman's speech. By now the number of clients had grown and equalled the number of employees. But Sir Sid had decided, I think – not having had the opportunity to meet those who sauntered in after the musical performance had started – that private banking was the only business of note in AbAd's Dubai office. He described the business as 'a brilliant initiative' and spoke highly of us and our clients. He promised to increase our budget within the region. He referred to Peggy as an 'exceptional talent'. He even said – he had probably had one too many by this time – that our clients and their families would be given free annual holidays to exotic locations.

He told the gathering that he had been most impressed by the quality of our clients. Too often, he said, private banking clients were boring old moneybags who couldn't think beyond the stock market and real estate. But here were highly sophisticated clients who were as knowledgable as they were wealthy and could talk freely of everything from World Cup football to alternative energy, from the intricacies of the auto industry to Indian classical dancing. He proposed a toast to them and predicted that the business would be a thundering success. Finally, he promised that before the end of the year he would arrange to invite to Dubai to meet with our clients, any Indian film star of our choice. 'Maybe Shahrukh Khan,' he said impressively, 'Amitabh Bachchan or…' – he paused for effect – 'even the queen of Bollywood and Big Brother,' – another pause, hands spread wide for maximum impact – '… Shilpa Shetty!'

On that note, Sir Sid left for London, but not before presenting to each of our clients a gold coin with the AbAd logo on it. These had been earmarked for certain key NRI/investment services/premier banking clients, but at the chairman's suggestion it was given to all the private banking clients instead. Each of our clients had a picture taken with the chairman and the fifty-gram gold coin, some of which appeared in the papers the next day.

At about half past ten, the head of the NRI team, the premier banking head and the head of investment services sidled out sheepishly along with the head of compliance and the head of finance. The regional CEO stayed back to pump our hands and wish our clients a very good night. The chairman shook hands with all of us. He and his wife extended an invitation to Peggy to visit their farmhouse in the UK on her next visit. They left on a high, waving at all of us and blowing kisses in Kitty's direction.

We had pulled it off big time!

On the day of the function, we had actually opened only seven accounts. Two of them lived abroad. Of the five who lived in Dubai, one was Kamal Lalwani, whom we had decided not to invite. He was too full of himself – both literally and figuratively – very cocky and not the type of chap you would want your chairman to meet. The second was a client of Kitch's who, notwithstanding his wealth, looked like something the cat found in the bin. The third was Sunny Singh, who had been invited and who attended, dressed in all his splendour, looking like an erstwhile Maharaja of

Punjab. We had also invited our clients Saxena and Harsh, who were old friends and well-wishers from my Myers days. Others were relatives and friends, chosen for their personality, their ability to speak English and their general reliability. Two of them were, of course, Kitty and Shree, who had stopped in Dubai on their way to South Africa to see the FIFA World Cup. I had promptly roped them in, much to Peggy's discomfiture and to Kitty's delight. The idea of fooling the chairman of a multinational bank appealed greatly to Kitty. While Shree initially dragged his feet, he was fine once he found that the suit he had borrowed from Kitch fit him perfectly and that the chairman was a football fan. Others included Kapoor at his flamboyant best, Rachel looking gorgeous, and her fiancé Tim, who held his own with Sir Sid with his ideas on solar energy and wind farming.

Flushed with our success, we left the hotel to find some place to celebrate with our distinguished group. I was delighted. Shree had kept the chairman enthralled with the latest on the odds that bookmakers were offering on Brazil, England and the others. My dear sister Kitty, looking charming, perhaps even stunning, in a black and orange salwar kameez with mirror-work, had so enchanted Sir Sid with stories about the dance school she was running in India, that he wanted to send his grand-daughter to India to 'learn Indian dance and absorb the great Indian culture'. Then there was Kitch's cousin Ravi, a Dubai-based social worker of sorts, who looked like an Indian version of George Clooney. Kitch's brother Andy had wanted to come to the party as well, posing as a rich man's son, but Kitch wouldn't hear of it.

'Let's go *home* and celebrate, guys,' Kitch said. 'I'm starving. The décor and the music were lovely, but somehow the bigger the hotel, the less I like the vegetarian choices. I've got plenty of drinks at home for everyone and I can eat some curd rice.'

'With VK,' Galiya added.

Andy joined us at home with a young Filipino lady in tow, and promptly proceeded to have a go at the scotch. The kid was really living it up.

'I love this bank,' Kitty announced as she raised a toast to the private banking team. 'It's such fun. I thought banking was a boring business with forms and documents and numbers. But see how easily we impressed your chairman. I had him eating out of my hand. I think, after dancing, banking is the thing I like best.'

Peggy smiled. 'Darling,' she said, 'believe me, the banking I have always known is all about business and fourteen-hour days. I have never seen banking as it exists in this bank. It's all about meetings and hype. But you look terrific, sweetheart. Any chairman would have been taken in by you today.'

In a corner of the room, right next to the corridor that led to the bedrooms, Andy was sitting on a two-seater sofa, smooching the young lady and simultaneously kneading her bare calves. I shuddered at the audacity of today's younger lot, and remembered his mother holding my hand a few months ago, fervently pleading with me to take good care of her son. 'Please teach him to be responsible like you,' she had said. And I realized that I hadn't so much as given the guy a second thought in all these days.

Suddenly a small figure with tousled hair and sleepy eyes appeared from the passage. It had a thumb in its mouth. The other hand clutched a fluffy pink rabbit. It was Olga Dharini Krishnan, the pretty little daughter of Kitch and Galiya. She stood just behind the smitten couple who were deeply absorbed in their task, and registered a formal complaint with an abrupt announcement.

'Too many people. Too many noise!' she said in her squeaky two-year-old voice. I know you will say that it is not possible for a sitting person to jump and I will admit that this is true in most cases. But if a person is taken completely by surprise when he or she is totally engrossed in something, it can happen. Andy and the girl rose as if a bomb had exploded under them. For a brief moment, they seemed to rest in midair, like a couple of levitating, embracing yogis. Then they came crashing down.

There was a stunned silence. It hadn't occurred to us that we had been making far more of a ruckus than was appropriate after midnight in an apartment with a sleeping child. We stared at the kid. The kid stared back. 'Too many noise,' she repeated. Then, replacing her thumb in her mouth, she walked back to her room, with Galiya jogging after her. The rest of us tried hard not to make the sound of a dozen adults doubling up with laughter.

The heady success of the chairman's do lasted several days. In the aftermath of the glow, we sauntered around like my former colleague Philippe used to do at Myers. Philippe was then the top revenue producer there and he spent most of his time sitting in his office with his feet up on the table and a wireless device stuck to his ear. When he did swagger around the office, the others hurriedly got out his way for fear of being snubbed or barked at.

Now it was our time under the sun. Peggy showed us an email that had been sent to the various heads of departments. It contained a stern rebuke from Fergs for failing to bring in the required number of clients and compared them unfavourably with us. Peggy got promoted to the mancom, the revered and greatly feared management committee, an all powerful body that could make or break ideas, products and careers.

Peggy couldn't believe that an issue as ridiculous as this had catapulted her into the limelight. I knew she had never felt too comfortable in this new setup, where office work consisted predominantly of a series of meetings, almost all of them with colleagues. Clients were rarely met by senior employees. Indeed, the heads seemed to shy away from clients, neighing like a frightened horse and running for cover if a client so much as approached them. They were very uncomfortable with clients, especially if there was a chance that they may have a grouse. They kept proudly busy with internal back-to-back meetings. That was their zone of comfort and they liked staying there. Of course, when a client offered his yacht to the senior management of the bank for a weekend or put their families up at his resort complete with booze, food and spa, they lapped it up. But they drew a clear line at meeting a client face to face or listening to his ire. That was left for the minions, the officers and front office soldiers. That's what they were paid for.

If there were more than two participants at a

meeting, they were referred to as 'conferences'. Poor Peggy had to spend a good four to five hours a day on these. 'I have never attended such unproductive meetings,' she told us. 'Many of the decisions made at these hour long meetings could just as easily be made over a quick phone call or a couple of sensible emails. Sometimes no decisions are made at all. It *kills* me.'

Nevertheless, the meetings continued and, if nothing else, it gave the secretaries of the heads a sense of importance. They took immense pleasure in informing callers that their calls could not be returned by their boss as he or she would be in a series of meetings all day.

While nothing much changed at the grassroots level or in the well-enmeshed bureaucracy across departments, our considerably better standing with CEO Fergs helped us win approval for four more private bankers to join. They were in place in a few days, which goes to show how easy it was to cut through red tape once the CEO had signed off on a document. The entire circus at AbAd revolved around pleasing the CEO. So there we were, more than twice our strength almost overnight. Who would have thought that a seemingly small matter of getting together a few guys for the chairman's event would yield such positive results?

The new members of the team were Rachel, Harry,

Gavaskar and Omar. Harry Bauffeurhaugham (pronounced Boffam) was an Oxford boy, tall, well-built and usually serious. He was a former colleague of ours from Myers, a man of few words and a fitness freak. He was the type of Brit one associates with the likes of Alistair Cook rather than, say, Graeme Swann. There was a time when Rachel and another former colleague Melissa vied for Harry's attention, but now Rachel seemed to be happily teamed up with her scientist fiancé.

For young Gavaskar it was a homecoming, in a sense. For the last two years he had been working with a sheikh in Abu Dhabi, after he was sacked from Abbott (prior to the merger) at Nathan's behest. The finance head had apparently been scrounging around Gavas's desk and had discovered in his wastebasket a caricature that Gavas had drawn of him. He insisted that Gavas be fired. Getting him back in a second time was not easy but once Fergs okayed it, Nathan timidly buckled down.

And that wasn't the first time Gavas was fired. At his first job at an American bank in Abu Dhabi several years ago, he had been asked to leave after a very senior diplomat made a sarcastic remark about him to the head of retail. What happened was that Gavas had presented the gentleman with a diary. Just the previous week, Gavaskar's Dubai-based colleague had presented the diplomat's junior in Dubai with a similar diary but with his name embossed in golden letters. The senior diplomat had noticed his junior colleague's diary during a visit to Dubai. He himself had been presented with one *without* the gold embellishment. He considered this not just a personal affront but something in the nature of a breach of protocol. He called the top man at the bank and gave him a piece of his mind. The next day, young Gavas was given marching orders.

Of course, we had no doubts about Gavas's ability to bring in clients and mesh well with the team. He had been sacked twice before the age of twenty-six but according to us, he had just been plain unlucky. If anything, his little scrap with Nathan endeared him to us. He was an interesting character, prone to talking philosophy and always tending to fast. He fasted on Monday for one reason, on Thursday for another. He fasted for nine days during Navratri and did not eat dinner, ever. It was not good to eat after the sun set, he claimed. That was how the yogis of ancient India lived till they were a hundred and twenty. All in all, a very likeable guy but one who sometimes made you feel fat, flabby and unspiritual.

Omar Kazmi was a Pakistani; suave, friendly and impeccably dressed. He joined us from HSBC, where he had worked for several years, focussing mainly on the Pakistani and expatriate Pakistani segment. He had a few Indian accounts as well. He was very brand-conscious – everything he wore and used, from his shirts, pens and glasses to his socks and probably even underwear, was a well-known brand.

The winds were clearly blowing in our favour. I recalled something a colleague told me soon after I joined. 'In this bank,' he had said, 'it is difficult to simply put your head down and work. There are different camps and you have to commit yourself to one of them. Camps either win or lose. If you are on the winning side, you prosper. If not, you wither and die.'

It wasn't just the camps. I had also noticed that at the senior levels, almost every email sent out had two meanings. One would be obvious and the other hidden, its meaning clear only to the one concerned. Every email that had the potential to boost oneself or nail someone's folly, snigger at someone or demoralize another was suitably cc'ed or bcc'ed to the appropriate persons. At Myers, it was considered poor email etiquette to bcc anyone. Here, I suspected, more emails were bcc'ed than not. It was as if the sender took perverse delight in doing so. Business remained firmly on the backburner. As Shakespeare might have put it, what held centre-stage were 'treason, strategems and spoils'.

7

Pati, Patni and Vow

I pushed Minnie Mouse's nose and Kitch came to the door. On the dining table was a map of Karnataka that Kitch had been poring over.

'Kitch, there's something I want to talk to you about.'

'Yes, machan?' he said distractedly.

Kitch was planning a short trip to Chennai to see his folks and check on the restaurants. A friend had suggested he go across to neighbouring Karnataka. He knew a godman there, a rich guy called Putla Baba who, Kitch had been assured, would be keen on an off-shore account with a large European bank like ours.

He looked up at me. 'Don't tell me to remove that L-O-V-E photograph from the wall. Galiya has moved it to the living room because she wants people to see it. She loves that picture.'

'No, no! Not that. She can make a wallpaper of it, if it makes her happy. I'll just turn the other way. Er… it's about Andy and that young girl he brought with him the other day.'

'What about her?'

'Well, I mean, who *is* she? Is there anything you and I need to do? Your folks have left him under our care, haven't they? So…'

Kitch folded the map and scribbled down some names. He looked at me and grinned. 'She is a waitress.'

'A waitress!'

'Yes,' he said with affected nonchalance. 'At a pizza place. With every bite of pizza, his love for her grew. Such an idiot he is. But there is nothing to worry about. Here he is in person. Let him tell you the story himself.'

'What story?' asked Andy, who had just entered the room. 'Oh, *that*!' he said, guessing correctly, probably from the bemused look on my face. 'It's okay, Jai anna. That's off!'

'Off! I thought it had just started. Have you left her already?'

'Actually, no. *She* left me!'

'Oh, I'm sorry!'

'It's okay. But it wasn't really my fault. Hazel's sister looks so much like her and, well, you know, many of them look alike, anyway. Besides, they share the same apartment. It was an honest mistake.'

My heart turned a somersault. 'You mean you flirted with her sister thinking it was her?'

'It was more than flirting, actually.'

'Good heavens! B-b-but, this is... this is terrible. I mean, didn't the sister try to stop you or anything?'

'No!' he said with feeling. 'That's the thing. She found it all very funny. But Hazel didn't. So she chucked me.'

'Good lord!' I said, shocked to the core and trying hard to digest this piece of news. But I recovered quickly enough. With Andy, one had to. 'Well, don't worry about it, mate,' I told him. I didn't want the lad to fret and pine. 'Maybe it's all for the best.'

'I'm not worrying,' he said with a dismissive shrug. 'I should have stuck to Svetlana right from the start. Anyway, we are back together now. She is Russian. She's really nice.' He walked into the kitchen even as Kitch and I stared at each other, aghast. Kitch buried his face in his map. Suddenly the nonchalance was gone.

A week later, I was back in Kenya on a two-day trip, again with Mina. This time it was to attend her cousin's wedding and also to meet Madan Dodhia, another client of mine from Myers. Kitch and Galiya decided to take a short break and come with us to check out the African wildlife.

Dodhia had shifted from Kisumu to Nairobi, after starting a real estate development project there. He still went over to Kisumu on weekends. We had a good meeting at his house, laughing as we talked about the old days and recalled a conversation we once had about Barack Obama.

I first heard of Obama – in early 2007, I think it was – from Dodhia's African driver and I had genuinely believed the man was off his rocker when he mumbled something about a man from the Kisumu region becoming the President of the United States.

'Do you know, Jai bhai, the first time Obama came here, he actually went from Nairobi to Kisumu by matatu, public bus, can you believe it!' Dodhia gushed. 'Of course, in those days he was just a young man trying to find his roots, nothing more. I think that was 1988. When he came back many years later as a senator, things were so different. I shudder to think what will happen if he comes now as President. The entire country will come to a standstill.'

Dodhia's Kenyan wife walked in just then. She looked at me through half open eyes, creased her forehead and then smiled. She had a lovely smile, like in a toothpaste advertisement. 'You're from the *baank*!' she said in her East African accent. 'Welcome *baack*!' She placed two plates of samosas on the table. 'These are mariakani,' she said, pointing to one plate, 'and these are lamb. I get you some tea.' She flashed her million-watt smile at me again and went into the kitchen. Her bum left a few seconds later. She had the biggest bum I'd ever seen.

On the wall separating the room from the kitchen, I saw a large framed photograph of Amitabh Bachchan with somebody. 'Who's that?' I asked.

'That is a superstar from Hindi films. His name is Bachchan.'

'I know that! I was asking about the other guy.'

Dodhia laughed. 'That is one of my best friends. He went into partnership with Mr Bachchan on some media business, a TV channel it was. But it didn't do too well and they had to sell it off. If only he had hung onto it, it would have been worth well over a hundred million dollars today. But my friend is making a film now, along with my son Chimpu. Some Bollywood movie... I forget the name. They want to launch a film with umm... oh yes, Mahadevan.'

'Mahadevan? Shankar Mahadevan, you mean?'

'Yes, yes, he is a south Indian star in Bollywood.'

'But he is a music director,' I said. 'He must be composing the music for the film.'

Dodhia looked confused. 'I'm sure he is acting in it,' he said. 'My son told me he is. Maybe he is doing both. These guys like to do different things, you know. They are very creative. I don't know anything about films but my son is very interested.'

That evening Mina and I were at the Oshwal Centre with our relatives, serving food to our guests. It is a custom at Gujarati weddings for the guests to be served by family members rather than waiters. It was the reception of Mina's cousin, a Gujarati Patel girl who was marrying a Gujarati Shah boy. Earlier that day, I had spent some time with the boy's uncle who lived in London now, after spending fifteen years in the US. 'One can't be too fussy about these things,' he confided in me. 'In this day and age parents have to be happy as long as their son marries a girl.'

Kitch and Galiya missed the garba and dandiya dancing before dinner. When Mina and I saw them walking in looking rather sheepish, we beckoned to them and handed them plates piled with food. A few minutes later, Mina noticed them picking at their food and shouted out, 'Eat well, guys!' She despatched a relative to go over to their table and serve them some more. I think Indians like to force-feed. It's our way of making guests feel welcome.

Towards the end of the function, we noticed Kitch and Galiya huddled in a corner, looking rather unwell. It turned out that the two of them had initially strayed into the adjoining hall – there was a Gujarati wedding going on there as well – where they had been ushered into the dining area at once. They had enjoyed a full meal there. It was only later, when they asked for us and no one seemed to know who we were, that they came out and noticed a second wedding party in the next hall. Kitch and Galiya were both lovers of good food, but two Indian wedding feasts in half an hour had done them in.

'But why didn't you tell us?' Mina asked later as we escorted the now distinctly green couple to their hotel room.

'We thought it would be rude,' Galiya said, smiling ruefully. 'We had planned to get away with eating just a little bit, but you forced us!'

A minute after entering the room, Kitch threw up.

Thankfully, there were no after-effects of these excesses the next day. Kitch and Galiya looked bright and raring to go, as we all went together to attend the traditional wedding ceremony at a place called Karen. It is named, I was told, after a Danish lady by that name. She lived in Kenya in the early twentieth century and married a Swedish baron, but was apparently best known for her affair with an English hunter – a real life story that was later made into a Hollywood film starring Meryl Streep and Robert Redford.

The wedding took place on the green lawns of the Karen Blixen museum. The bride was delicate and pretty and made to look all the more so by the hundreds of bubbles floating all around her, created by half a dozen kids armed with small buckets of frothy water and a bubble blower. The match was obviously a case of opposites attracting because the groom was a stocky and decidedly tough-looking specimen with a shaved head.

Mina's mother nudged me and whispered, 'Earlier, people used to shave their heads only at funerals. Now it has become a fashion and grooms even shave their heads for weddings.'

'Nowadays so many grooms get married in their thirties that there's not much hair left, anyway,' I conjectured. 'Maybe that's why they shave it off.'

'Thank god *you* had a head full of hair at your wedding, Jai,' my mother-in-law said, 'otherwise I wouldn't enjoy watching the video so much.'

The wedding went off well, with romantic Hindi film numbers wafting across the lawns and flower decorations lending a delightful touch to the proceedings. There were tens of young girls with freshly straightened and blow-dried hair imagining themselves as close substitutes for reigning Bollywood queens. Of course, where you have teenage beauty queens and wanna-be beauty queens, you also have a necessary evil, that abhorrent species: the gawky teenage male, complete with gelled hair combed from both sides to form a ridge in the middle, and an earring to boot.

There were two small hitches, though. One was that when the bride and the groom were asked to light a lamp at the beginning of the ceremony, the groom – probably unused to such bending and stretching – pulled a muscle, with the result that he spent the next two hours clutching his side. The spectacle jarred on the romance a bit. The other was that the power supply went off towards the end. But without much ado and with the ease of those who have dealt with such things in the past, people placed half a dozen cars at various angles near the mandap, and left them there with the headlights on. The rest of the ceremony was completed as scheduled.

Kitch had his own perspective on the wedding and I was copied in on the email he sent his parents that night and on the reply he received the next day.

Kitch comes from an orthodox Tamil Brahmin family, so I didn't quite understand all of it but it just shows how we all have a different take on life.

I'm reproducing his email. It went like this:

Dear appa and amma,

You won't believe what fun these Gujarati weddings are in this part of the world. They don't have it early in the morning like we do. They choose a convenient time during the day (or night). The wedding took place in the evening at a sort of park near a museum. Moreover, it took place after *the reception! The groom's head was clean shaven and there was only one pandit, a jolly Gujju Brahmin chap who didn't know much Sanskrit. I think he was just a part-time priest. He seemed to know only the basic shlokas and even got that wrong. He kept saying 'bakshanam' instead of 'bakshitam' in the Gajananam prayer. And he kept repeating the same prayer every few minutes, he probably didn't know much else! The puja itself didn't take too long and it was interspersed with Hindi film songs. They also served alcohol for the guests, who incidentally were a varied group. There were black, brown, white and even a couple of Chinese people! By the way, the priest also wrongly translated – for the benefit of the lay public – the first line of the Gayatri mantra as 'Oh god! The one who can swallow the whole earth!' That's completely wrong isn't it, appa? And, do you know, the couple didn't have to sit in front of a fire for hours, so they didn't have their photographs taken with watering eyes. Nor did they have to sit cross-legged all the time. So how come they have all the fun, huh? How come* we *don't have weddings like this?*

Love,
Kitcha

In response to this outpouring of information, he got prompt replies from both parents. His mum wrote:

Dearest Kitcha,

I think you have not attended the wedding.

You must have attended the reception or some party after the wedding and thought it was the wedding itself. No Indian wedding can be like that. And how can they invite Chinese people and all, I cannot understand. They won't even enjoy our food. I am glad you enjoyed it. But Kitcha, when I hear all this, I feel more and more worried about our Anand.

Kitcha, you and Jai have to take good care of him and make him more responsible. These days girls are so bold that he may easily be led astray. He is very innocent and trusting. Of course, we could not have wished for a nicer and more beautiful daughter-in-law than Galiya but it will be nice if Anand gets married to someone from our community. If he ends up with a Chinese or any such woman, that will be the end. Even thinking about it makes me faint. Looking forward to seeing you when you come here on Friday.

Yours affectionately,
Amma

His dad had sent only one line in reply.

How come we don't have such weddings? Well, Kitcha, all I can say is 'Thank god for small mercies'.

Appa

8

The Haunted Hotel

My client Lalwani had decided that he wanted to start trading currencies. He had also decided that he was pretty good at timing and with his choice of currencies and didn't want to rely on anyone's advice. He wanted to buy British pounds. 'But I don't want to buy at over 1.50,' he told me. 'Two days ago, it was about 1.49. If it goes back to those levels, I will pick up sterling for a million dollars.'

'It's very volatile,' I warned him. 'Would you like to leave a limit order at say 1.4950?'

'No, I don't like limit orders,' he said. 'Let us wait and watch.'

It was nearing dinner time and I was at the hotel. Mina had gone home to spend some time with her family and I had decided to relax at the hotel and take a reflexology treatment at the hotel's spa – something that had strongly been recommended by Kitch. Kitch, who two years ago was hesitant to so much as inhale the euphoric and sedative vapours that surround a spa, was now a much sought-after client at spas worldwide. He rarely saw a spa nowadays without getting his muscles kneaded, his head oiled and hammered, his body poked and prodded and having mineral rocks placed on his back.

While Kitch moved from one extreme to another, my own approach to spas had always been one of cautious curiosity. But I submitted myself to the reflexology treatment at the hotel spa. As I lay on my back in a sufficiently darkened room, a lady in uniform informed me that she would work on the soles of my feet. Nerves from all over the body ended there, she said, and manipulating them would cause positive ripple effects all over. At least that is what I understood from her rather jumbled explanation, in which tenses collided liberally and Swahili words mixed freely with English ones. Then she asked me which my right leg was.

'Why?' I asked, not unreasonably. It is not every day that adults ask you such a question.

'Because, for this treatment, I have to start with your right leg,' she said chirpily. 'So which one is it?'

I pointed, but my confidence in this lady had plummeted several notches. If she didn't know left from right, how would she know which nerve to manipulate? What if those ripple effects were negative instead of positive?

As it turned out, I need not have feared. She may not have known her right from her left but she knew her nerves. After a few minutes of doing something that felt remarkably like my dog nibbling at my toes, she did a series of moves from toe to heel that left me feeling happy and lazy.

I was lying in my room in much the same pleasant stupor, waiting for Mina to return, when the phone rang and Galiya's anxious voice sounded through the wire. 'Jai! Can you come to our room quick? *Now!*'

Still in my boxers and tee, I turned into a man of action. Damsels in distress never had to wait for long when Jai Patel was around. Galiya had sounded quite frightened, as if she had seen a ghost. I smiled to myself. Girls will be girls. It was probably some inconsequential thing. I hoped it wasn't a lizard, though. I had barely knocked once when the door opened and Galiya stood there. The entire room seemed bathed in some kind of eerie, mystical haze. Her face was white.

My heart turned cold. She pointed at the bathroom door to her right and turned to me. Even as she opened her mouth, the door creaked open and a large, shapeless white figure emerged from the bathroom and stood threateningly behind Galiya.

A shiver of fright went through my spine. 'G-gug-gug-goat!' I stammered. 'Run, G-ghastliya!

G-gug-ghostliya! I mean, r-run! *Run!*' I screamed. Grabbing her by her wrist, I dragged Galiya halfway down the corridor before I realized that the reluctant girl was not cooperating to the extent a chivalrous knight might expect from a distressed damsel.

'Run!' I shouted again, unable to think of any word beyond that. As far as I was concerned, the first step to dealing with the current crisis was to put as much distance as possible between us and the ghost. Then we could chew over the problem at leisure. There were a zillion things we could do. Check out of the hotel, stay at Mina's parents' house for the night, go to the airport, whatever. But all that would come later. At a time when I needed discipline and complete obedience, this imbecile girl was tugging at me and whining.

Then I realized what had happened. Numbed by the sudden appearance of a ghost in the bathroom, she was not quite herself. What she wanted was a bucket of cold water poured over her head. Pending that, I chose the next best option. It's how strong men save drowning novices; when the novice panics, flails her arms and starts screaming, the recommended remedy is to deliver a stinging slap to bring her to her senses before hauling her out of the water.

I swung my hand backward. Bringing it down on her bare shoulder, I dealt her a resounding blow. You cannot win a war without spilling blood. Ask Winston Churchill or anyone. 'Run!' I hollered in my most commanding masculine voice.

She burst into tears. 'G-go back there,' she sobbed. 'That's K-k-kish.'

'What?'

'Kitch.'

'Which?'

'That!'

'Where is Kitch? Is he still in the room? Is he hiding?'

'K-k-kitch in there.'

'I know that. But there was a thing behind you.'

'W-which?'

'It's not a witch, dumbo! Witches fly on brooms! It was a *ghost*. Didn't they teach you anything in Kazakhstan? That's a ghost!'

We were back outside their room now, Galiya pulling at my reluctant arm. The door was slightly ajar. The bathroom door was shut but the apparition was standing near the bed and had buried its head into a pillow. I watched, transfixed, standing gallantly in front of Galiya, holding her hand tightly. Somehow, we needed to find Kitch and get him out of the room.

The ghost raised its head from the pillow. Portions of a human face emerged from behind the white form. It was the face of my good friend Kitch.

'Kitch!' I yelled. 'What on earth are you up to?'

Kitch opened his mouth and made a frothy sound. A bubble formed around his lips and then burst.

'Jack b-beat me!' Galiya sobbed.

A cautious but closer look at Kitch revealed that the man – for reasons best known to him – had covered himself from head to toe with a mass of bubbly lather.

'Why don't you use a towel, you ass?' I said.

More frothy sounds came from his direction, accompanied by frenzied hand movements. Broadly, I understood that, for some reason, he couldn't go into the bathroom.

I decided to inspect things firsthand. I put my hand on the bathroom handle.

'Don't open it!' Galiya shouted. But I had already turned the handle.

If Kitch was a ghost, the bathroom was the mother of all ghosts; a mass of super-hot, volatile, silvery cloud, like some deadly volcanic lava. It was filled with steam and soap from top to bottom. A wave of heat slammed into me and water gushed towards me, threatening to scald my feet. I hastily shut the door and stared at the two of them. They looked back at me sullenly.

A thought struck me. 'I know what happened!' I exclaimed. 'You two have been making out in the bathroom!'

'Don't be an idiot, Jack,' said Galiya crossly. 'We were just watching TV!'

I looked at her incredulously. 'And that has wreaked such ruin? Such utter and complete devastation?'

'Kitch wanted to have a bubble bath.'

'I did not (pop) want a bubble (pop) bath!' Kitch protested. He was talking a little better now. Small bubbles still poured out from his mouth when he opened it and burst one after another, but his speech was clearer.

'Then what did you want?' Galiya asked him sharply. 'Niagara Falls?' Caustic, but I could understand her plight. Close to midnight after a long day, first her husband almost turns into a ghost and then, when the rescue team arrives, she gets slapped and shouted at.

'It wasn't *entirely* my fault,' said Kitch a little angrily, giving her what can best be described as a knowing look. He turned to me. 'I just wanted a regular bath,' Kitch said in an injured tone. 'There was a bottle which said "bath essence" so I poured it in. I thought it would give a nice scent, like in a spa.'

Bubbles fizzed and popped randomly at regular intervals all around him, revealing more and more of him like a slow, aquatic, foamy striptease. With every mini explosion, he looked more human and less like a giant, white, spitting, crackling amoeba.

'All of it?' I gasped. 'You are supposed to use a drop or two.'

'Well, how was I to know? I poured it in, turned on the tap and shut the door, meaning to get back after a few minutes. But there was something interesting on the pay channel and I forgot all about it.'

'Hah!' I said triumphantly. 'I knew this had something to do with sex!'

'We were watching *Cloudy with a Chance of Meatballs,*' Galiya informed me coldly.

'In that case,' I retorted cleverly, suddenly turning into a deadly combination of Sherlock Holmes and George Barnard Shaw and mixing deduction with sarcasm, 'perhaps that condom decided to take a little walk along the carpet by itself.' I pointed at the spot.

The couple looked at each other, aghast.

'Don't know how that landed up there,' Kitch mumbled. 'Anyway, when I remembered after about half an hour, I went to the bathroom to turn off the tap, but by then the whole place was filled with this… this stuff and I got completely covered with it. That's when you came in.'

'And got scared to bits,' Galiya added, not to be outdone in the sarcasm department. 'But please tell me, Mr Patel, do you propose to be of any help at all, or will you just stand there making wisecracks?'

'Watch me,' I said.

I went into the corridor and summoned a housekeeper. She entered the room and pushed open the bathroom door. 'Oh, no!' she exclaimed and pulled it shut. Eyes wide open, she looked at me and said, 'This has to be dealt with at a much higher level.'

'God?' I whispered in awe.

'My supervisor,' she replied and came back in five minutes with a small, wizened gentleman, veteran of many a watery faux-pas, no doubt. He suggested we leave the room – which we were happy to – and told us he would fix it in half an hour. Taking a change of clothes for Kitch, who now looked almost human, we trickled off to my room, even as Lalwani called again.

'Jai, what is pound at now? Quick, quick, quick!'

'1.4860,' I informed him after checking. 'It's below the level you were looking at. Shall I buy for you?'

'See, it is a very good thing that we did not leave a limit order. If we had, it would have been done at higher rate. Now we can buy it at lower.'

'So shall I place the order?'

'No no no!' he said firmly. 'I think it will go to 1.48. Let us try to buy at 1.48.'

Mina returned just after midnight.

'Jack saw a ghost!' Galiya giggled before Mina had even sat down.

Mina raised her eyebrows. 'That's a new one,' she said. 'So, what is the colour of an African ghost? Black or white?'

We took turns at telling her the story, three different versions of it. Each of us downplayed his or her role in the story while exaggerating the actions of the others.

Once Mina gets tickled by something (and it doesn't even have to be extraordinarily funny, it just has to appeal to her mood of the moment) she tends to laugh like she is having a fit and finds it impossible to stop. This was one of those occasions. She laughed till she spilled buckets of tears and it ended with her getting a stomach cramp.

Kitty called minutes later, filling me in on all their activities. The FIFA World Cup was in full swing and they had seen three matches already. They had booked some tickets earlier and our uncle Kaushik had arranged a few more. 'Jai, why don't you come along as well?' my uncle asked me, taking the phone from Kitty. 'There's a really festive atmosphere here this month.'

'I don't want to take a vacation just now, uncle,' I told him. 'If I had some prospects to meet, I could swing a business trip, but not otherwise. I did get a referral from a chap called Prospero Pindoria to his brother, but going by what happened with Prospero, I have no hope on that one.'

'Would his brother be Pedro Pindoria, by any chance?'

'Yes! Do you know him?'

'Then you simply must come, Jai. Pedro is a multimillionaire. I know him personally. He is crazy about just two things: women and football. Come over, Jai. We'll try to do something.'

'But big chief, I am not a woman and I know nothing about football.'

'Jai, just come! I'll help. These kids are having a great time. It will be wonderful if you join them. I will send you an invitation. I don't think it will take more than a day or two to get visas for both of you.'

Just before I went to bed, Lalwani called again. 'The pound has shot up to 1.51,' he said, fuming. 'They are just manipulating the price, all these hedge fund operators and speculators! Scoundrels! Criminals! But let us keep watch. If it touches 1.50 again, I want to buy quickly.'

'Should I leave a limit order at 1.50?'

'No,' he said firmly. 'I don't believe in limit orders.'

Back in Dubai, there was football fever in the office. There was a lot of group betting going on with everyone pooling in. I called Kitty's husband, Shree. 'Hey, Shree, I need to place a bet on one of the FIFA teams, who should I put my money on?'

'Well, Spain was my favourite,' he said, 'but they are struggling. I think Brazil will pick up steam.' So I scribbled 'Brazil' against my name on the betting sheet and, as history would show, bid permanent goodbye to a hundred dollars.

Compliance and finance approved my South Africa trip within a day of my submitting it. Clearly, we were still the golden boys.

Meanwhile, Peggy had been called to London to attend a global meet. Select members of the bank's managing committees worldwide had been invited for a top-level powwow. When I spoke to Peggy on the phone, she sounded rather low.

'It's all about football out here,' she said. 'I wish I knew more about the damn sport.'

'You took the words right out of my mouth,' I told her. 'I am leaving for South Africa in two days to meet a multimillionaire who is a football fan. My uncle tells me I will have him eating out of my hand if I talk football to him. Or if I turn myself into a pretty lady. Women and football are the two great loves of his life.'

'You should get Kitty and her husband to accompany you,' she suggested. 'One is a pretty lady and the other can talk football!'

I made a mental note of this. They were going to be there anyway. You never knew how these things worked; they might well come in useful.

'There's a huge power struggle going on here

at the top, Jack. I think it will be good for us if the British group grabs power. Both Mr Fergusson and Mr Weatherford strongly support us. Even the chairman thinks the world of us. But if they decide to have a Dutch CEO globally, it could change power equations everywhere and things could go against us. We are going to be here another ten days. Teams from each location are making a series of presentations. It's a real pain in the ass. Wish me luck, darling.'

'Kitch and I will take care of everything in Dubai,' I reassured her. 'You just focus on what you need to do out there.'

Among the other things I had to do on behalf of Peggy before I left for South Africa was to do a draft half-yearly appraisal, redo some of the job descriptions and submit the resume of each member of the staff for the central database. Peggy asked me to ensure this was done for all the members of our team. The last one I was sending out before I left for the day was Gavaskar's. I looked at the form he had completed. I was a bit puzzled. His first name read 'Gavaskar' and his surname read 'Tendulkar'. Both were surnames that belonged to two of Indian cricket's most famous sons.

'Hey, Gavas,' I beckoned to him as he walked past my room on his way out. 'Is this a mistake? Or a joke? I have to send out this information to London.'

'It is a joke,' he said sadly, 'and it's on me.'

'What do you mean? Is this really your name?'

'Okay, I'll tell you,' he sighed. 'You are probably the millionth person to ask me this.'

'You can skip the story if you like,' I said. 'I just wanted to be sure there was no mistake.'

'It's okay. If I don't tell you, you will not be at peace nor will I. But this should be a lesson to all parents not to indulge in personal whims while naming their kids.' He let out another heavy sigh and the room took on a gloomy hue. 'My father was a big fan of cricketer Sunil Gavaskar,' he began in a dull, hollow monotone. 'I was born on the day Gavaskar scored his thirtieth test century in Madras in 1984. As a mark of respect to him, my dad decided to name me after him. He could have named me "Sunil" like most people would have done, or even "Sunny" which is the cricketer's nickname. But my father decided that would not be sufficiently respectful to him, because Sunil is a common first name. So he named me Gavaskar. Our family name is Tendulkar. I became Gavaskar Tendulkar. Of course, at that time we had never heard of Sachin Tendulkar. He came into the limelight five years later and complicated things for me right from kindergarten. Expectations from me were sky high. In school, my classmates would get applauded even if they scored just twenty runs. But if I scored fifty, I was considered a failure! So in high school, I refused to play cricket. But then they insisted on making me a sort of manager-cum-coach, almost like a non-playing captain. I hated it. I spent most of my time signing autographs for younger children and the rest of it either explaining my name or answering snide remarks. At my first job, my clients refused to take me seriously because of my name… It's been tough, but I've learnt to take it in my stride.'

He turned away, shoulders drooping, head bowed, and I was left feeling like I had been drenched by a tidal wave of incredible sorrow. Like those tragic tales from history that envelop you in sadness and make you shudder. Or like the London Dungeon.

'Don't worry,' I told him, hoping to cheer him up. 'Think of Kitch! Kitch's name is Brahmadesam Balasubramaniam Krishnan. Once, he shortened it to B.B. Krishnan on a Thai Airways frequent flier form, and they mistook the dot after the initials for an 'o' and sent him a letter addressing him as Bobo Krishnan! And in the Arabic computer system here, they have left out the name Krishnan altogether and misspelt the rest. It's recorded as Bramesam Balasubra. The government officials look at him suspiciously if he says his name is Krishnan.'

A faint smile lit up Gavas's face and he walked away with his head tilted at a slightly optimistic angle. It was my turn to sigh, this time in relief. I had done my good turn for the day.

There had been a few other developments of note in the last few days. Rachel had, well, not exactly broken up with Tim, but it was becoming increasingly clear that they were drifting apart. Tim was busy with his work in Abu Dhabi and Rach had opted to stay back in Dubai. Tim was on the verge of teaming up with an Abu Dhabi-based sheikh to start a solar energy venture. Unlike Peggy and her Abu Dhabi-based boyfriend Dan who made it a point to meet at least a couple of times a week, these two had let nature take its course and gently floated away from one another. No heated words, no argument; in fact, nothing was said at all, just quietly understood and accepted by both sides.

Rach was beginning to get into the groove at work. It helped that we were around to help, because this bank took some getting used to. It also worked in her favour that our team was currently riding a wave of popularity. She had lost a good bit of weight in the last couple of months and she was looking as becoming as she did two years ago. This had won her a few fans around the office. People went out of their way to talk to her or do her favours.

Meanwhile, Harry, always fitness conscious, persuaded me to shift allegiance to his gym. I was quite happy to do so because Kamal Lalwani went to my current gym around the same time as I did and kept talking shop. I hate discussing currencies and stocks during my workout. Besides, he had this annoying habit of letting out self-motivating shouts while lifting weights and even on the treadmill. He moaned and groaned like a porn star. 'Aaah!' he went. 'Oooh! Oh, yeah! C'mon, Kamal, faster!' At first I found this amusing but it soon got irritating. So I was quite relieved when Harry suggested I join his gym.

Both at work and in the gym, Harry got going with his methodical approach. He was a stickler for punctuality and discipline. He was at the gym at exactly the same time every evening and his routine was clearly structured. Even at work, he was extremely systematic and regular. His clients always knew exactly what to expect from him. He had several prospects, most of them senior executives. His database and spreadsheets generated regular updates, portfolio charts and clients' birthday letters.

Omar, on the other hand, did things his way. First, he took the rather liberal auto loan that the bank provided and bought a BMW 7 Series.

Then, he took the housing loan, put in a million of his own, and bought a 6 million dirham place at the Palm Jumeirah. Once he had set up these 'basic' things, he brought in the account of one of Pakistan's largest industrialists, initially with remittance of 25 million dollars. It was the biggest account we had opened so far. That was Omar's style. He always focussed on the big fish.

Kitch had opened a couple of large accounts from Dubai and also met and cut some ice with someone from Tanzania.

It was good going. But minor irritants were multiplying at the same time. While compliance had relaxed their grip, facilitating easier account opening, the internal audit chaps were beginning to gnaw at us. Three months after Sunny Singh's account was opened, I got an email from them saying they had rejected his account because the account form had been filled up as 'Satwinder Singh Bali' while the passport copy read 'Satwinder Sing Bali'. I tried convincing them that it was just a clerical error at the consulate office and showed them copies of the previous passport which had the correct name. But they refused to consider the previous passport because 'the old passport is not a valid document any more'. Then they said I should either get a new set of account opening forms from him or get the spelling of his name changed on the passport. Since the latter could be a lengthy process, I troubled Sunny and his wife for six more signatures each and changed his correct account name to match the wrong passport name.

'Your bank people have no brains,' Sunny told me as I adroitly deflected the blame to my colleagues in audit. 'If they are asking me to sign so many papers because of this small thing, your well-paid senior colleagues are no different from the clerks in the passport office. In fact, they are far worse!'

A stream of frustrating issues followed. 'MILK' Shah's account got frozen because while I had submitted a utility bill in Mr Shah's name with their residence address, they wanted one in Mrs Shah's name as well. My plea that a husband and wife living together would not have two different bills didn't move them an inch. I had mentioned in my accompanying note that Madan Dodhia had been the governor of the Lions Club in Kisumu. A young upstart from audit sent an email asking me to outline the activities of the Lions Club in Kisumu. I told them that the activities of the Lions Club were irrelevant to the opening of the account. The reply came in double-quick time. It said: if the information was not relevant I should not have mentioned the club in the first place. Since I had mentioned it, I had to jolly well give all details asked for. I lost my cool. I sent a stinker copied to Peggy, Fergs and the head of audit.

'Is this audit or is this farce?' I queried, sounding like a Shakespearean character. 'I simply mentioned his governorship in the Lions Club to emphasize his standing in society. What does it matter what the club does? What is the Lions Club supposed to do, anyway? Promote drug trafficking? Conduct midnight orgies? I am all for audit. But it needs to be meaningful. It must make sense in the context of our requirements. We cannot afford to waste time in the name of audit.'

As I clicked the 'send' button I felt a sense of triumph. The next second, I got a severe bout of cold feet. As I re-read it, the feet got colder. No one wrote such directly nasty mails in this bank. Everything was couched and worded in an appropriately roundabout way. At any moment, I expected something to explode. I wished I could talk to Peggy. But she'd still be in bed; it was 5.30 a.m. London time. Luckily for me, the suspense lasted only forty minutes. Fergs sent a mail to the upstart copied to all of us. It simply said, 'The Lions Club is an international organization whose activities are well-known. We ourselves have been associated with them in the past. If there are no other issues, I suggest we proceed with the opening of this account.'

I had won this round. It filled me with exhilaration. I could feel adrenalin sloshing within me. For the rest of the day, I walked about with a swagger.

That night I was a tiger in bed.

9

A Quick Trip Home

It was Friday and I could only apply for my South African visa early the following week. So when I got a call from Kitch asking if I could spend a day or two with him in Chennai, I jumped at the offer. He wanted me and a few other friends to be mystery diners at his three restaurants – Kitcha Hut, Kitcha Inn and Kitcha Corner. I was quite excited about indulging in this rather novel experience. The idea was to act like a regular customer and use the opportunity to observe how well or badly the system functioned, something the owner himself might not know since employees tend to behave differently in the presence of their employer. Mina was still in Kenya. She would fly down directly to South Africa from Nairobi.

On the flight to Chennai, I noticed the airhostess paying particular attention to a passenger sitting on my right. I took a closer look. It was Shankar Mahadevan! I started. What a coincidence! It was just a few days ago that my client told me he had signed him up for a film and now here he was. I was a fan of Shankar's and was glad to have a chance to tell him that. The last time I was with a celebrity on a flight was when Katrina Kaif sat next to me on a flight from London. At that time, while every cell in my body urged me to strike up a smart conversation with her, I couldn't for the life of me think of anything to say. I didn't want to tell her I was her fan, because I had seen all of one film of hers. Once, I did think of something to say but when I turned and saw her long legs, my mind went blank. So I spent the entire journey discreetly eyeing her, but not exchanging a single word. On another occasion, I found myself just behind Amitabh Bachchan as we were walking out of the aircraft. As I walked towards the luggage area, I thought of a few bright things to say to him, including a point about Abhishek's acting in *Guru*. But he never came to the luggage area. It was only then that I realized that the luggage of superstars is probably handled separately.

But this was different. There had not been a single day in the past few months when I did not listen to the 'Iktara' song from *Wake up Sid*. All of last year, my favourite had been 'Sapno se bhare naina'. So I rather fancied we had this 'bond'. Besides, we had a common producer friend.

'Hi!' I said suavely. 'I'm Jai Patel.'

He smiled. Not in that cagey, wary manner

that most celebrities adopt while dealing with a potentially chatty fan inside an aircraft, but crisp and matter-of-fact. 'I'm Shankar,' he said.

'I know!' I gushed in a rather silly way and suddenly couldn't think of anything else to say. I think I simply have a problem when it comes to celebrities. I am just not at ease.

I struggled for a few moments. He busied himself with a book.

'I met Mr Dodhia last month,' I blurted out.

'Sorry?'

'Mr Dodhia.'

'Who is he?'

I was discouraged. How could he not know his producer's name? That too, of the first film in which he was to star as a hero. Then a thought struck me. Maybe it was still under wraps.

'It's okay,' I told him with a half wink. 'Mr Dodhia told me about roping you in as a hero in his film.'

He stared at me blankly.

Suddenly I started having all kinds of doubts. 'Er… maybe not as a hero…' I mumbled, desperate to see some trace of recognition on his face. 'Mr Madan Dodhia… he… er… his son is making a film starring you? That's what he told me. Mr Dodhia from Nairobi? Used to live in Kisumu,' I concluded unhappily. All I could see from the expression on his face was that he was getting irritated.

He shook his head. 'My name is Shankar Mahadevan,' he said sharply, like he thought I had mistaken him for someone else.

'I know, but this friend of mine said his son was making a film with you in it.'

'Where is this guy?'

'In Kenya,' I replied. 'His name is Chimpu.'

'Chimpu from Africa!' he exclaimed. Then he clammed up, put on his headphones and closed his eyes. I decided to give it a break. I slipped over to the back of the business class section to pick up a magazine. Behind me, I could hear Shankar talking to the airhostess. I chose an *Economist* and walked back to my seat. The renowned music director, stage performer and singer was once more immersed in his music. But not next to me. The airhostess had accommodated him elsewhere, a good three rows and fifteen feet ahead of me. Any further and he would have been seated in the cockpit.

Later, in the middle of the flight, our eyes met once but he quickly looked away, as though afraid that I would again start talking to him about my African filmmaker friends. It wasn't a happy flight and it was a disturbing half an hour after the flight. England had crashed out of the FIFA World Cup, beaten by Germany. Netherlands, on the other hand, was going strong. Peggy called to tell me that the English mancom members were so crushed after the team's performance that they had lost the will to fight for management control. The Dutch, boosted by their team's unexpected performance, were gung-ho about their presentations and were clearly getting the better of the Englishmen in every debate. It looked like some of the plum posts at the senior levels would go to the Dutch. If that happened, all the good work done by us so far would be undone.

I needed something really good to pull me out of my depression and I found it: bingeing on my favourite comfort food at Kitch's restaurants. I loved it. In fact, I would have no objection at all to making this a full-time profession – pigging out at restaurants and coming up with some important sounding comments at the end of the day. In this case, however, I think we managed to put together some pretty useful feedback at the end of day two. We agreed that two of the waiters were pulling down the ambience with their approach. We found that a very slight change in the arrangement of the tables would help accommodate four more chairs, always useful during peak hours. We calculated that the time spent bringing the bill to the table took up to seven minutes on average. This reduced the turnover as those who didn't find a table immediately tended to walk across to 'Raman Idli', the restaurant located just opposite Kitch's. The food there was not as tasty as Kitch's, the place was

not air-conditioned and the waiters tended to be sloppy, but they had much more space and many more tables. We spent some time working out numbers on a proposed profit-sharing arrangement with the waiters and the cooks. We also considered a few common tricks followed by some of the other eateries in town, like leaving bottled water on each table. The margins on drinks were much higher than on food. Getting customers to drink water, juice or milk-based drinks would raise profits significantly. We knew of a restaurant that charged separately for milagai podi (a specially blended chilli powder which many North Indians refer to as 'gunpowder') and oil if they wanted that along with their idli, sambar and chutney. We also considered keeping the price per idli low and charging for every serve of accompaniments.

'I wish I could buy out that restaurant opposite ours,' Kitch said. 'Then all the restaurants on this road would be ours. Maybe we will not air-condition that one. If it's too comfortable, people just hang around longer and the spend per minute goes down. There is no point air-conditioning a restaurant if it keeps potential customers waiting outside.'

On the second day, we had dinner at Kitch's house. His parents weren't too bucked about our new business ideas. 'You make all kinds of high-flying plans,' Kitch's father admonished him.

'And we have to spend most of our time trying to implement them.'

There was more berating and his father wondered aloud whether sending Andy to Dubai was the best thing that could have been done under the circumstances. 'Maybe we should have encouraged him to help run the restaurants,' he said. 'After all, what is the point of having two sons if both of them live abroad?'

Kitch's mother turned to me. She seemed to find me a more sympathetic listener than Kitch, whose only response to whatever his parents said was to keep eating and say nothing. 'I go to the school behind our house thrice a week to distribute fruits, nuts and sweets. Anand insists I go personally. Uncle has to go to Kitcha's restaurants every single day, sometimes twice a day. If the manager is not well, he has to spend several hours a day there, leaving his own work aside. I hope you boys will come back next year. After that you can make all the plans you want. We cannot have all the good children leaving the country! Our neighbour's daughter has just left to study in the US. I think it is all because of the government's silly reservation policy. They reserve seats for hundreds of communities, win all their votes, come into power and then make enough money for the next seven generations. And our children suffer and go abroad.'

The next day, I managed to spend a few hours with my own parents, when there was more conversation along similar lines. 'You have spent two whole days in Chennai,' my mother said, 'and I have spoken to you only as much as I do when you are in Dubai. Free food doesn't mean you should forget your own parents!'

'Mum!' I protested. 'It's not that! I'm here to advise Kitch on how to improve the business. I'm a highly regarded consultant, not a free loader.'

Later that night, I called up Madan Dodhia's son to clarify something that had been nibbling away at me for the past two days. 'Chimpu! Listen, tell me, who is the hero of your film?'

'I'm thinking of that hero from Chennai, Madhavan. Y'know, the guy in *3 Idiots*?'

'*Madhavan!*'

'Yes, why?'

'Your father told me it was Shankar Mahadevan.'

'Pappa doesn't know anyone beyond Amitabh Bachchan. He does not even know Aamir Khan.'

'What's the film about, Chimpu?'

'Oh, it's a period film, man. It's on Emperor Ashoka. I know it has been made before, but this script is too good, yaar. Mind-blowing! Only problem is, I am told that after *3 Idiots* Madhavan insists on a plane scene in every film. It is like his lucky mascot. But how can we have a plane in a period film? If you have any ideas, let me know.'

'I will. Good luck, Chimpu!' I rang off and swore silently at his father.

10

Fooled by a Football

I had a day and night in Dubai before I had to catch my flight to the Zuid Africaanse Republiek (that was the day I realized why the South African currency was referred to as ZAR). It was a good feeling not having to pay a visa fee. It made me feel very welcome. There aren't too many countries where you don't have to pay a fee as an Indian national. It's not exactly a travel-friendly passport, though I dream of the day it will become one.

Emirates had introduced a direct flight to Durban, the city that Kitty and Shree were now visiting. Mina was at the King Shaka airport to meet me along with Kaushik uncle, Kitty and Shree. Also greeting me was a large banner of Nelson Mandela holding the golden World Cup trophy and another of President Zuma. There were numerous pictures of a footballer in silhouette against a swirling backdrop of South African colours – red, orange, yellow, black and blue – the tournament logo. A large printed message in front of me said: 'Welcome to the land of the Zulu. Your soul may remember being here before'. Well, my soul couldn't remember anything from the past, but it was already beginning to get a sense of things to come.

Kapoor had fixed a breakfast meeting with Prospero Pindoria who, coincidentally, was in SA for the World Cup. I was dreading the meeting. It was one thing meeting him along with Kapoor and have him fill in the blanks, dot the i's and cross the t's as required. But the thought of being on my own in a coffee shop with a deaf, eccentric old man with a high-pitched voice filled me with horror. But Kapoor had decided that the way to Pedro was through his brother, so that was that

The magic of the World Cup was everywhere. You couldn't miss it. Everyone was in football t-shirts. Billboards spoke one language. There was one that read: 'The World Cup's coming to Africa. Let's keep it here'. Another one said: 'Kick out Malaria. Africa 1, Malaria 0'. There were many others along similar lines. 'Fan Fests' were being organized in private by various groups of people, complete with giant screens and free eats. Dutch supporters were travelling all over in their 'Oranje' caravans. Waiters at restaurants had a picture of a football stitched onto their uniforms and a little message underneath: 'South Africa can'.

I was sitting in the coffee shop at Hotel Beverley Hills, located in an upmarket suburb of Durban called Umhlanga Rocks (I will tell you later how the word 'Umhlanga' is pronounced), where Prospero had a permanent suite. I was told by my aunt that this was where Shahrukh Khan had stayed during a part of the IPL in South Africa. I was staying at the Oyster Box, which was just adjacent.

Smiling brightly and trying to erase the memory of my last meeting with the gentleman, I started off chirpily. 'So!' I said. 'How was Spain?'

'The pain in my feet has subsided,' Prospero replied, his voice echoing around the place, 'but I have got a frozen shoulder.' He made a couple of bird-like movements with his arms, bending them at the elbow and turning them in a circle. 'I can do this,' he said, 'but it hurts to do this.' He showed me a few more exercises. He had already got the attention of a good number of customers in the coffee shop. 'For my feet, I dip them in warm water three times a day. Morning, afternoon and...'

The others stopped eating midway as they eagerly waited for him to complete his timetable for soaking his feet in hot water.

He had put two sugar cubes in his tea by mistake – apparently against his doctor's strict instruction to stick to just one – and was busily engaged in fishing one out with a spoon. 'It has got half melted,' he said, unable to hide an element of glee from his voice. 'Morning, afternoon and evening,' he concluded loudly. 'The doctor says it is good for my feet.'

The waiter hovered around, asking us if we would like bread. He seemed concerned that Prospero wasn't replying. But Prospero's mind was elsewhere.

'I was there at the bull run at Pamplona last week. I go every year. It is…' He gestured with his hands, eyes closed, trying to think of the perfect word. 'Magic!' he said, spreading his hands wide like one who has just conjured up a trick. 'It makes me feel young, strong, masculine! *Viva Espana!*'

'Er… would you like some bread?' I asked him, trying to save the waiter from further embarrassment. 'Bread!' I repeated, raising my voice.

'Red? Oh, yes, red. It is supposed to attract the bull. But you know what, young man? The red colour is just to make it attractive for the spectators. The bull is actually colour blind. It makes no difference to the bull if it is red or yellow.'

Towards the end of the meeting, I desperately tried to bring up the subject of his brother, but he simply refused to even acknowledge the Pedro motif in the conversation. The meeting turned out to be a complete waste. Later, I called my uncle, who turned out to be far more enterprising.

He fixed up a meeting with Pedro that very afternoon.

Pedro owned a large resort overlooking the Indian Ocean at Umhlanga Rocks, close to where I was staying. One part of the resort, Kaushik uncle told me, was reserved for the parties he frequently and famously held, usually for footballers, cricketers, diplomats and the well-heeled. But I met Pedro at a sprawling mansion in another of Durban's prosperous suburbs, Lalucia Ridge. I was guided to his room – or den, as he called it. It was in the basement, a large hall at least 50 feet long. At one end was a 56-inch television. He sat at the other end, sporting the air of a reigning monarch. He was a tall man – by my standards – just over six feet perhaps, and sat comfortably on a bulging sofa. What was particularly striking about him was not his height, though. It was his build. If you asked an eight-year-old to draw a 'muscleman', the kid would probably end up drawing a body like Pedro's. He was wearing a t-shirt and track pants. His rippling muscles beat any steroid-pumped film hero's. Unlike his elder brother, who was distinctly European in appearance, Pedro was fair but with very Indian features. I wondered where his loyalties lay, what with an Indian father who had settled in Uganda, a Spanish mother and a lifetime split between Spain and South Africa.

On the two long walls were several frames which contained t-shirts signed by – as far as I could make out – football players. There were several other pictures of the football players themselves. One large picture was that of several elderly African women playing football. I wondered what that was about. Behind him were pictures of women, some known to me, some unknown, some of them posing with Pedro, some by themselves, but all of them dressed somewhat uninhibitedly.

'How's it, man?' Pedro asked, stretching out his hand. Deducing correctly that this was some form of greeting rather than any real intention of gathering information on 'it', I smiled and stretched out my hand to shake his. What followed was a bit of unintended comedy not unlike what happens sometimes when Western Heads of State meet the Japanese Prime Minister. I stretched out my palm in the regular Western style at waist level, while he swung it in from his right, chest high, fingers pointing upward, all bluff and hearty. Just as he switched to my style, I changed to his, resulting in some mild embarrassment, never a good thing to start a meeting with.

With a light smile and an air of imperiousness, he gestured to a sofa by his side. My uncle had told me that Pedro was better known in Durban as 'the Don' and at that moment the name seemed apt. I perched at the edge of the sofa. The sofa was so deep that if I leaned back, I would be practically lying down.

'You like football?' he asked.

'Yes,' I said guardedly. 'But I'm... er... still learning about it.'

'What do you mean, learning?' he rasped sharply. 'You're old enough to know all about it.'

I felt my heart sinking. It seemed to have reached knee level already. This guy was not going to be easy. He might not be hard of hearing like his brother but he seemed downright nasty, which was worse. A pang of self-pity shot through me. Why couldn't people open accounts based on one's knowledge of investments? Why did football have to come into it? And why did I keep bumping into eccentrics? Why not normal people? Maybe because, I answered myself, normal people had only normal amounts of money. And that was not something private banking businesses were interested in.

'But you do *like* football?' he said suspiciously, with the air of one all set to treat me like one if I replied in the negative.

'Absolutely!' I said, more confidently this time. And added, rather cleverly, 'The beautiful game!'

His face lit up. 'Ah!' he said and closed his eyes as if in complete agreement. 'So you would like to open my account at Abbott bank.'

'Very much,' I said. I liked it when people came straight to the point. But could it be this easy?

‘I have four accounts with four banks. At least 10 million dollars each. All those bankers are huge football fans. Maybe I can open a fifth account with you.’

I smiled brightly and respectfully. Also, I hoped, endearingly and winningly.

‘Who is your favourite player?’ he asked.

‘Pelé!’ I said at once. I knew very few footballers, past or present, but I knew Pelé as one of the greats and that was the first name that came to mind. Then, noting a slight look of surprise on his face, I added, ‘My all-time favourite player.’

‘Who is your favourite 2010 World Cup player?’

I blanched. The only two current footballers I knew of were England’s David Beckham and Bhaichung Bhutia of India. I understand enough football to know that India did not compete in football at this level, but I had no idea if Beckham was playing in the World Cup. I decided to take a chance. ‘Er… David…’

‘Viya!’ he exploded. ‘Yes! Daveed Viya! He is one of *my* favourites too!’ He pointed to a picture of a chappie wearing a red shirt. On it was written ‘DAVID VILLA’. I smiled weakly.

We looked at each other. He seemed to be sizing me up. I decided to change the subject.

‘Are you in the construction business, sir?’ I asked.

‘I am,’ he answered, ‘but all that’s handled by

other people. Nqobile takes care of my business and Govinder handles the finance and investments. In terms of time spent, you can say I am now, for all purposes, in the football business. My main aim is to promote football, particularly African football. For all of us on this continent, especially in South Africa, FIFA 2010 is a dream come true.'

We were back to square one. Football. Now I knew how Peggy must be feeling out in London.

'All I do for the construction business is to sign cheques. How it takes care of itself I don't know. Maybe He plays a role in it.' He pointed upward.

Sudden a flash of brilliance passed through my brain. I had remembered that infamous goal of Maradona.

'The hand of god,' I said, feeling terribly pleased with myself. Even a genuine football fan might not have caught this cue, I thought vainly.

'Do you know what we call the South African men's team?' he asked.

Much to my delight, I remembered this question from a recent quiz at my friend Harsh's place. Unfortunately, I couldn't remember the answer very well. I knew it was not 'banana banana' but it was very close to that. Could it be 'bamana bamana' or 'bawana bawana'? I decided to take a chance. 'Bawana bawana,' I said in a low voice, hoping he wouldn't notice the mistake even if there was one. It worked.

'Correct!' he said, beaming with pleasure. 'Bafana bafana! And our girls' team is banyana banyana!'

I smiled nonchalantly, intending to convey that this was basic stuff.

'Our football stadium in Durban is called Soccer City, agree?' he asked.

I didn't have a clue, so I nodded. It must have been the typical Indian nod, the one in which the head doesn't move up and down as in the West, but bobs about in a general sort of way which only a person whose parents are both Indian can ever hope to decipher. Pedro, not having this advantage, misunderstood.

'Correct again!' he shouted excitedly. 'You are shaking your head! So you know that Soccer City is in Johannesburg, not in Durban! Here it is called Moses Mabhida Stadium!'

I laughed happily, if a little nervously. This, I was beginning to realize, was one of those days when everything went right, even wrong things.

He pointed to another picture – a middle-aged face that conveyed nothing to me. 'What did you think of his performance in the last match?'

'Brilliant,' I said, taking a chance.

'That one, close to the interval…' Again he closed his eyes as if in reverence.

'What a goal!' I said. I was feeling confident now. This football interview was actually working in my favour. If my luck held out, in another minute I would have this fellow eating out of my hand.

He turned to me sharply. 'What goal?' he asked, returning to that nasty rasping tone with which he had begun this conversation.

I turned cold. There was a 10 million dollar account at stake.

'The goal he scored,' I mumbled.

Pedro Pindoria looked at me with contempt. 'Iker Casillas does not *score* goals!' he sneered. 'He *saves* them. He is Spain's captain and goalkeeper and, in my opinion, the best goalkeeper in the world.'

Pedro was eyeing me keenly. His gaze seemed to go right through me, making me sweat profusely.

'Let me ask you one last question. If you get this right, you get my account. If you don't, you don't.' He had now picked up a football and was spinning it around on his index finger. To my inflamed senses, he resembled Lord Vishnu with his chakra, all set to aim it in the direction of my neck. 'We have seen a lot of Jabulani in this tournament,' he said. 'Who is he? Is he a goalkeeper, scorer or defender?'

I looked him in the eye, hoping the correct answer would, in some miraculous way, be mirrored in them. But his eyes held no clue. My heart was beating fast. I was thinking hard. This seemed to be a trick question. Could it be somebody other than these? Who else was involved with the game? Could it be some minister? An official? No. A referee maybe? Possible. Or say, a coach. *A coach!* That was it. A coach. Not a goalkeeper, defender or any star scorer. It was some celebrity coach.

'None of them,' I said.

I had caught him squarely in the jaw, I could see that. All the ebullience, the zest had gone out of him in a jiffy. He collapsed on the sofa like a limp rag, a deflated superman. I knew I had given the correct answer. My confidence soared. I stood up and looked at him triumphantly. 'It's a coach,' I said with the air of a boxer delivering the final knock out punch.

Suddenly, he sprang to life and rose like a cobra. 'It is not a coach! Jabulani is the ball being used in this tournament! *This* ball!' he screamed, holding it up, his eyes glinting with the joy of having savoured an unexpected victory. 'You are a fraud! I have caught you, man. You are a *fraud*!'

I remained rooted to the spot. I was angry, but I had lost fair and square. There was nothing to keep me here. Who on earth knew they would name a dumb ball? I silently cursed the game and everything connected to it. Fool game! Grown men running around in shorts, kicking a ball. There was nothing to do but go back to my hotel and knock back a couple of whiskies.

Pedro quietly escorted me to the door. 'I cannot give my account to a man who does not breathe football,' he said, 'but if there is anything else you would like, let me know.'

'I would like to headbutt you,' I told him, 'like Zinedine Zidane.' And feeling rather proud of my riposte, I turned and walked off. I had no intention of staying in South Africa a day longer.

A refreshing sleep later, I was a changed man. To hell with Pedro, I thought. If nothing else, I would get some fun out of this trip. I went to bed that night after tucking into a quarter loaf 'bunny chow'. From taste and appearance, it seemed to be a local version of the Indian pav bhaji, except that here they scooped out the insides from a loaf and put the bhaji in the hole. During the meal, I also found out from the waitress why the word 'bafana' was repeated twice to describe the football team, something that had been puzzling me. The reason was simple. It was the plural in local lingo. One bafana, eleven bafana bafana. For some reason, it never occurred to them to use the dull and colourless 'bafanas'. I think they prefer to leave such things to the Brits.

I was all set to ignore Pedro for the remainder of my stay in SA, but Kaushik uncle persuaded me to keep an open mind. He had thought of something, he said, and promised he would get me Pedro's account if I hung around till the World Cup final, which was just four days away.

In the meantime, he had arranged to take all of us – my aunt, their two children, Mina, Shree, Kitty and me – on a safari to a place called Hluhluwe, in the Kwazulu Natal area, some four hours away. Their kids were thirteen-year-old Munna, a tubby, quiet fellow with a somewhat supercilious air about him, and his eight-year-old sister Dolly. Now I'll tell you how these typically ZAR words are pronounced. The syllable 'hl', for reasons I have not been able to fathom, is pronounced 'sl' except that you have to say it with a bit of a lisp. So 'Hluhluwe' is 'Slu-slu-way' (don't forget the lisp along with the 's', it's important) and likewise with Umhlanga (where I stayed in Durban). But the expats simply pronounce it the way it comes most easily to them; for many of them, 'Hluhluwe' is simply 'Shishloowee'!

Kaushik uncle told us that there were about a hundred lions and leopards in the area, which got me, Kitty and Shree very excited. While Mina had done this kind of thing before, it was quite a novelty for us.

'Papa took us on a safari last year but there were no lions,' Dolly complained. 'We saw only deer and giraffe.'

'It is all a matter of luck,' her dad explained.

'Sometimes you spend days here and see nothing. At other times, you can see a whole pride when you casually drive out in the evening.'

The next morning, we left at half past six, a good hour behind our scheduled time. Within the first hour we were rewarded with some delightful views of a whole family of giraffes including a baby – a little beauty that looked like eyelashes on stilts, so pretty that I couldn't move the camera away from her. I was sure she was female – no male could look so sweet. Later, we saw some rhinos, deer and warthogs. So many warthogs, in fact, that we quickly lost our fascination for them after the first few. For the next hour or so, however, we saw nothing and the kids started whining.

'Papa, where are the lions?' asked Dolly. 'You said we will see lions and leopards.'

'The first thing you kids must learn is patience. Look at that deer. It is known as the "McDonald's of the forest" because of the M-shaped black line on its behind.'

'I don't want to see the backside of a deer,' said the tubby kid loudly. 'Mama, where are my burgers? I want to eat them.'

'I've brought one for you now, beta. The other one mama will give you when we go back, okay, sweetie?' I always feel a little green when I hear huge kids being called such names by their mothers. I wonder if only Indian mothers do it.

We decided to give it another couple of hours and kept our eyes peeled on either side of the forest path.

'A leopard! I see it!' Dolly screamed suddenly.

All of us craned our necks in the direction she was staring. Kaushik uncle reversed the car a little. 'No, that's just a bush,' he said. 'The brown colour sometimes gives it the appearance of a cat. And those dry leaves in front make it seem spotted.'

We continued our hunt for the big two.

'Look!' I ventured, pointing. 'There!' I brought my voice down to a whisper. I didn't want the lion to slink away. 'There, on the ground, behind that tree.' It turned out to be a largish deer.

From time to time, my uncle would stop the car when we were nearing a passing vehicle and ask, 'Seen any cats around?'

'Nothing,' would be the standard reply. 'But we saw some buffalos (or deer or zebras or rhinos and, of course, warthogs) back there.'

At various points, everyone except Mina and my uncle discovered lions and leopards. Only, it turned out to be a tree stump, a fallen branch, a heap of sand, a bush or, increasingly towards the end, just a figment of our imagination.

'Look at those lions.'

'Where? *Where!*'

'Not lions, lines,' my uncle clarified. 'On that deer. White lines. That's a nyala. This is a female nyala.'

The car stopped again. 'Those,' my uncle said, pointing at a couple of tiny black dots by the side of the road, 'are dung beetles. They roll elephant dung into a tiny ball and bury it and lay eggs in it for the young ones to feed off. These tiny insects play a vital role in soil enrichment. It is important to understand how the entire ecosystem works. Everything here is a thing of beauty and wonder.'

'I am not interested in dung beetles,' Munna announced. 'No need to give us so many details.'

Mina and I exchanged glances. 'What a spoilt brat!' her eyes told mine.

'I'd like to throw the brute out of the car,' mine replied.

'Shh!' her eyes cautioned. 'It's not your car, it's his!'

Dolly continued to whine. 'Can't we see some lions? When I went with my class to that place in Jozi, we saw lions every minute!'

'That was a park, baby. They monitor animal movements and share information with other guides so the tourists see what they are looking for. This is the animals' natural habitat. It's not stage-managed.'

The tubby one made a rude noise.

'I'm tired,' Dolly whined. This was her constant refrain every twenty minutes or so. 'My eyes are paining from looking for leopards.'

'They should stop calling leopards spotted animals,' I said, trying to lighten the mood. 'Nobody ever spots them.'

'Ha, ha, joke,' said the eminently dislikeable teen. The chap had, I sensed, been nursing a grudge against me ever since his dad made him get up from the front seat (to make way for me) and join his sister at the rear of the SUV.

Just then we came out of a loop and hit the asphalt again. As we got onto the road we saw a car reversing rapidly. Almost immediately, we figured out why.

'Elephant!' we cried in unison. Just some thirty feet in front of our car, an elephant was walking towards us, looking distinctly angry. He lifted his trunk as if warning us to move back and waved his ears menacingly.

'Daddy! Are we going to die?' Dolly cried.

The elephant was huge. One gets slightly constrained in describing a very large elephant because you can't use the words 'mammoth' or 'elephantine'. We started reversing too, but the elephant continued to amble towards us. Suddenly, Uncle K stopped the car.

'What are you doing, Bablu? Go, go!' my aunt cried out.

My aunt calls my uncle 'Bablu'. This is bad enough in itself, but what is worse is that my uncle calls her 'Babli'. I suppose these things start early, perhaps during the honeymoon, and before you know it, the name has stuck and there's little anyone can do about it. You can't suddenly change these things when you are fifty or sixty. I'll let you into a little secret here. Kitch will kill me if he sees this in print, but I'm pretty sure he and Galiya call each other 'Kuku'. (Both of them! The same name! What sense does that make?) Of course, he stoutly denied it when I asked him, but his denial suffered from a lack of conviction and confidence that one associates with truth.

'Bablu' had stopped for good reason. An even bigger elephant was strolling towards us from the back. 'Good lord!' I said in a hoarse whisper. 'That must be the father! Gosh, he looks angry! And b-big.'

'Matriarchs, both of them,' my uncle replied. 'Males rarely remain with the family once they become adult. Keep absolutely quiet. I think the rest of the herd must be around here, and almost certainly some calves.'

The first elephant came right up to the car and pushed the car with his trunk. *Her* trunk, if one was to believe my uncle. It is kind of difficult to believe that an animal of that size could be female. Besides, I thought only males had tusks, but apparently that is not the case.

The car rolled back a couple of feet. 'We are going to die!' Dolly moaned.

Shree started murmuring Sanskrit prayers in a last attempt to get us out of this jam. We silently egged him on. Anything that might work was welcome. I hoped he was praying to the elephant god. The elephant kept pushing and Uncle K let her do so quietly, without starting the car. I was terrified but, to the elephant, it seemed to be a very natural thing to do. She was going about her task with a sort of casual disdain.

The elephant at the back was relatively passive; it seemed to be waiting for something. Suddenly there was a rustle and a crash, and a few small trees fell like bowling pins as a whole herd of elephants crossed the road in front of us. There were elephants of every conceivable size, about a dozen of them, including three or four little ones. One of them gambolled playfully on the road in a brief canter, before being gently but firmly guided on its way by an adult. The matriarch then casually joined them without a second glance at us. We drove away slowly.

'We are not going to die!' shouted Dolly.

'Wow!' said Kitty, who had been as quiet as a mouse all this while. 'How exciting! And what a wonderful video we have to show everyone!' Everyone looked in my direction, the man who had been saddled with the responsibility.

'I... er... no. I'm so sorry. I didn't... I mean, I didn't want to offend the animal. It might have got angry or something... Okay, okay, I'm sorry. Listen! I just completely forgot about the camera. I'm *sorry*!' I said, faced with a howl of protest.

Munna, who had hitherto maintained a reasonable silence, now showed his true colours. 'What a waste of a great opportunity,' he said in a superior tone and in that irritating voice of a boy who is on the cusp of manhood. 'I think we should just throw Jai out of the car. The lions will come and eat him up and then we can see them.'

'Don't say such things, beta,' said his mother. 'We are all disappointed like you, but it is not nice to talk like this about your uncle.'

'I don't care,' the kid said. I was now developing very strong anti-Munna tendencies. 'He missed such a good chance for a great video. Now no one from school will believe my story.'

'That's enough, Munna,' said Uncle K firmly, coming close to appeasing my wounded feelings, 'or I will have to throw you out of the car.'

My feelings got a second dose of comfort later that evening. We were staying at a cottage in the area, thatched roof and everything. Outside, we were getting busy with the barbeque or *braai*, as they call it in these parts. We had the coal going nicely. We had roasted some potatoes and corn. Now we were doing the boerewors. My aunt had brought along a few packets of biltong for us and some vegetable samosas as well (*samoosas*, as they are known here in SA). A lot of Indian words and even names had, I noticed, undergone a change from their original over the decades. Naidu had become Naidoo, Kuppuswamy became Cuppasami and Mudaliar was Moodli.

The tubby teen was rather aloof, not even volunteering to help. He had just brought his burger out and sat down comfortably – greed and anticipation nicely blended on his face – when a monkey sprang down from a tree behind him, grabbed the burger and quickly climbed back, looking the adolescent clearly in the eye while steadily chomping down the burger like a man. A scream of anguish froze in the tubby one's mouth as he writhed in distress, his second chin almost touching his chest, even as a smile of pure pleasure lit up my face.

I heaved a sigh of relief when the boy and his whiny sister were dispatched home the next morning to attend school. The rest of us left for St Lucia for a spot of whale watching. A bus took us to the beach, where we were given an informative talk about whales and their behaviour.

'Jai, Kitty says she won't come,' Shree whispered into my ear. 'The captain told us we might get fully wet and Kitty has left her... umm... spare underclothes in Durban.'

'She can buy new ones later,' I hissed.

'She says she won't. She only buys them from a particular shop in Chennai.'

'What an idiot! She's becoming just like Peggy.'

'Your boss?'

'Yes.'

'Even she buys underwear from that shop in Chennai?'

'I have no idea about her underwear. What I meant was, she too is finicky about a lot of things. *You* talk to Kitty. You're her husband!'

'But... but can't you do it? You've known her for twenty-four years!'

In the end it was Mina who talked to Kitty and soon the six of us – along with a motley bunch of twenty-odd tourists – were clutching the sides of the boat for dear life as we sped through the waves. Twenty minutes later, we were well into the ocean, right in the middle of humpback whale territory. What a sight it was! There is nothing more remarkable than seeing this mammal, almost six times the size of an elephant, hurl itself out of the water – doing a breach, it is called – and dive back into the ocean. It was magnificent. And what's more, they did it repeatedly, almost like they were putting on a show for us. For variety, they did a flip, turned sideways and slashed their fins at the others. The captain told us this was a group of males on their way to a meeting place in warmer water, which they would turn into a mating place. During that long haul from Antarctic to African waters, the males seek to establish supremacy and eliminate rival males. At one point, there were about a dozen whales all around us, moving at breakneck speed, diving and slapping and slashing at one another. How a fifty-thousand pounder could move at that pace, heaving itself in and out of the water like that, beats me. It was heady stuff.

'I don't see any hump on the whale,' Mina gasped, clinging to the side of the boat.

I spat out the salty water that kept getting into my mouth as I was doused by the ocean spray. 'Maybe it's called that,' I said, raising my voice to be heard above the din of the engine and the shrieks of the twenty-strong group, 'because it goes to Madagascar to get humped before coming back.'

'Shut up, Jai,' Mina hissed fiercely in my ear. 'There are children around.'

Things were now getting fast and furious. Shree's camera almost slid off his shoulder and Kitty almost slid off the boat. My aunt alternately bawled, screamed, puked and raged against her husband for bringing her along. She didn't take to the waters one bit. I too was beginning to a feel a little queasy by the time they decided to turn back. 'Everyone still there?' the captain joked. 'Those who aren't, please put your hands up.'

On the way back, I overheard Shree admonishing Kitty. Shree, when he whispered, was more audible than when he spoke normally. 'Look at the female humpback whale,' he croaked in a loud, hoarse whisper. 'It travels thousands of miles to mate, going without food for months, delivers the baby and then returns with the baby to the Antarctic, keeping sharks at bay the entire time. And look at you! Making a big fuss about your underwear!'

I would have thought she would be suitably chastened. But Kitty was in a sulky mood. She hadn't enjoyed the trip. She had got wet, she had nearly fallen off the boat, and she screamed every time a whale came too close. I think she's a bit like Kapoor. Wildlife doesn't really tickle her. She would rather learn a new dance, watch a movie or play a round of Pictionary. Through a gap in between the seats, I saw her glare at Shree mutinously and show him the finger. Girls will be girls, I suppose.

Back on the beach, the captain told my aunt to drink some orange juice. 'It will help you feel better,' he told her. My aunt was a completely different person now, with the land firmly beneath her feet. She hugged the captain, hugged everyone in sight and giggled like a schoolgirl. 'Is there anything I could have taken before the trip?'

she asked, the green and yellow colour on her face rapidly morphing into her regular brown.

'Hmm… maybe strawberry jam.'

'Oh! Does that help?' she asked, surprised.

'No,' the captain replied. 'But at least it would have tasted good on its way out.'

11

In Madiba Land

It was the day before the final.

Netherlands was pitted against Spain. Out in London, the great big mancom jamboree was over and done with. The Brits had given up. Sir Sidney would remain chairman but a significantly weakened one. The group CEO would quit and be replaced by a Dutchman. In Dubai, Fergs had already submitted his resignation, miffed by the changes in London.

Wayne Rooney and the English team's lack-lustre show at the World Cup were having repercussions on us too. All over AbAd, Dutchmen and their supporters were circulating one-liners on email putting down English football. 'What will the English football team do after winning the FIFA 2010? They will put down their play stations.' Or 'Maybe the FIFA should replace the English football team with Indians. They won't play any better, but at least the game will attract more eyeballs.'

Out here, there was going to be a do of some sort at Jozi, as Johannesburg is locally known. Kaushik uncle had asked me to make sure we all went. He said he had a surprise for me. The sense of expectation was palpable and the energy all around was beginning to have an effect on me. There was so much pride among the South Africans at having hosted the World Cup, it was touching. Class distinctions seemed to have been cast aside. Apartheid, reverse apartheid and all other forms of racism had been – for a month at least – discarded. Football was the one common religion and you practised it either by kicking a ball, watching the game or blowing the vuvuzela. Even a guy who wasn't a football fan could not help being swept up in the euphoria of the World Cup tidal wave.

As we neared the Soccer City stadium, the city's latest prized possession, we could see quite a crowd. The fun and games had started a good twenty-four hours before the big final.

We walked from the car towards what appeared to be the hub of excitement. We saw a striking girl, clad in jeans and an off-shoulder shirt, being ushered into the stadium. For some reason, she seemed to have caused quite a stir.

'Who's that?' I asked a blue-uniformed chap – probably a cop – standing just next to me.

'Shakira,' he said, sending Kitty into raptures.

'Oh, I want to see her!' she squealed.

'You just did,' said Shree, who tended to get irritated if anyone's attention veered away from the main theme of football. He was still a little peeved about having to miss a couple of matches while he accompanied us to Hluhluwe.

'I want to see her knowing that she is Shakira,' Kitty reasoned. 'Do you think that was really Shakira, Jai?'

'I think so,' I told her. 'She was looking the other way when I saw her but I noticed her hips, and hips don't lie.'

Grabbing Mina by the hand, Kitty dragged her optimistically in the direction in which the Latino singer had disappeared. Meanwhile, the chap in blue seemed to have lost something. He was patting his various pockets and looking all over in the hope of spotting it.

The two girls resurfaced a few minutes later. They had managed to spot Shakira on the ground posing for pictures with a football (no doubt a Jabulani) but in the melee, someone had grabbed Kitty's rather ornate and favourite stole. It was cold too – July is winter in South Africa – and the stole was the only warm thing she was wearing.

'I'm going to complain to the police,' she said. 'They can't do this to their guests.'

She stormed off to the cop who was still wearing a rather hunted look. 'Hi, I'm Kitty,' she said loudly, trying to make herself heard above the noise. 'Can you help me, someone took my stole.'

The cop, in addition to looking disturbed, now looked puzzled. 'Someone stole your kitten?' he asked.

'No! They stole my stole.'

'A cat stole it?' the cop asked cautiously.

'What cat?'

'Where is the kitty?'

'I'm Kitty.'

The cop lost his cool. A third emotion got added to his repertoire. He was a multi-faceted cop – if he even was a cop, that is. He might have been a security guard.

'*Yini lombhedo owenzayo!*' he snapped, stamping his foot. 'I'm in no mood for jokes! How can anybody steal a steal? What is this nonsense? But someone has stolen my wallet. *My* wallet!' he growled, breathing fire. 'And when I find out who it is, I will… I will steal his *ass*!'

Mina pulled a slightly bewildered Kitty away from him and we moved towards a makeshift stage where some activity was taking place. There was a group of people dancing a well-choreographed series of steps, many of which involved football moves including kicks and headers. This, I was told, was South Africa's indigenous *diski* dance, the word being local slang for football. This was followed by a little boy singing 'Wavin'

Flag' which had been composed by a Somali-born Canadian artiste called K'naan. I had never heard this song before, but in my short stay in the country, I had already heard it several times. There was a brief pause before the next item and most of the attention shifted to a group of elderly women wearing identical t-shirts with 'Vakhegula Vakhegula' printed on them. I wondered what it meant. Hobnobbing with them was a large, suited figure with a face that looked familiar. It was Pedro! The Don himself.

He was in animated conversation with my uncle. Then I remembered. That picture in the Don's den. It must have been the same group of elderly women. I mused on them for a bit even as I got jostled from all sides. Suddenly I was yanked out of my thoughts as the whole place got electrified with the inspiring voice of Shakira singing the 'Waka Waka'. I looked around for her and then realized they were only playing the recorded song. The elderly women broke into dance and were joined by a few others. Mina and Kitty, always ready to dance, rushed to the middle and plunged into a Bollywood-style hiphop. A few men – such naturals, these Africans – followed Kitty's steps with so much ease and grace, it was a pleasure watching them. Some Western bystanders began to shake a leg or two as well. Mina shouted out to me to join the group. I had actually been dying to, but the sight of Pedro had put me off. But the enthusiasm of the participants and the mood were such that I could bear it no longer.

A sudden rebelliousness surged over me. To hell with Pedro, I thought. I'd show him I didn't care. Much to Mina's and Kitty's surprise, I did a 'Dada'. Like former Indian cricket captain Saurav Ganguly at that historic moment at Lords, I ripped off my t-shirt and swung it around forcefully over my head. Then I hurled it in the direction of Pedro in an attitude of defiance and stormed to centrestage, accompanied by cheers from the multitude. We did the song first in English followed by Spanish, dancing with increasing gusto.

My effort found support from some of the other women. A well-endowed young lady was dancing next to me wearing a t-shirt that read 'Check Out My Assets'. Inspired by me, she removed her t-shirt and threw it on the floor as she continued dancing. A few others followed suit and soon there were half a dozen of us in various stages of undress, with me, the only bare-torsoed male, as the centre of attraction. Mina, taken aback by this unexpected development and wary of what else might follow, was giving me dirty looks, but you know how it is when you get caught up on a high. It's difficult to climb down. So, with a whoop and a holler, I gave it all I had. From the corner of my eye, I noticed a banner going up behind the stage.

It read: 'Sponsored by UniFoods Margarine'. Below this was printed: 'Live, Laugh, Play! The Vakhegula Vakhegula Way!'

Uncle K beckoned to me. 'Pedro has been behind the team, encouraging them and spending his own money. He has been asking me to sponsor them for a long time now. I have now agreed. It's a quid pro quo arrangement. He will give you his account.'

'What team? You don't mean these old ladies?'

'Yes. They are the *Vakhegula Vakhegula* or The Grannies. They are aged between 50 and 85 and are quite a force, very popular in South Africa. They are seeking sponsorship to travel all over Africa and to Europe. Now that might become possible. It also helps my company because we are promoting margarine as a way to a healthier heart. What better way than sponsoring a team of active elderly women football players? It's a great fit. We are talking to an American company to sponsor them for a US tour for the Veteran's Cup.'

Soon my uncle and Pedro were both on stage making generous remarks about each other over the microphone. A couple of reporters asked a few questions and both of them responded in turn. I heard my uncle telling a reporter that he had been considering the sponsorship at Pedro's behest for a long time, but that his nephew, who had come all the way from Dubai, was the one who pushed him into it. He was going to great lengths to promote my case in all this and I was grateful to him. I just wish he could have avoided calling me onstage. But call me he did, and buoyed by all the dancing, the semi-dressed women and the electric atmosphere, I rushed up without hesitating. Show business really does go to your head.

Uncle K looked at me in surprise. 'Put your shirt on, idiot,' he said. 'They'll be taking pictures. Why are you still wandering around half naked?'

Suddenly I felt extremely silly. I had no idea where my t-shirt was. The initial high had worn off and my fellow dancers seemed to have either disappeared or put their shirts back on. I was beginning to realize the acute discomfort of being shirtless. I lied that it had fallen somewhere on the dance floor.

He beckoned to one of his guys and asked them to try and find my shirt.

'What colour?' they asked.

'Black,' I told them.

It took them less than a minute to throw it to me. The press had already started clicking, even as I was just about struggling to get inside the t-shirt. It seemed rather small. It also had some words printed on the front.

'This isn't mine!' I wailed to my uncle.

'Just wear it!' he snapped impatiently. 'It's only for the picture.'

So I did. When he saw the shirt with the words 'Check Out My Assets' neatly printed on it, he nearly fell off the stage.

'You moron!' he hissed. 'At least wear it the other way!'

Smart idea, I thought. In one swift motion, I peeled it off me, quickly turned it around, pulled it through my neck and down, trying hard not to leave a gap between the shirt and my jeans. A fresh wave of laughter emanated from the crowd and following the source of their laughter, I found that it was me. To my horror, I discovered that the back of the t-shirt had something written on it too, and it now adorned my chest. Hastily, I rushed off the stage, filled with shame. But the damage had been done.

The next day was a big day for South Africa, the day of the World Cup final. It was a big day for me too. I woke up bright and early. And almost immediately broke into cold sweat when I realized what was in store for me. Of course, not all the local newspapers had my picture on the front page. A few were considerate enough to put it only on their sports page. A glutton for punishment, I went through the agony of looking up my photograph in three of the newspapers. In all of them, the supremely well-built and flamboyantly suited Pedro shared the dais with my uncle, the director of UniFoods, almost as tall and elegantly dressed in grey chinos, a white shirt and a blue jacket. Standing between them, in the first photograph, was a sweaty and obviously inebriated young man of medium height, both of whose armpits were on display as he struggled to remove a tight black t-shirt. With his face half covered by the t-shirt and somewhat contorted by the effort, he presented a rather comical picture. In the second, the chap wore on his face a distinct sulk, and on his body the same tight t-shirt with an inscription in front that read 'Check Out My Assets'. In the third – this was on the front page – the same fellow, this time with a silly simper on his face, was, once again, wearing a black t-shirt that was several sizes too small for him. This one read 'I Have Two!'

It wasn't without its funny side, but it would have been a lot funnier if it had happened to someone else. But boy, was I glad this had happened to me in a foreign country. I briefly contemplated – my blood curdling as I did so – how I would have felt if this had happened to me back in Dubai or in Chennai. I would never have heard the last of it.

My thoughts were interrupted by a phone call from Kamal Lalwani.

'Jai! You know that zuluva?' he started, with no thought about anything in the nature of a greeting, let alone pleasantries.

'Zuluva?' The word was new to me.

'Yes, yes, yes!' he barked impatiently. 'You're in South Africa, no?'

'Yes. Are you referring to the Zulu tribe?'

'Zulu tribe? What nonsense,' he said sharply. 'No, man. What I want to do with Zulu tribe? I mean that thing, what they're all blowing there in South Africa. Pah pah pah all day long.'

'You mean the vuvuzela?'

'That is what I am saying. Vuzula! When you come, you bring one, okay? Don't forget. I am thinking to manufacture in India. I think it will get too popular, here, there, everywhere. In India, there is very good scope for this lazuva.'

'Vuvuzela.'

'Yes, yes, yes! That is what I said. I tell you it will catch on like wildfire. I want to tap the market. Very important for me, Jai. Don't forget, okay? I think very big margin in this vuzulala. Too big, too big. Okay, okay. Now bye'.

Once more I read the article and looked at my pictures in the papers. Then I folded them, tore them up and threw them away. It might be an interesting, even entertaining story to tell one's grandchildren. But one hoped that when the time came, there would be a stock of other stories, refined, dignified and more likely to instil in them appropriate values and a sense of pride in their grandfather.

That evening the Soccer City stadium looked like a brilliantly lit, giant UFO. There we were – Shree and Kitty, Mina and I, Kaushik uncle with family, Pedro with a team of red-clad supporters and tens of thousands of football fans. Munna and Dolly wore on their cheeks the colours of the Dutch flag which eager hands had painted outside the stadium in exchange for a hundred rand.

If you were at the stadium that day with your eyes closed, you would have been forgiven for thinking that you were in a land of a million monster mosquitoes, such was the effect of the myriad vuvuzelas being blown at the stadium, a loud, persistent and insanely nagging buzz. Two giant video screens flashed the countdown, and the ceremony, a kalaeidoscope of colour, began to a cacophonous roar. Thousands waved their flags, raised their hands, clapped and screamed. This was a night that carried with it the hopes and aspirations of millions of people in a young country with a chequered past.

The light effects were spectacular and the next half hour was sheer magic. A quartet of aircrafts suddenly appeared over the stadium and in the middle a helicopter hovered in midair, flashing a series of pictures on the ground in an incredible slide show, pictures that traced the history of the FIFA World Cup, combining it with frozen frames of poignant FIFA 2010 moments, with newspaper headlines flashing the choice of South Africa as the host, the flags of the participating countries and more recent clips from the matches – moments tracing ecstatic heights and gloomy depths. The effect was electrifying. Africa had hitherto always remained on the sidelines even as the rest of the planet basked in the glory of growth. This was one event that put Africa in the spotlight. The whole world was watching.

Thousands at the stadium and millions glued to television sets across the earth were enjoying Africa's impressive ability to turn on a party. Members of the African band Ladyship Black Mambazo played a song, keeping the spectators enthralled by coordinating foot movements magnificently on pictures of keyboard keys that were projected on the ground by the overhead helicopter. Shakira was in impressive form and had the crowd on its feet and screaming for more. There was a beautifully choreographed piece with hundreds of performers dancing and forming the shape of a vuvuzela. There was another where stage dancers representing participating countries held coloured flags and, after a series of superbly arranged moves, left just the two finalist teams 'facing off'. The crowd's energy levels remained at a perpetual high, their enthusiasm infectious. All of us screamed, cheered, jumped, whistled and then, just a little later and in complete contrast, we silently rose as one and cried. For those few moments, we stood dumbstruck as we recalled the sacrifices that the man in front of us had made for the people of his country. He waved at the crowd as he was driven in a vehicle around the ground, this man who had displayed courage, compassion and conviction as few men ever have and few ever will. I joined the rest of the stadium as they chanted his name. 'Madiba, Madiba, Madiba!' We could not be like him but we could show him how much we appreciated and valued his sacrifices and his contribution, not just to South Africa but to humanity. We got an opportunity to do just that, that day. And I think he heard us.

I didn't see much of the match itself. In any case, there was nothing I found particularly noteworthy. No head butts or hand of God, nor any spectacular overhead reverse kicks. In fact, the only overhead kick was landed by a Dutchman on the chest of a rival. I was too busy watching the people around me, some shouting with almost inhuman energy, others screaming with uncontrollable frustration, all equally passionate. Shree wore an orange t-shirt that he had picked up the previous day. It read: 'Paul on the Ball'. Just behind me, a big red-faced Dutch supporter wore an orange one that said, 'To Hell with *Paul*p Fiction' and beneath it, 'Go, Dutch! Go!' Well, the Dutch tried their damnedest. But

they couldn't get going. Towards the end of the game, the Spaniards managed to sneak the ball in. As the Spanish captain – the guy who nearly put paid to my chances with Pedro by being a saver instead of a scorer of goals – broke into tears and covered his face. Pedro himself, standing two rows ahead of me, clenched his fists, pumped them over his head and let out a roar that was heard by every Spaniard (or half Spaniard) the world over.

The next morning, Pedro asked me to meet him at his hotel so he could sign the account documents. When I called him from the lobby, he asked me to come up to his room. The door was half open. I knocked, entered and almost stepped on the toes of the longest pair of legs I had ever seen. They were bare and smooth and shapely and... well, in short, they were quite sensational.

Coming my way as they did when I was expecting Pedro, my heart can be forgiven for behaving in an unusual fashion. First it stopped beating. Then it beat rapidly, and finally in fits and starts. I excused myself and was about to rush out when the owner of the legs began to purr. In a low husky voice, she told me to sit down and said that Pedro was in the bathroom and would be out in a minute. I sat stiffly on a chair while she lounged comfortably on the bed.

When I mustered up enough courage to look up, she was sitting there, her legs crossed, all poise and queenly dignity, and smiling at me – or perhaps at my obvious discomfiture. She was, I could see now, actually fully dressed and not in her birthday suit as I had presumed. But it was one of those flimsy, minimalist dresses no doubt designed in Paris or Milan and probably costing a bomb. Back in Chennai, still the bastion of traditionalism, most women would have hesitated to use it even as an undergarment.

The outcome of that morning's meeting with Pedro was the signing of the account documents and a promise to remit 20 million dollars. That in itself was enough to take my mind off my front-page splash the previous day. It did, however, cross my mind during the occasional black moments that I lapsed into, that there ought to be some kind of t-shirt censorship. It appeared to me that t-shirt makers carried their slogans a bit too far. If you wouldn't print something in a newspaper, I felt it shouldn't be on a t-shirt. But the others didn't seem to agree. Kitty and Shree took a far too flippant view of the matter, seeing nothing but humour in the whole regrettable incident. Mina, on the other hand, took a narrow, prudish view and insisted that if I had not removed my t-shirt in the first place, none of this would have happened.

That evening, I had the honour of being invited to dinner at Pedro's house along with my uncle, aunt, Mina, Kitty and Shree. My aunt chose not to come – she was not comfortable with Pedro's parties. She didn't like the way he paraded his trophy women and disliked the way he behaved when he got drunk. I knew what she meant about the trophy bit. And I'm not talking about the photographs in his room.

As we huddled together and chatted, many fair women and strong men – no doubt Durban's leading lights – walked in to enjoy the Don's hospitality. Pedro was at his ebullient best, taking great pains over every guest, every spouse and every partner. Wine flowed like South Africa's Orange river, much of it of local vintage. Pedro had arranged for a team of masseuses who went around kneading necks and tweaking toes as the guests sat smoking cigars or sipping wine.

An hour into the party, Pedro put his arm around me. 'Alcohol is an incredible thing,' he told me. 'A little while ago, none of these women seemed pretty to me. But now,' he said, giving his glass an appreciative look and a congratulatory shake, 'now, after a few drinks, they all look beautiful.'

A few minutes later, Pedro produced his partner for the evening, a woman of bewitching beauty. He seemed to like them tall. This one was taller than me, and looked even taller in her heels. She wore a long black cape – at least I think it was a cape, it was this Batman-like thing – which stretched behind her from her neck down to her heel. It provided an interesting backdrop to her delicate curves and served to accentuate the shortness of her dress and the exquisite pearly white of her skin.

Shree, who happened to be talking to me when the woman was ushered in, froze completely. Halfway through a sentence on how Beckham gets the ball to bend, he stopped and never completed it. In the wake of such beauty, he probably felt speech had no meaning. Even the words that he had already uttered appeared resigned to their fate – unwanted and incomplete, they broke into tiny fragments and crashed to the floor.

And it wasn't just Shree. All around, people had stopped talking and started staring. Only, some did it more discreetly than others. 'Jai!' Shree whispered, finding his voice. 'Look at her. She is the most beautiful woman I have ever seen in my life! Better than any supermodel! Just look at her, Jai… Oh, my god!' For a moment I thought he would swoon and pass out. Not that I was immune to human emotions, of course. My mind too was in a whirl.

'Is she the same one you met in the room?' Shree asked.

'No, that one was taller. Those legs almost came up to my chest.'

The girls walked over in the meantime. 'You guys are disgusting,' Kitty said.

'One look at that vampish woman and you two are behaving like besotted schoolboys,' Mina added.

'Which woman?' said Shree bravely, looking everywhere but the right direction.

'Oof, stop it!' said Kitty. 'You can't even lie properly.'

Around midnight, Pedro changed tack. His decibel level rose. He became less cheerful. Small things started to irritate him. He found fault with the food. He seemed to take a sudden dislike to one particular waiter. He called his butler (whose name, believe it or not, was Lovemore) and asked him to bring the loo to him. Lovemore, no doubt an old hand at this kind of thing, held him gently by the arm. 'I'll take you there,' he cooed.

'No!' Pedro thundered. 'Bring it here!' There was a pause. Pedro appeared to be grappling with some puzzling issue. 'Look,' he said. His tone had changed from angry to forlorn. 'There is Pedro and there is the loo. Why should Pedro go to the loo every time? Bring the loo here! Fair's fair!' he concluded a little tamely.

Lovemore's kind, experienced and firm hands finally led Pedro to the loo, much against his desire. Upon his return, his mood had undergone another change. He seemed to be eager to share something with his public. He stood up on a chair. 'Friends!' he shouted. 'F-friends and countrymen! Lend me your ears!' He turned around slowly, heaving gently, trying to establish eye contact with the audience. 'Ladies and gentlemen, friends and Romans and most importantly, fellow South Africans. Let us today raise a toast to the host.'

There were a few sycophantic claps.

'No, not me,' he clarified. 'The host of FIFA 2010. Africa, my friends and dear women, is no more the dark continent. It is a beacon of light. A ray of hope. Friends and South Africans and glorious Spaniards… *Viva Espana!* Lend me your ears.' He spotted his partner, the 'vamp', and his mood changed from patriotism to romance.

He got down from the chair unsteadily and beckoned to her with his index finger, curling it slowly and repeatedly. 'Come here, baby, and lend me your ears.'

Which she did. Attracting every eye in the room, she sashayed her way to Pedro, her dazzling smile lighting up the place like the beacon that Pedro had spoken of. And when she reached him, she lowered herself into his lap and lent him her ears. For the rest of the party, the Don busied himself nibbling at her earlobes and whispering sweet nothings into her ears. One by one, the guests excused themselves and started leaving.

I found myself talking to the man who was

in charge of Pedro's construction business. He presented his business card to me. It read 'Nqobile'.

'N-q-obile,' I read out. 'Are N and Q like initials?'

'No,' he said. 'It is part of my name. Like this.' He said his name.

I stared at him incredulously. He repeated it, making a noise like that of horse trot intertwined with 'Nobeelay'. Of the letter Q there was no sign whatsoever.

'Why are you making that sound?' I asked. 'That horse trot sound. Surely that's not part of your name? And where is the Q in this?'

'There is no Q sound,' he said. 'The N followed by Q indicates a click consonant.'

'A what consonant?'

'Click consonant. It is part of some South African words or names. It is pronounced in different ways. Like *Xhosa*.'

'Hosa?'

'No, Xhosa,' he said, pushing his tongue against his upper teeth and making a clicking noise from the sides of his mouth before proceeding with the rest of the word.

'So the full word is actually that click sound followed by hosa? What does it mean?'

'Don't ask so many questions. Just repeat after me. Xhosa.'

'Khosa?'

'Xhosa.'

I shut my eyes and gave it a shot.

'No!' he exclaimed. 'Not Tik-khosa, silly! *Xhosa*. Less of your tongue. Bring more teeth into play. Watch my mouth. Xhosa!'

'Xhosa?'

'Yes! You got it! *Xhosa!* That is the community of Nelson Mandela. It is spelt X-h-o-s-a.'

'But what about the horse trot sound in your name?'

'Oh, that is a different click. There is a third click as well which goes like this.' He pressed his lips together and made a noise. 'See?'

We were now joined by Govinder, Nqobile's colleague and Pedro's finance guy. 'It is like calling a puppy,' he said helpfully.

'In Mumbai, they call people like that,' I told him. 'But fancy having a sound like that as part of a name!'

'Okay, now say my name!'

'Say it to his satisfaction,' Govinder drawled, 'and I will ensure that we double the funds in Pedro's account with you!'

I attempted it.

'No. Here, the click is not separate,' said Nqobile. 'It should form part of the name.'

I tried several times.

'No! Not click-nobile. Like this, man! Nqobile! Nqobile!'

I repeated it.

'Wrong! It should start with N, not with T!'

Feverishly, I kept trying. I was getting a little desperate. I wasn't going to let a thing like this come between me and another 20 million dollars.

'Not in fits and starts. Smoothly, casually, man. Remember it's just one word. Nqobile!'

'Like this?'

'Where is the N sound? It's not just the click followed by obile. It is Nqobile!'

'Nqobile!'

Nqobile narrowed his eyes and tilted his head. 'Say it again.'

'Nqobile!'

'Again!'

'Nqobile! Nqobile! Nqobile!'

'Very good! Fantastic!' Nqobile exclaimed, downing a quick peg in celebration. 'You are now one of us!'

'I did it!' I shouted excitedly.

'You did, man, you did!' Nqobile said, looking equally pleased. 'That is what my name means, Nqobile – to triumph, to succeed.'

I beamed and turned to Govinder. 'I did it!' I told him, all pumped up. He didn't reply. He was sprawled across the sofa just behind us, mouth open, snoring gently every time his stomach swelled up and and letting out a teeny wheeze when it subsided.

'Jai,' Mina whispered in my ear, 'I think we should leave. Pedro's asleep and most of the guests have left.'

I wished Nqobile goodnight and we trooped past our host, who was sleeping peacefully on the left breast of his friend. She winked at me and blew me a kiss. Pedro stirred and came to life.

'Leaving, Jai?' he asked. '*Et tu Brute*?' He looked around at the almost empty room and shook his head in a resigned way. 'No friends, no Romans, no countrymen.' Then, quickly shrugging it off, he resumed his nibbling, this time on another part of the young lady's anatomy.

12

'Coz Love Has No Season, No Reason

July 2010 was South Africa's time in the sun. To a man, the country cheered like they had never cheered before. First for Bafana Bafana. Then for Ghana, the sole African nation remaining in the World Cup. Then for Soccer City, and finally for themselves, the super successful host country. But now the party was over. And it was time to move on.

Our new regional CEO was a chap called Peter van Hart, a Dutchman. The new compliance man was Jan Kahn. Nathan had so far managed to cling on, though there were rumours that he was on his way out. The top guys in corporate bank and treasury were also preparing to leave. As if the existing confusion in structure was not enough, the CEO had set up an NRP team akin to the NRI team to cater to off-shore businesses from resident and non-resident Pakistanis. To run that team, we had yet another head, a former colleague of mine,

Ahmed, whom I had not particularly liked when I first knew him. It wasn't just he I objected to, but the fact that in addition to premier banking, investment services, NRI team and private banking, we now had one more dimension to add to the whole 'wealth management' scenario. It was apparently Jan, in his capacity as the new CEO's close buddy and trusted advisor, who had been instrumental in getting Ahmed in and wrangling a good position for him.

'Ahmed's not a bad sort, Jai,' Kitch told me. 'Once you get to know him, he's pretty decent.'

'The creep sent me an invite on Facebook yesterday,' I told him. 'You should see his Facebook page! Ahmed talks quite well, but he writes a lot of rubbish. He's always been like that. I have kept a couple of his emails from Myers at home in my "funny file". On Facebook, he's put up a picture of himself wearing just a pair of unbuttoned denim shorts, bare torso and all. He seems to think he's some kind of love god. He's thirty-five and has three kids, but on his info page he has the gall to say he's interested in women and is looking for dating and relationships. He's put in a little bio... here, let me show you.'

I logged in and went to Ahmed's profile. Under 'About Me' he had written: 'I'm smooth. I'm sexy. I value my skills. I respect my intelligence. I act on my feelings and think for my beliefs. Believing is doing. I love what I am. Life is nasha. Live with junoon. DIL DIL PAKISTAN!'

'Can you believe it? Such nonsense!'

Kitch stifled a laugh. 'I know, Jai! But that's just the way he is. A lot of bluster and bravado, a bit immature perhaps, but he's all right. Do you know I took him to see a Tamil movie once, while we were at Myers.'

'What!'

'Yeah, we happened to bump into each other in Deira one evening. He was at a loose end and decided to join me at Galleria. He enjoyed the film, actually, and kept repeating some of the punch lines later. He's okay, Jai. Don't worry. You're getting too tensed about these small things. Take a chill pill.'

But I did worry because over the next few weeks, it became obvious to us with sickening clarity that we were no more the bank's blue-eyed boys. We probably never were, but it had been nice knowing that the chairman and regional CEO thought highly of us. Now the chairman had been reduced to a puppet and Fergs had left. The new guys didn't know us and didn't seem to care.

Ahmed's position of strength even before opening his first account was obvious because he had been given a car parking slot, something that Kitch and I still didn't have. The bank was in a very busy location on Khalid Ibn Al Waleed Road and space was at a premium. A parking slot was the ultimate test of power at AbAd – or AdAb, as it was now called. (Apparently, the Dutch management felt that since they were the stronger faction now, the name Adriaan should appear before Abbott. Hence, AdAb). Our team had three slots which we shared. Peggy could have kept one for herself, but she was gracious enough to allow all seven of us to share the three. It helped if some of us were travelling, but there were times when all of us were in Dubai and on those days parking was a nightmare. Traditionally, the regional CEO had always had two parking slots to himself and it was a matter of pride for Fergs – and now Peter – that he could park in comfort across two slots.

At Myers, your pay packet determined your standing. Here, the remuneration was quite hush-hush. Nobody knew anything for sure, although everyone kept talking about it all the time; about how much money Alpha made or how Beta was done in by a scheming management coterie which was rumoured to have kept a substantial part of the bonus pool for itself. So, for all practical purposes, parking slots determined the hierarchy for the grapevine. In keeping with this, therefore, Ahmed had already edged past us. It was not an easy thing to digest. Still, there was little I could do about it, frustrating as it was.

To get over all this, Kitch and I tried to pack in

as many things as we could outside of work. We checked out the view from near the top of the Burj Khalifa, we tried parasailing and we camped out in the desert a couple of times.

We also met at each other's houses from time to time. That week, we, along with some other friends, had planned to get together at Galiya's and Kitch's for dinner and Galiya had asked Mina and me to stop on the way to pick up some freshly made kuboos, which are like large, thick chapattis, very popular in these parts.

'Let me get a parking ticket,' I said as we got out of the car.

'Oh, you don't have to. It'll just take five or ten minutes,' Mina replied.

'That means nothing. I can see that khaki-clad guy hovering around, waiting to pounce on someone and sock him for a fee. That's jolly well not going to be me, after what happened this morning.'

What had happened that morning was this: Mina and I had, for a change, decided to have a buffet breakfast at a hotel in town. I had wolfed down sausages, toast, omelettes and muffins neatly washed down by some coffee, while Mina had tucked into fruit, hash browns and pancakes. I had bought a one-hour ticket and placed it under my windshield. Just as we were stepping out of the hotel, Ahmed appeared from nowhere and rushed up to us in a bit of a panic, wanting to know if I had three thousand dirhams in cash.

'I don't think so,' I told him. 'Can't you use your credit card?'

'No, no,' he said emphatically, looking behind him a little nervously. 'Cash! I need cash. Can you check please? Quickly! There's no ATM nearby and I just realized I have no cash on me. I need three thousand.' I had less than a thousand, but luckily for him Mina had enough. Between the two of us, we gave him the money. He grabbed it, mumbled a quick thank you and rushed off.

As a result of this little encounter, we reached our car ten minutes late, just in time to find an employee of the Road Transport Authority punch my car number into the little machine he carried. No amount of persuasion could make him change his mind. It turned out to be a rather expensive breakfast.

Luckily, our evening stop was more smooth. We picked up the kuboos from the little shop in Bur Dubai that Galiya had insisted on. Mina kept looking the other way deliberately, so she didn't have to see the man use his sweaty hands while making the stuff. After that we were on our way to Kitch's house.

For dinner, Galiya had to cater to all kinds of tastes. Four of us – Mina, Kitch, his cousin Ravi and Gavas – were what would technically be described as lacto-vegetarians. Then there was Andy who was a lacto-ovo-vegetarian. Harry ate only fish and chicken. The rest of us – Rachel, Peggy, Galiya and myself – pretty much ate everything.

Galiya had made several gallons of the VK stuff, some of it with manathankali and the rest of it with lamb. Then there was fish fillet, grilled paneer, cauliflower and lots of beer. Andy had brought along what he called 'Bengali Biryani', a rice dish with baby potatoes and whole eggs dipped in some tasty vegetarian masala gravy.

'I have tried to cater to everyone's taste,' Galiya announced. 'There's more in the kitchen, so please help yourselves… Andy, I'm gonna kill you! You've outshone me completely! Your biryani is the best part of the meal.'

'Non-vegetarians are always at an advantage,' Kitch grumbled. 'They eat up the non-veg stuff and also dig into the vegetarian food. So we get only a small portion of what was meant for us!'

'Kitch! You are not being a very good host today!' Peggy remarked.

'No, no! I didn't mean it that way. But it's true, we vegetarians always get a raw deal wherever we go.'

'And not just literally,' I added.

'Yesterday,' Kitch continued, ignoring me, 'we were at a buffet where there were four non-veg dishes and only one vegetable dish. Even that was a dry one, so what do we eat the rice with? The problem is that chefs are non-vegetarian. They can't think from a vegetarian's point of view. Look at airlines! Most airlines seem to believe that vegetarian food consists exclusively of salad, zucchini, brinjal and mushroom.' He had hit upon his pet peeve. He kept going on along these lines for quite a while, while the rest of us kept eating.

In the middle of all this, I got a call from Lalwani. 'Jai! This damn thing, this zuvulala,' he began, striking a complaining note straightaway. 'It's not working! Useless, kaput!' he said. 'I'm blowing, blowing, blowing, but no sound is coming!'

'You are not supposed to blow like in a pipe,' I told him. My brain had been much enriched in the last few days. I had learnt about a variety of things from dung beetles to football, from click consonants to the right way to play the vuvuzela. 'You have to keep your lips pressed together and then blow like you are spitting.'

With the entry of the Lalwani motif, the topic gradually veered to the office. 'You'd have thought,' said Peggy wryly, 'considering the profound impact the World Cup had on those London meetings, that Netherlands' loss in the final would have shaken them up a bit. But no, they are far from being chastened. It's like, as far as they are concerned, the World Cup was played only between England and Netherlands.'

'I think one reason why we are finding things a bit difficult to cope with is because this place is so big and unwieldy,' Harry chipped in. 'So many employees, so many grades and so many positions.'

'And such a complicated structure,' said Kitch. 'I believe that Peter chap was just an HR guy in Rotterdam with no business experience. Derek from treasury says he is long on theory and short on everything else. And a fellow like that gets two parking slots!'

'As they say in Hindi, *time time ki baat hai*,' Gavas added.

Rachel raised an enquiring eyebrow. 'What was that again?' she asked.

'It means,' Kitch replied, 'that it's all about being in the right place at the right time.'

Rachel nodded in agreement. 'Oh, it is. It always is, isn't it, dear?' she said, leaning to her left. The next moment – I'd been tilting my chair backwards and sipping my beer – I toppled over and dropped the bottle. At the same time, Kitch uttered a hoarse cry and his jaw dropped. And for good reason.

Rachel had just planted a kiss on top of Andy's head and was folding him in a long, slow embrace. The object of her affection responded with a wide smile, the lovelight shining in his eyes and on his face, the unmistakably intoxicated look of a young man deeply in love.

We had this practice at office of meeting every Monday at noon to discuss what we had done the previous week and how best we could coordinate our efforts in the week to come. Sometimes we decided to pair up to accomplish select goals, if we felt that would make quicker progress. In this we were unique within the organization, because in most other teams in the bank, there was a lot of infighting and ego tussle. But our faith in Peggy and her sense of fairness helped immensely in keeping our team working in unison.

Omar and Harry had opened one account each that week. Omar's client was an Iranian who owned a chain of craft and curio stores. Harry's client, he told us, was an Indian businessman who sold Arab men's underwear. This statement was greeted with a long pause. Some of us looked at each other and the others looked at him.

'What do you mean, Arab men's underwear?' Rachel asked. 'Don't Arabs wear the same underwear we do?'

Harry stared at her incredulously. 'You don't expect them to wear what *you* wear?'

'Well, okay, I mean, like... *you*.'

'What will you pay me for this information?' Harry asked, tongue firmly in cheek.

Rachel pretended to throw something at him.

'Well, they probably do wear what I wear...' Harry continued. 'Frankly, I'm not sure, but what

I'm referring to is this thin white cloth that they wear under their robe. That's what this guy sells. He imports it from a town called Tirupur in south India.'

'Guys, if I might digress for a moment from this theme that seems to be holding you all spellbound,' Peggy interrupted, 'we desperately need an Arab private banker in the team. I have spoken with Aliya, our former colleague, but she is getting married soon and is not too sure how things are going to shape up. Let me know, please, if you think of anyone. Someone with experience preferably, because they need to be prepared for the sales part of the job. I met two or three very good Arab nationals in the last month, but they want only a managerial job. So keep your ears open.'

I then told the group about Pedro's account. The money had come in the previous Thursday. I had called Pedro that morning to tell him that everything was fine. 'It may be fine with you, young man,' he had told me, 'but not with us. The World Cup is over, and now we don't know what to do. It seems like suddenly there's no energy, no purpose. It is very important for a country to have a common short-term objective, something everybody is passionate about, that will unite everyone. Not something vague like GDP growth, but a clear ambition that they can attain quickly.

Like the game of football itself. There is one clear purpose. To shoot the ball into the opponent's net as many times as possible in ninety minutes. Our goal was FIFA 2010. That goal has disappeared for us, Jai. Now it is like living in a vacuum. Life has lost its meaning.'

'Jack is lucky,' Gavas said after I had told them about the account. 'He meets the most incredible people. The rest of us have just been meeting textile merchants, jewellery shop owners and underwear importers.'

'Is this Pedro chap short and cute?' Peggy asked.

'No! Far from it. Why?'

'Oh, somehow, that's the way I picture him, going by his name. Pedro Pindo – whatever. Like Dudley Moore.'

'He's tall and well-built with rippling muscles. More like a cross between Arnold Schwarzenegger and Popeye.'

We went on to talk about products and the relative absence of good quality in-house research. 'The brand is brilliant,' Harry said. 'People are willing to move money in, but then what? We don't have our own brokerage arm, our research is too macro. Clients like specific product ideas that they can act on. I reckon that's where we lose out.'

We got around to discussing Ahmed and the newly proposed NRP team. There was talk that

Ahmed was in the process of opening a 200 million dollar account. There were rumours that it was 'political' money being channelled through an offshore trust. Omar, who had some common friends with Ahmed, told us that the new compliance chap, Jan Kahn, was a family friend of Ahmed's and that he was a Pakistani too, or at least of Pakistani origin. His original name was Jansher Khan and after a stint in Europe, he changed it to Jan Kahn and went to the extent of pronouncing his first name as 'Yan' rather than Jan, to make it sound European.

'I'll let you in on a secret,' Omar told us, a little hesitantly. 'I learnt this from a friend of mine who works at a hotel in town. You won't believe this, but on Thursday, Ahmed had arranged for both Peter and Jan to be put up at the hotel with some, er... escorts. He had booked rooms for both of them and they checked out the next morning. I was shocked when I heard this. I can understand Ahmed arranging this kind of thing for Jan, but for the CEO! It's crazy, I know, but I heard this from a senior hotel employee. He said a cleaner had called him that morning after they checked out, saying there was blood on the carpet, but it was only some ketchup. The girls had ordered burgers very early in the morning. It's ridiculous, I know, and I'm sure you don't believe me.'

Everyone laughed except me.

'The ketchup story is droll,' Harry said. 'It's the funniest thing I've heard all month. But I say, I mean, really! The hotel chap must have been pulling your leg, Omar. I think it's just a lot of poppycock. It can't be true.'

'It *is* true,' I announced, remembering my encounter with Ahmed at the hotel the other day. 'I believe Omar entirely. I paid for the escorts – three thousand dirhams!'

I told them my little story, enjoying their rapt, open-mouthed attention.

'Well, there you go, sweethearts,' said Rachel at her caustic best, stretching out her arms. 'That's the moral of the story. If we want to be stars, we should spend less time on business and turn into pimps. Quick results. Watch out for Ahmed's bonus next year.'

'But this is insane!' Harry protested.

'Peggy, I don't think this is the place for us. Maybe we should all look for another job. Perhaps an investment house will suit us best. Can't we talk to Goldman Sachs or Morgan Stanley? They've both got offices in Dubai.'

'Peggy, they took two months to approve Harsh's perfectly legal three million dollar account. And now, they see no problems with a 200 million account? One that stinks of corruption from a mile away? If the colour of money does not matter, we can open our doors to Indian black money. I'm sure we can rake in billions.'

'We thought we were joining a British bank. It's turned into a Dutch-Pakistani outfit!'

'Listen, guys, girls. There's nothing wrong with the bank. It's just that we've got ourselves into a bind out here. Look, I'm alive to all our problems. In fact, I've been working on something for a few weeks now. But there is nothing that can be done right now. So can I just ask all of you to put your heads down and keep working hard. Keep your clients in good humour and look after them well, as always. They are your assets and always will be. And now, I'm afraid I must share with you some bad news. This is hardly the time to be telling you this, but there is probably never a right moment for this. Look, the bank has not made any massive staff cuts anywhere in the world and none at all in Europe. European governments have been pressurizing all banks to cut costs. AbAd... I mean, AdAb, has decided that there's going to be a salary freeze across the globe. So, come January, we hold onto our existing pay packets, but get no increment.'

There was a silence. 'And bonuses, Peggy?'

'I don't know, guys, to be honest. I did ask, but they are not used to direct questions over here. They looked at me like I had committed blasphemy. But I'll find out, I promise, and I'll let you know. But please, let's stick together and keep the faith. Good things will happen.'

'Like the Bhagavad Gita says,' Gavas added, adding a touch of the spiritual to this sordid discussion on money and sex, 'do your duty. Excel in what you do. Don't waste your time expecting results.'

I always found it funny when Gavas said such things because he was so young; in fact, he was quite the baby of the team.

'Well, there's a man who always practises what he preaches,' said Peggy, smiling at him. 'Are you eating anything today, Gavas? I can see lunch coming in.'

'No, I'm fasting,' he replied. 'I've ordered my lunch separately.'

So while the rest of us ate biryani with tomato and onion raita, Gavas ate a plate of French fries, a packet of walnuts and almonds and a double scoop of butterscotch ice-cream. It was a moot point, who was eating and who was fasting.

'There are two other bits of news. One, Jack, do you remember that Sir Sid had initiated moves to bring in Shakira Kan?'

I stared at her blankly, waiting for something to register.

'Or is it Shakir Kan?' she muttered, eyes closed, forehead creased, trying hard to recollect the name. 'Shakoor Kan?'

‘Oh, you mean Shahrukh Khan!’

‘Sorry, Sharook Khan. Or that other star, Amitabh. By the way, is his surname pronounced Bacon or Bayshun?’

Kitch waved his hands impatiently. ‘Doesn’t matter. We understand.’

She continued, ‘Our budget has been reduced to less than a quarter. You know how things are nowadays. Jai, honey, do you think we can get either of these guys for about forty thousand dollars?’

‘For that amount, Peggy,’ I replied, ‘we would only get lookalikes of those two. There are lots of star lookalikes in India, you know, like your Elvis impersonators. Amitabh Bachchan and Shahrukh Khan are huge, Peggy. Forty thousand dollars must be like peanuts to them.’

‘Damn! We’ll have to see what to do about that. The other news is that the bank has decided to go ahead with this year’s off-site at Udaipur as originally planned. But they have decided to cut the proposed cost by half. All staff from grade 2 downwards – that means all of us – will be travelling economy. We also have to share rooms.’

‘*No!*’ All the occupants of the room rose as one in protest.

‘Peggy! This is awful!’

‘The last time I shared a room was when I was doing my articleship during my CA!’

'Wow! Can I share a room with Rachel?'

'I want that hot green-eyed babe from investment services!'

'What misers they are!'

'Losers!'

'I know a joke about a Dutch guy.'

'I'm not coming!'

'I snore in my sleep.'

'Will Peter and Jan also have to share rooms? Then they won't be able to have all the fun they want.'

'Maybe they can have fun together!'

'Guys, please! Stop. You are behaving like a bunch of schoolkids. This has nothing to do with the Dutch or anyone else. Can we please not bring individual nationalities into this discussion? Thank you. Listen! Being a Dutch institution is a matter of pride and strength. No two ways about that, as far as I'm concerned. Unilever, Phillips, ING, Ahold, UniFoods, Rabo, Adriaan... these are rock-solid names. The management says they are doing this to encourage people from different cultures and people from the two banks to bond together. It's not a bad idea at all. If we behave sensibly, I don't see why we can't get some serious fun out of this. Now chin up, please, and if you've finished your biryanis and fries and... Oh, my god, Gavas! Don't tell me you finished that ice-cream all by yourself,

sweetheart! I thought you were going to share it with the rest of us!'

As we were leaving the room, Rachel tugged at my shirt. 'Wait,' she hissed. I stopped.

'Jack!' she said. 'I need your help. It's about Andy and me.'

'Hmmm,' I said, trying to remain non-committal. I wasn't sure where this was going. I had spoken to Kitch about it earlier and he didn't think it was worth giving it a thought because, knowing his younger brother, it wouldn't last very long. Andy and Rach were both at loose ends and that was probably what brought them together, he felt.

'Don't say hmmm! I want help, Jack. I want you to talk to Andy's parents for me.'

My knees gave way and I collapsed into a chair. 'Rach, you must be joking! I mean, c'mon, Rach! You can't be serious about this, surely!'

'Why not?'

'But the two of you, Rach! I mean you are so, well, so mature and...'

'Are you saying I'm too old for him?' Her eyes were blazing.

'No, no, of course not,' I said quickly. 'But we can't deny Andy is a good four or five years younger than you.'

'Well, how about Sachin Tendulkar, then?' she asked, her chin up. 'He married someone five years older and look how the whole country worships him!'

'How do you know about Sachin Tendulkar?' I said in surprise. Rachel had never had a clue about cricket.

'Andy told me.'

I looked at her earnestly. Her eyes were cold, grey and forbidding, like the weather in London. 'Rach, he is only twenty-three and just a few years out of college. He's a kid. You have to give this relationship some time to test it. It isn't that serious.'

She grabbed the front of my shirt, tie and all, hauled me off the chair and shook me. Gosh, this girl was strong. '*I'll* be the decider of that, Jack Patel!' she hissed. 'I'm *very* serious about this. I'm more serious about this than I have ever been about anything in my life.'

I adjusted my tie and my faculties and stood a little distance away from her. This was not the Rachel I knew. I fixed a thoughtful eye on her. In return, she singed me with hers.

I tried again. 'Listen, Rach, honey, this is not a movie. You are a mature girl. *Not* old, just mature. Andy's a kid. And he's a kid with conservative parents who are so concerned about him they've made me a guardian of sorts. They sent him here so he could make something of his career. From what I know of him, he's nowhere near the settling down stage.' I paused to see how she was taking it. She wasn't angry, but she looked saddened, disappointed.

'I don't have much of a family, Jack,' she said quietly. 'There's my mother, who couldn't care less, and her sister, who is well meaning but little else. I've been on my own for ten years now. But I know that Indians like you and Kitch and Andy are all about family. His parents wouldn't accept me if Andy or I went to them. I hoped... in fact, I was sure you'd help. I love Andy terribly. I'm crazy about him. I've seen a lot of him these four months. Believe me, he's not a kid, Jack. He may be a bit of a baby in some ways, but he's actually very spiritual.'

'Rach, please! Give me a break.'

'I don't mean in a religious sense. But he understands people. He knows how to handle people. He can empathize. And he can give. Do you know that maid who works in my house, that girl, Sarla?'

'Er... yes,' I mumbled, wondering how she came into the picture.

'When she went to the airport about a year ago to go back to India, she found that her visa had been cancelled. There was a misunderstanding between the Arab sponsor and her agent and the sponsor cancelled her visa without even telling her. Since then she was living here illegally because she had no choice. Her young children are in India and were waiting for her to get back. I knew all this but simply accepted it as one of those things. When Andy heard her story a few weeks ago, he was almost in tears. He went and met the sponsor, the consulate office and the immigration officials and he sorted the matter out for her. He's young, Jai, but he's not a kid. Do you know he once slapped his lecturer in college?'

'No! And you want to associate with a man like that?'

'I've never been more sure of anything in my life. He slapped him because he was flirting and laughing with another teacher while your national anthem was being sung.'

I remained quiet.

'Jack, I need your help. Do this for me. *Please!* You are the only one who knows both me and his parents well.'

'But sweetheart, what's the hurry? You can see how things go for the next couple of years and then, you know, figure out what you want to do.'

'That would have been fine; only, Andy's parents are about to foist some Indian girl from the US on him next year. Andy said both Kitch and you know the family. He says he doesn't mind just going ahead and getting married to me right here right now, but I don't want to do that, Jack. I don't want to break up his family. I have been without roots all my life. Now I feel I've found something I want to hold onto. He's given me a completely different perspective of life. He has so much time for others, so much compassion, it's incredible. He sends ten per cent of his salary every month to a charity in India. He has arranged for a collection centre in his building to give to Rashid Paediatric every month. And I've spent the last few years in bars and clubs and parties, thinking I was leading the good life. I won't let go of him, Jack. I love him so much. I feel so secure, so comfortable when I'm with him. He is the horse I'm riding now...'

'Rach, please! Let's keep it clean, shall we? I mean, this is a family book!'

'Don't be daft, Jack! I meant my rocking horse. My father died when I was very young and I used to spend hours sitting on my wooden horse, crying and rocking myself to sleep, day after day. Now that rocking horse is Andy. You haven't really spent time with him, Jack. For you, he's just Kitch's kid brother. But you know what, Jack? He's a wonderful human being with great depth of character. Andy doesn't just look at people, he sees inside them, Jack. *Jack!*'

'Yes?'

'Help me, damn you! Andy says you and Kitch know this US girl – they are family friends, he says. You bought your farm from her father.'

'Oh! That girl! Krishnaswamy's daughter!'

We stood in silence for a while. I could feel her eyes piercing through me, trying to get inside my brain – perhaps seeing *inside* me, like Andy, and not just looking at me.

'You may be the better choice,' I said at last.

Her features relaxed. She smiled.

'And if you are *this* serious, Rach, then yes, I'll do whatever I can.'

She fell on me in a heap and hugged me hard, crying like a baby. She was very strong, this girl, I thought, even as I struggled for breath; as strong as a… well, for want of a better word, a horse. A real one.

13

A New Day, A New Experience

Kitch and I had a day together in Dubai. I was leaving for Tanzania and he had just returned from a visit to Muscat. So we decided to spend some time catching up and babysitting Olga at his house while Galiya and Mina went shopping. Mina needed a few things for the house and she took along our new cook-cum-man-about-the-house, Juma, whom she had 'imported' from Kenya last month. Juma had worked at Mina's house in Kenya for several years. I had got a nasty jolt when he showed up at the Dubai airport wearing red trousers and a t-shirt that read 'Doggy Style's da Way to Do it' but had recovered substantially since. The chap was a terrific cook and kept our place looking so spic and span that you could have eaten off any part of the house, no plates needed. He spoke only Swahili, though, and unfortunately my Swahili had never progressed beyond 'Jambo'.

'Anything interesting in Muscat?' I asked Kitch, settling comfortably on the sofa. Galiya had fixed us a pitcher of a lime-and-mint drink, while Kitch had dug out half a dozen thattais. Kitch ensures a perennial supply of some snack or the other from Chennai.

'Just a four-hand tandem massage at the spa,' he replied.

'Four-hand tandem massage!' I exclaimed. 'You mean two people massage you simultaneously?'

'Obviously! It can't be one person with four hands!'

'That sounds interesting. How was it?'

'Like being pummelled by two sumo wrestlers.'

'Good lord! Er… men?'

'Women. But they were like sumo wrestlers.'

'You mean, big?'

'Very.'

The soprano voice of young Olga wafted into the room. 'Poppa! Potty's not coming!'

'And these women… what were they wearing?' I asked.

'Not what you're thinking. They wore regular white uniforms. My body is still aching and my chest and arms are pink and painful. When you go to Tanzania, are you meeting that Myers client of yours whose wife hits on you?'

'Potty's *not* coming, poppa!'

'Did you say "potty, potty, come come"?' Kitch

shouted back. 'How will it come if you don't tell it to come?' He looked at me, eyebrows raised.

'Er… no, Kitch. I think I'll skip that family. Don't want to reopen that case. But never mind all that! Listen, have you spoken to your parents about Andy and Rachel?'

'I did. They wouldn't even listen to me, Jai. They just want to speed things up with that US girl.'

'Hell! Listen, Kitch, I've met her just once. But I was rather put off by her ways. She's only been in the US two years and she couldn't think of a single good thing to say about India. She takes malaria tablets whenever she goes to India and complains about mosquitos, humidity, water, powercuts, all with this American accent… and, well, I don't see Andy with her, somehow.'

'Potty's still not coming, poppa!' Olga screamed. 'I said "potty, potty, come come" but it's not coming!'

Kitch ran his fingers through his hair, grimaced and glared at me. 'You have no younger brother and no two-year-old. You don't know how lucky you are. Listen, Jai. Can you talk to them? We'll go to Chennai together next week. They might listen to you. I didn't have a problem with Galiya, but this one is going to be difficult. In return, I promise I will persuade Galiya to put that L-O-V-E photograph back in the bedroom.'

I hadn't had time to get my visa for Tanzania, so I had to get it done at the airport. Much to my dismay, I realized I wasn't carrying any dollars, only pounds and euros. They insisted on dollars as visa fee. There was no forex house at the airport, but there was one just outside. They let me go out to exchange some money and come back in to make the payment. Immigration officials always fill me with dread. In fact, all uniformed people do. Cops, customs people, immigration guys, even air hostesses to an extent. They seem to have this uncanny ability of looking deep into you and unravelling your innermost secrets. Like Andy.

I stayed at a new hotel in Tanzania. My usual one was not on the bank's approved list. I met three prospects that day and one of them clicked.

'I want service,' Kishan Patel told me. Kishan was about fifty, with a paunch that protruded so much I couldn't see the top of his trousers. With a twinge of remorse, I promised myself I would start exercising regularly. I had been a little remiss the last few weeks. Kishan looked at me through half closed eyes. 'I don't like to call my bank and be put on hold or be made to talk to a machine. You know, for thirty years I had this account with the same bank. Last month, I wanted to transfer some money and they told me that before remitting it they needed to know the source of funds. Thirty years and *now* they want to know the source of the money?!'

Kishan insisted on taking me out for a drink that evening. 'The Chinese are everywhere in Africa,' he whispered with a nod at an adjoining table that seated a few Chinese diners. 'Africans like the Chinese. Westerners also give them money, but those guys want bills. They ask for transparency. Chinese don't want transparency. They don't want bills. Just oil and minerals. It suits both sides.'

He took me to a sort of Indian club, where three or four girls danced to Bollywood hits. From time to time, someone would come around with a plate of garlands. If you liked any of the dancers, you could select her and let the guy know. He would go over and garland her, indicating the benefactor. She would bestow a charming smile upon the guest and dance for the next few seconds facing him, a sort of exclusive privilege. They billed you separately for the garlands. I noticed that some of the dancers got garlanded repeatedly by loyal fans. I chose a glum-looking girl who seemed to be ignored by the audience and brought a smile to her face. I felt rather pleased with myself. This was my good turn for the day.

My thoughts strayed to Andy. I wondered what he would have done in the same situation. Perhaps he would have tried to find out more about the girls. Were they happy? Did they earn enough? Was I, Jai Patel, doing anything for society? Or was I leaving it to the Andys of the world? Wasn't I doing just what Rachel had said she had done most of her life? Eating and drinking and partying? Was I shallow? Uncomfortable thoughts, but I couldn't keep them away. That bugger Andy was beginning to haunt me.

Interspersed with these thoughts, I was also dealing with Kishan Patel's genius theory of stock picking. 'My strategy is very simple,' he told me. 'When the price is low, buy. When the price is high, sell. Simple.' He looked in my direction as if waiting for appreciation. Then he continued, 'I don't have time for all this, otherwise I could have made big money. I would have bought Barclays during the crisis when it had gone down to 60p. Today it is three pounds. I would have made 500 per cent,' he said smugly. 'Or I would have bought gold at 300 dollars ten years ago. Today, it is 1,300 dollars.'

'What would you buy today?' I asked him, a little testily. I get irritated when people boast about what they would have done but never get around to doing.

'Today it is not possible,' he told me decisively. 'The market is too volatile.'

When I went back to the hotel, I noticed three women sitting together in the lobby – a large, middle-aged, fashionably dressed woman, accompanied by two younger women. As I stepped inside the lift, one of the younger ones quickly nipped in. As the door shut, she smiled coyly and said, 'So, are you alone?'

'Yes,' I answered without thinking. Then I pressed the button for the third floor and looked enquiringly at her. She shrugged her shapely shoulders. 'Wherever you are going,' she replied. A mild chill went through me. One is so unused to these things. As I walked to my room, the young lady followed me. 'I give you company,' she said.

'No, it's all right,' I replied, walking in and trying to close the door without being too rude.

She stuck a dainty foot in the door. 'Okay, no company. Massage only?' she asked.

'No, thank you,' I mumbled. I wished I wasn't feeling so nervous. Why should I? I mean, she was the one who should be nervous. And yet, there she was, cool as you please, while I was sweating through every pore.

She pouted. 'You don't like me?'

I refrained from giving a direct reply. 'I... er... have to go out now to meet someone,' I told her. Idiot! I told myself. Why do you have to do this? Tell her politely and firmly that you are not interested. Why this diffidence? Just ask her to go.

But these things are always easier in theory.

When you are confronted with the unexpected, it's damn hard to say the right thing.

Anyway, it seemed to work. She left. I heaved a sigh of relief, watched some TV and then decided to go down for dinner. The first thing I saw when I got out of the lift was the girl. I had to turn right to go to the restaurant, but I turned left. Somehow, I felt obligated. I had told her that I had to go out. So I did. I left the hotel building. I could sense her eyes following me and then heard footsteps. I hurried off. She broke into a run and came up to me and placed a light arm on my left shoulder. I was just shaking her off when a strong arm placed itself on my right shoulder. I whirled around and saw to my horror that it was the arm of the law. The girl said something in rapid-fire Swahili and left. The cop shook his head sadly. 'I have to arrest you, sir,' he said.

'No!' I croaked. 'I didn't do a thing. That girl followed me from the hotel.'

'Ah!' said the cop. 'That may be. But that is for the judge to say. On Monday perhaps. Now it is Friday evening so you have to spend the weekend with us.'

'No, officer!' I cried out. 'There must be something we can do! Please guide me!'

'Maybe we can settle something,' he said in a less official tone. 'Come this way.'

I took out my purse. 'How much?'

'Twenty thousand shillings. But I am just doing this to help you. You look like a good man.'

'Thank you.' I stretched out twenty thousand.

He stepped back and stared intently at my wallet.

'Better you give me those dollars,' he said. 'I think the shilling will weaken.'

While Kitch was away, Mina and I called Galiya and Olga over to spend a night with us. We called some more friends and decided to host a quiz at our house. My clients Harsh and Joi came too and we were expecting Andy, Bharat Saxena and his wife and two other couples.

Little Olga was getting to be quite a delight. She had brought some picture books and without any prompting, came up to me, plonked herself in my lap and said, 'Uncle Jai, read this book Olga.'

I was awfully pleased. My interaction with kids hitherto had been limited and I found it rather gratifying that she seemed so naturally comfortable with me.

The book she had chosen for me to read was titled *My Little Potty Book*. I had to read loudly to her how the little girl in the book had a pink potty and how one day, she was playing in the garden after drinking a lot of juice, but she was so clever that she managed to sit on the potty just in time. I was tickled to bits but had to keep a serious face because Olga was so absorbed in the story. Every time I read a page, she would look up at me with large eyes and explain it to me in her limited vocabulary, pointing at the pictures and gesticulating liberally. It was a unique experience.

'Did Kitch tell you his parents are trying to get Vidya and Andy together?' Galiya asked me. 'I believe you don't like her very much.'

'I've met her once, yes, and I didn't particularly care for her. I can't see Andy with her.'

'We looked her up on Facebook,' she said. 'Kitch thought she was quite hot.'

'Kitch would find anyone hot. Even a penguin.'

'What do you mean by that!'

'Actually, penguins *are* hot!' Harsh grinned, walking up to us and nudging me. 'They are certainly warm-blooded. They have to be to weather the cold.'

But Galiya was not to be distracted. 'Mr Patel, what exactly was that last remark supposed to mean?' she queried, her eyes narrowing and starting to smoulder. Girls were beginning to make a habit of destroying me with their eyes.

'Not what you think!' I said hurriedly. 'What I mean is that he is such a gentleman that he doesn't speak ill of any woman. Anyway, he scored bull's eye with you. You were the hottest girl at Myers.

When guys saw you approaching, their hearts stopped.'

'Hmm…' she said, considering the statement. 'Okay, I guess I can forgive you then.'

'Jai says he's going to try and get Rachel and Andy together,' said Mina.

'Well, he'll have to do it on his own. I doubt if Kitch is going to do much talking. He doesn't seem very confident of Rachel being a good prospect for marriage. Nor does he think his parents will listen to him.'

I shrugged. 'I guess I'll just give it a shot. I feel like it might work. And Rach seems very sure of it. Anyway, I promised her I'd try.'

Andy walked in just then. After the preliminaries, I took him aside. I decided I was going to try out some psychology on the kid. Deep stuff. If he was just playing around with Rachel, I would put a stop to it rightaway. 'Look, Andy,' I told him. 'I'm sorry to be talking to you like a grandfather and I know it's none of my…'

'Anna, it *is* your business. You're just like Kitch to me. If you have any advice to give me, please do.'

'Well, Andy, you probably know that Rachel has spoken to me about you. Frankly, I'm not sure about this whole thing. I mean, surely you don't think this relationship will last a lifetime? You two are poles apart. Maybe it's time to move on, you know. Besides, just between you and me, aren't you too young to get married? You've got years of fun ahead of you.'

'I am ready to get married to Rachel, anna. But I'm just as happy to wait for her. The problem is, this has to be tackled now, because the way things are moving, Vidya is definitely in the picture. I don't want it to come to the point where I have to rebel. My parents have had enough of that from me. Rachel's the one for me, anna. I've never been more certain of anything in my life. But I don't want to hurt or disappoint amma and appa. So when you go to Chennai, please bat for me. You won't regret it, anna, I promise. I won't let you down.'

I looked at him long and hard. Rachel was right. There was a kind of openness about this boy that was quite disarming. 'I'll do what I can,' I told him, patting him on the shoulder. Suddenly I felt very responsible and grown up. I, Jai Patel, was getting youngsters married.

The evening ended with a Bollwood music session. Sunny Singh took us all by surprise by belting out the latest item number, replete with vigorous pelvic movements. He made it his own by replacing one of the words in the lyrics with his name. Balancing a glass of beer on each of his palms, he danced in front of his wife to the tune of '*Sunny* badnaam huwi, darling tere liye'.

Not to be outdone, Bharat sang and danced to a modified version of another recent hit, 'My name Saxena, Saxena ki jawani…'. But the highlight of the evening was a performance by Pammi, Sunny's wife. She labelled herself 'Sikhni' Chameli and did an impressive little item.

Before leaving, Andy grasped my hand. 'I'm very grateful to you for taking the trouble. I think my parents might just listen to you,' he said.

Less than twenty-four hours later, I was at Kitch's house in Chennai.

'Have you gone mad, Jai?' his father asked me. 'You are asking me to let my son get married to a British woman five years older than him, whom he has known for just six months?'

'We did not expect this from you, Jai!' his mother said accusingly. 'You were smart enough to marry a girl from among your own! Now you want us to welcome this… this divorcee girl? We thought you will give Andy good advice, Jai. Instead of that, you are trying to ruin his life!'

'Aunty, I didn't marry Mina because she was a Patel! That was incidental. Look, aunty, uncle, I've known Rachel for years… She is a lovely girl. I have seen her and Andy together many times and they make a wonderful couple.'

'So that's what he has been doing in the Gulf,' his father said, raising his voice a notch, 'becoming a *couple* with this woman? I am desperate for someone to help me run my business, but still I sent him there to get some exposure and stay out of trouble. And this is what he does. That black sheep! He has always created trouble for me. Always!'

'But uncle, Kitty married Shree and see how happy they are together. And look at Kitch and Galiya. What a lovely pair! And little Olga, the apple of your eye! Look at it this way. No other couple combination could have produced Olga just the way she is!'

'There is no issue with Galiya, Jai. She is not older than Kitcha and is very understanding of our culture and customs. If Anand marries this British girl, all of Chennai will be talking about it. She does not even seem to have a proper family. What can we expect from a girl with such a background?'

This seemed to be a suitable cue to win some pity points. 'Rachel lost her father when she was just three, aunty,' I said solemnly. 'For months, she was in tears.' I felt like an actor who had been handed an extremely powerful scene. I hoped I was getting the right amount of pathos in my voice. 'In *tears*!' I continued, striving for the emotional touch and aiming to break my voice suitably. 'For months and months. Her mother turned into a recluse. She was an only child.

Her only friend in the whole world was her little rocking horse...'

'I don't care, damn it!' Kitch's dad shouted. 'Rocking horse or flying elephant, what does it have to do with us? Po da!'

Kitch's mum stepped in. 'And even worse, she is a *divorcee.*' She seemed determined to harp on that theme. 'What guarantee is there that she will not leave my son after two months?'

'Aunty, Andy is a wonderful guy, but he is no saint. We can't deny that. There is an element of chance in every marriage. Andy is young but in some ways, very mature. So is Rachel. They have given it a good deal of thought and seem to know what they are getting into. And they are both adamant that they will get married only with your blessings. As for the divorce, aunty, it wasn't her fault. She didn't leave him, he left her.'

'Why? Maybe she was not a good wife.'

'She was the perfect wife! But h-he was an alcoholic,' I said, letting my imagination flow. I had no idea why Rachel had divorced. 'For two years, the poor girl tried her best to help him. She even appointed a nurse and used up all her personal savings. But that man, that shameless beast! He... he ran away with the nurse.'

There was silence. I racked my brains for something positive to say. 'Even Mina simply adores Rachel. And you know Peggy, our boss.

She really likes her as well. She thinks she's a good worker and a terrific human being.'

'But Jai, please try and understand. She is almost *five* years older!'

'So is Sachin Tendulkar's wife!' I replied promptly, grateful to Rachel for this point.

'Sachin Tendulkar's wife is not a British divorcee!'

'And Andy is no Sachin Tendulkar either. So we're quits! Besides, come on! It's not fair to hold her age against her. There's nothing she can do about being twenty-seven, just like Andy can't do anything about being twenty-three.' I could see that I was grinding them down with my remorseless reasoning. 'But the important thing is they are both mature and very fond of each other. I'm sure they will go all out to make this a success. Look, uncle, aunty, you've known me for so long now. If I wasn't so sure, I would not be pleading their case. Please give them a chance. Ask them to come here. That way you will know how well she will fit in. In fact, Rachel is almost Indian! She is friendly, respectful of elders, understanding and humble. And,' I added, suddenly remembering something, 'although Andy and Rach have known each other really well only this year, they actually met during Kitch's wedding. Do you remember a lovely girl wearing Indian clothes at the wedding? The one with Peggy and me? That's Rachel. You would

remember her from the video. And I promise you this: their baby will be as beautiful as Olga!'

His mom said something to his dad in rapid Tamil. I was pretty sure it was about the video. Suddenly the sullen look disappeared from Dharini aunty's face. I could tell Rachel had been noticed in the video *and* in a positive way. I could make out the words 'red dress'.

'Yes, yes!' I said with enthusiasm. 'Red and white. She looked very pretty. She really enjoyed Kitch's wedding. She loves Indian weddings and Indian families.'

'We will discuss again with you and Kitcha when he comes tomorrow, Jai,' his dad said. 'Then we will see. I am not promising anything.'

Kitch didn't have to do much the next day except nod his head in approval. Watching a pretty Rachel enjoying herself at their son's wedding seemed to have mollified his parents greatly. But Rachel would have to come to India for a final approval, they said.

That night, Kitch came over to my parents' house for dinner. There was my father and mum, Kitty and Shree, Kitch and I. Kitty was gushing about her dance school and how well it was going. She had just opened a branch in Bangalore and started yoga classes in Chennai.

Kitch had been planning to go to Zambia the following month. 'You go instead, Jai. Africa is not for me. The last time I went there, I got arrested for a visa-related problem. This time in Tanzania, I almost got arrested for molesting a woman.'

'You *molested* a woman!'

'I didn't molest anyone! She came and grabbed me just outside the hotel. Then a policeman appeared out of nowhere and said he had to arrest me. I paid him off.'

I stared at him, aghast. This was obviously a ruse between the girl and the cop, a ploy to fleece unsuspecting tourists. It dawned on me that he might not even have been a cop. 'How much did you pay?' I asked.

'Thirty thousand shillings.'

'Thirty!'

'Why? Is it too much?'

'Well, the market rate for not molesting that girl,' I told him, 'is twenty thousand.'

14

Trapped Between Two Women

'I don't know what today's children are coming to,' Sunny Singh told me in a low voice, nodding towards his son's room. 'My son Monty… he is going to prom night, so he wants to wear a new suit and go in a limousine. Arre, what nonsense is this! When I was his age, I was working as garage assistant during the day and as dhaba cleaner at night. After more than thirty years of hard work, today I own sixty trucks, twelve vans and five cars. But I have never been in a limousine. And this munda wants to start his life in a limousine, bloody hell! Any idea what they do at this prom-shrom, Jai? Is it a party?'

'I think so. I've never had one myself. I believe it's a farewell organized by the school, but Saxena's son told me that the real party starts only after the formal school party, when the teachers leave.'

'You mean there will be drinking-shinking, boy-girl everything?'

'Something along those lines, yes.'

'I have no faith in this new generation. Of course, with every generation, we have only made this planet worse. But at least in our time we worked hard. We valued things. We respected elders. But look at these gadhe. My father has been staying with us ever since we came to Dubai, as you know. But these two boys, they don't even know what to talk to him about. They have nothing in common. And they don't even know when he is talking to them because they are always wearing those damn earplugs.'

'Headphones,' I offered.

'My other son is good at studies, but Monty is at the bottom of his class. He says the teacher is not good. I told him, oye duffer, it is the same teacher for everyone. Then why is it that only you come last? Behind all the other Indians and whites and Arabs? Damn shame!'

Meanwhile, the cause of shame waltzed across the room swaying to music and left the house. Sunny looked up and raised his hands in despair. 'Okay, let's forget all this. Let us talk about your Zambia trip. I have a customer there called Sartaj Singh. He is a sweet man, very godfearing. I supply auto spares to him. He wants to open an account with you. It will help me also, because every time I sell to him, he can just ask you to debit his account and credit mine. Transaction becomes ekdam simple.'

Kitch's client was based in Chingola, a mining town. Sunny's friend Sartaj Singh was in a place called Ndola. People pronounce it in various ways – Ndola, Undola, Andola, Endola, Dola. But apparently, the right way to pronounce it is exactly the way it is written. Very close to 'dola' but with just that touch of the letter N. It's not easy but it comes with practice, unlike the 'zh' syllable in Tamil, where even practice rarely works. They say you have to be born a Tamil Brahmin.

Reaching Ndola was not easy. There was no direct flight from Dubai to Ndola or even to Lusaka, the capital of Zambia. I had to go to Nairobi and then take the connecting flight to Lusaka. I spent the day at the Taj Pamodzi hotel, located on a road lined with trees of pretty jacaranda flowers – or so a hotel employee told me – and took an evening flight to Ndola.

It was the smallest aircraft I had ever been in. I needn't have worried about getting an aisle seat, because I found that every seat in the plane was both an aisle seat *and* a window seat. Basically there were just single seats with the aisle running down the middle. Even at its peak altitude – which, I suspect, couldn't be more than a thousand metres – I could see plants and trees on the ground below. I also discovered, to my discomfiture, that there was no toilet in the aircraft.

Kitch's client drove down to the Ndola airport, which resembled the pavilion of a small, rundown cricket stadium. He told me he had brought all the forms with him and was ready to open the account. 'Very difficult getting all signatures, Jai bhai,' he said. 'You won't believe, it took me three whole months. Maara mota bhai, my elder brother, London ma che; his wife is in Australia with their son and my wife is in India for first baby. Finally I managed to get all four signatures. Oof! Bau mota kaam che, Jai bhai.Very big job.'

He needed a couple of hours with me to run through the mountain of product information that Kitch had supplied me with. We sat at a little café in town where I tucked into a burger and a sundae.

When I was done, I called Sartaj Singh, whose vocabulary seemed to be primarily limited to 'thank you'. 'Oh, thank you, ji, thank you, Jai ji, thank you for coming ji, shukar hai Rabba ki, thank you very much,' he started and continued along similar lines. I gathered subsequently that he had got held up somewhere and if I could get his wife's signature on a form, he would meet me at the airport closer to the flight's departure to complete the forms. 'My wife name Cynthia ji, thank you ji, Cynthia in Sartaj Auto Spares on Mkuma Street, thank you very much ji, thank you.'

I hailed a cab and was on my way. As soon as I entered Mkuma Street, I saw a building that had several shops on the ground floor. A modest sign on one of them read Sartaj Tyres. I stood at the counter and smiled at the plump Punjabi woman who was sitting inside, fiddling with the cash box.

'Good afternoon, Mrs Sartaj Singh?' I asked.

She was. I briefly explained to her the purpose of my visit and she readily filled up the form and gave me a copy of both her and her husband's passports. I was just about to put the papers in my folder when I noticed that her name on both the passport copy and on the form which she had filled was 'Prakash'.

'Is Cynthia your pet name?' I asked. 'Mr Singh referred to you as Cynthia.'

She glared at me. 'No!' she shouted. 'I am not Cynthia. There is no need to go to that bitch! I am his one and only wife, you understand? Not that black chudail. Now go straight to the airport and get Sartaj's signature and open the account. Go!'

I didn't need to be told twice. I rushed out of the shop and clambered into the car. As soon as I was out of sight, I called Sartaj Singh. 'Mr Singh, I got the signature but I am confused. I got it from your wife Prakash. Who is Cynthia?'

'Oye!' he wailed. 'What have you done? I told you Sartaj Auto Spares ji, not Sartaj Tyres. Oye hoye, sirji! Hai Rabba! Now Jai ji, you please quickly go and get another form signed by Cynthia please, thank you ji. I have already told her you will be coming, I don't want any problem, koi panga shanga na ho jaye sirji, Rabba na kare. Sorry ji,for this double trouble, thank you very much ji, thank you.'

Sartaj Auto Spares was at the other end of the street. I still wasn't sure who Cynthia was – second wife, mistress, girlfriend, business partner? I didn't know who to ask and how to ask. Cynthia appeared suddenly – she was short, black, ordinary to look at except for her bright red lipstick. She got down to business at once. 'Where do I sign?'

After she had finished, she told me firmly, waggling her finger under my nose, 'Mr Singh wants to open the account with *me*, understand? Not anyone else. He is very clear on that. There should not be any mistake. Are you going to the airport now?'

I put this form too in my folder and headed to the airport. I would just give him both forms and let him decide what to do. Sartaj Singh was waiting for me. 'I don't know how to thank you, sirji. I have already got accounts with Prakashji and I had promised Cynthia new account will be with her. Now I don't know what to do with this other form, ji!'

Suddenly I heard a shrill voice right behind me, making me leap several inches in the air. 'I will tell you what to do! Bloody man, what the hell do you think? You jolly well open account with your wife who has taken care of you all these years, whose father helped you start your first business. You swindler, scoundrel, scavenger!' Prakash had entered the scene and was swinging her handbag at her husband.

Even before I had time to close my mouth, I heard Cynthia's voice. 'Stop this nonense! I am also his wife, younger and better! I have every right to open the account. How many more accounts will you open, you greedy witch?'

'You! You dare call me witch! *You* are a witch! And you are a bitch! You steal my husband from me? I curse you! I put on you the curse of all my ancestors!' She swung her handbag at her, but it slipped out of her hand and caught me on the solar plexus.

I picked it up and turned towards Mrs Singh. But bags meant nothing to her at this moment. To my shock, she grabbed her rival by the hair. She gave it a sharp tug, making Cynthia squeal and step down hard on Prakash's toes with her high-heeled shoes. From the corner of my eye, I caught sight of Sartaj Singh, cowering in a corner.

'Oww!' Mrs Singh cried, hopping on one foot. 'Ow, ow, ow! This woman is the devil himself. Did you find no other place to go to, you disgusting female? Could you find no man other than my husband to ensnare?'

Sartaj Singh took a tentative step in our direction, where all the action was taking place. 'Oye, please ji, please stop it, thank you ji. What crime have I committed that my Rabba is punishing me like this in the middle of the airport? The confusion is utter. Please ji, both of you, I will tear up both the forms ji, but let us stop this tamasha. Jaiji, please can you give me both the papers… thank you so much ji,' said Sartaj, as I pulled out the forms from my folder. He grabbed them from me and tore them forcefully into two. Then, with greater effort, he managed to rip them into four and after trying hard but failing to tear them into eight, he marched to the nearest dustbin and hurled them in.

'Zambia Air to Lusaka, Zambia Air to Lusaka,' a lady announced just then. Still in a daze, I picked up my small suitcase and slunk off towards the aircraft, hoping to leave unnoticed. 'Thank you ji, sirji,' shouted Sartaj Singh from behind me. 'Thank you for coming. Please come again ji. God bless you ji, thank you very much!'

I found my seat, sat down and closed my eyes. Idiot, Sunny Singh. What a waste of a trip. But at least I had managed to get that one account for Kitch even if the other one ended in such tragic farce.

Suddenly a terrible thought struck me. With trembling hands, I opened my folder. My worst fears had come true. In my haste, I had inadvertently handed over all three account forms in my folder – including Kitch's client's – to Sartaj Singh for him to destroy. Almost as bad, my left hand was still holding Mrs Singh's handbag.

15

European Holiday

When I got back to office the next day, I was greeted with the dumbest piece of news I had heard in a long time. Our budgets had been further slashed and the bank had decided to forget about Shahrukh Khan and Amitabh Bachchan, and even Shilpa Shetty for that matter. Peggy told us that CEO Peter had decided to rope in 'Pickle'.

'Pickle?' I repeated blankly when I heard. 'What do you mean, Pickle? Is he a pop star? Rap prince? Or a drag queen?'

'No, Jack! I'm surprised you haven't heard of him. He appears to be a well-known entertainer from Mumbai. I'm sorry about this, Jack, but Peter says he's all we can get at this stage.'

'But Peggy! We'd rather not have anyone then. *Pickle!* We'll be the laughing stock of Dubai. And there's no one called Pickle, anyway. So it probably doesn't matter. This must be Peter playing a joke on you, or someone playing a joke on Peter.'

Peggy looked at Gavas helplessly. Looking sheepish, Gavas turned towards me.

'It's not my fault, Jai,' he said. 'Peter asked me if I knew any Indian entertainer who would perform for 5,000 dollars. Our budget is 40,000 dollars. He said the venue, food and drinks will cost 35,000 dollars. That left only 5K for the perfomer. So I suggested a relative of mine who mimics film stars and politicians. It's not my fault!' he said defensively. 'Who else will come for this little money? I thought I'd do him a good turn by getting him a Dubai trip. He's not bad, actually. There's this act of his where he sort of mimics God and does a take on international celebrities. It's quite popular in Mumbai. By the way, his name is not Pickle, it's P-i-k-l-e, pronounced Pik-lay.'

When I mentioned this half-jokingly and almost apologetically to a few clients,Saxena burst into uncontrollable laughter and was still laughing when I left his house.

Sunny Singh was most disappointed. He was a Bachchan fan and had been looking forward to an evening with the Big B. 'If not our Bachchan, you could have got Bipasha, Katrina or Malaika. They would have gone crazy for a chance to dance with your Sunny Singh Bali. You could have had banners saying *Bollywood meets Baliwood*! What will we do with this Pikle-shikle? Your bank is a loser. Better you leave, Jai, and start something on your own. I will support you. Let us do some business together. Don't associate with these cheapos. You will also go down with them.'

Kochar was even more forthright. He came over to my hotel when I visited Nairobi later that week. 'Babaji ka ghanta! Screw them, I will not come. Who does your bank think we are? Hume kya paagal kutte ne kaata hai? Have we been bitten by mad dogs that we will think of leaving our business and golf and wasting time on some buffoon? Do they think we can be bought with alcohol and food? Kanjoos, miser bank. Bunch of lafoots. I will close my account. You tell them I will show them…'

What he would have shown them will remain a mystery because, at that moment, Kochar suddenly stopped mid-sentence. He was staring at a brochure he had been reading in my hotel room. He let out a sharp cry. '*Ayee!* What's this? They are giving you *free* wife!' He spoke as much in envy as in shock. 'Now it has become legal in hotels? Fantastic! Kamaal hai, bhai!'

I took the brochure from him curiously.

'Not wife,' I told him. 'It's w-i-f-i. Wifi. That means internet connection.'

When I got back to office on Sunday – the first day of our working week in Dubai – I found the place abuzz with talk about Jan and Peter and their night out at the hotel.

'Yaar, Jack,' Ahmed asked me, 'did you tell anyone about that incident in the hotel that day? When I took that cash from you? Did you know I had arranged for some entertainment for Jan and Peter?'

'Actually I learnt about it only later from someone else.'

'Damn it, yaar, you Indians are all hypocrites, just like the goras. What is the big deal in this? I had submitted my claim for the hotel bill and other expenses to finance. That guy Nathan has gone and rejected it. He has sent it to London and Amsterdam, creating a big hue and cry. Who the hell is *he*? If he had a problem he could have just talked to me, yaar. If he was feeling left out, I could have arranged something for him as well. What is his problem? Sab hypocrites hain. What is the harm in some simple entertainment? Everybody does a little buttering of their bosses. *Thhodi bahut spot-fixing kar di to kaunsi badi gunaah ki hain humne?* What's wrong with a little bit of spot-fixing? It's all in the game.'

He left in a huff and I took a deep breath. This, I told myself, was one heck of a bank. There was always something or the other happening. And very little of it was actually connected with business.

Kitch too was feeling a bit low. A few days later he, Kapoor and I met for a bite at a café at Bur Juman. 'It's such a fucking mess,' he mourned. 'The management is all mixed up, we don't have any clarity, the structure is unclear, everyone has his or her own agenda. On the business side, Europe is sinking deeper into shit by the day. It's beginning to look like another 2008. Everything seems so insecure. I don't know what to hold onto and there's no relief in sight.'

Kapoor grinned. 'You just hold onto that,' he said, pointing at Kitch's crotch and making a crude hand movement. 'It will give you relief. *Apna haath Jagannath.*'

I left for London on training the next day. Mina decided to come along too, as a treat. It was her birthday in less than a week. Since the time she had done her studies in London, she had never gone back and was looking forward to it. She would catch up with friends while I was at the programme and then we could take a few days off to tour the English countryside and a bit of Europe.

The training course, which the new management had made mandatory for all those connected with investments, was abysmal. The trainer was a Scotsman who spoke with a thick accent that made listening a strain and gave me a throbbing headache. He went on and on about definitions of various investment terms, about sales theories and several tedious cases which we had to read and then answer questions at the end. I could not even muster up enough enthusiasm to read the cases, let alone answer the questions. On the third and final day, the new CEO of the bank came over to meet us. We thought it was just to say hello, but no. He had brought a presentation on what he called the 'push-pull theory'. It was something to the effect that a client would shift to a new bank if he faced problems with his existing bank while simultaneously being attracted to the other. This he explained to us over three hours, with the help of several flow charts, a hundred slides and a good bit of theory.

Consequently, it was doubly refreshing for me to rest my head in Mina's lap the next day, watching dreamily the clear blue sky above and listening to the sound of the ducks as they splashed and waded in the lake in front of us. We were at Windermere in the Lake District. The setting was calm, soothing and picturesque. If Mina hadn't been talking to me most of the time, I might have tried my hand at poetry that very day. After all, Wordsworth's residence Dove Cottage was just around the corner from where we stayed. How could one not be inspired to try and get some words to rhyme? Lakes, birds, ducks, grass, trees and delightful weather; it was sheer bliss. We did almost nothing for three full days and derived immense pleasure from it.

Our stay in Europe was more eventful. We did a Eurail trip, including a night train ride during which my beauty sleep was ruined by the fact that the train authorities took away our passports. I have always been a little paranoid about losing my passport and have this habit of patting my pocket every few minutes just to make sure it's there. To have to hand it over to a stranger and, worse, be told that someone else would give it back to me the next morning was enough to keep me up all night – though Mina insists I was asleep every time she woke up during the night.

Mina's birthday dawned fair and bright in Salzburg and we were pleasantly surprised when the staff of the hotel presented her with a bottle of champagne at the breakfast table; they had noted her date of birth from the copy of her passport. They stood there waiting for us to open it, so we did. They clapped and seemed genuinely happy – they must have been either extraordinarily good people or extremely talented actors.

After we popped open the bottle, there was a problem. I didn't feel like drinking champagne at eight in the morning and Mina doesn't drink in any case. So while the staff was looking elsewhere, Mina poured a good bit of it into the milk which remained in the cereal bowl.

The next thing we knew, there was a loud fizz and a mild explosion. The champagne had some sort of chemical reaction with the milk and, having bubbled over out of the bowl, was rapidly spreading across the tablecloth. Some of the staff screamed and others laughed, but all of them rushed to our table.

'I dropped the bottle by mistake!' I told them, my brain fizzing like the bubbly itself. As we left the room a few minutes later, they gave us another bottle and wouldn't take no for an answer.

That night we went to an Indian restaurant where we had the most expensive Indian meal we had had in a long time. 'The chapattis were so small!' Mina complained when we were on our way back to the hotel. 'And their portions of vegetables were like pickle.' My mind went back to Dubai and I wondered what had come of our proposed client 'do' and Gavas's cousin.

The poetic inspiration from Windermere lingered on and in honour of Mina's birthday, I managed to put a little thing together. It will not compare favourably with the works of our good friend William Wordsworth, but before you start smirking and giving it one on ten, see if you can do any better in twenty minutes. I did it while Mina was in the shower. In any case, she loved it when I presented it to her that night along with a rose and – I might as well admit it – a heart-shaped box of chocolates. For those readers who are not easily nauseated and who don't mind rhyme, it went like this:

What Have I Done to Deserve You?

No lands have I conquered
Nor battles have I won
No claim to fame have I
Nothing under the sun.

No Napolean am I, for sure
Nor a patch on Churchill
In fact, if you ask me
I'm pretty much a pill.

I'm not the Earl of Emsworth
Nor the Mayor of Winchester
Between you and me
I'm just a silly blister.

I can't paint like Leonardo
Nor can I, like him, act
I'm just a regular bloke
This I know for a fact.

But God has been great
And Cupid's been kind
They dropped you from the heavens
And made it easy for me to find.

Like a dewdrop on morning grass
You sud'nly came into my life
What a lovely treat it is
To have you as my wife.

Waca waca, have a nice day
Saminamina, oh Mina!
Saminamina, Saminamina
Tere bina bhi kya jina!

That last line, for those who need to be told, is Hindi for 'What is life without you'.

That night Mina was in a pensive mood. Thoughtful, even tense. But she brushed aside any signs of solicitous concern from me. I found out the reason the next morning.

Mina is one of those people who struggle to find words that rhyme. If my attempts at poetry are bad, hers are pathetic. On my twenty-eighth birthday, she sent me a bouquet of flowers with a poem so terrible that if she had not turned up in person shortly after, looking like an angel in a tight sweater and miniskirt, I might have been tempted to let the matter of our love story drop then and there.

On this occasion, she had decided to reply to my poem with one from her side; hence, the frown at night. When I woke up the next morning, I found a note from her. Don't get me wrong. Mina is a wife to die for. She is a great friend, a good cook, kind to animals, loved by everyone in my family, has a green thumb and is terrific in bed, but she cannot rhyme. This is what she had written:

You are not a pill
Also not a silly blister
You are the best man in the world
Mira agrees with me (my sister).

Yes, I know what you're thinking, but I can assure you that she was not dropped on her head when she was a baby. She's very bright in all other aspects of life. It's just that the moment she tries to make something rhyme, her mind kind of goes blank, like how I freeze if there are more than six people in the same room as me.

News trickled in from Dubai. After much deliberation, our off-site was going ahead as planned. We were still going to Udaipur, but they had reduced it from a three-day off-site to a two-day one. Since it was off-season, the bank was getting special rates from the hotel. But the economy class and the room-sharing rule stood, despite waves of negative feedback from staff. If spouses came along, they would have to be paid for by us.

The other irritant for me was that Nathan had kicked up a bit of stink about my taking days off after an official trip. Granted, I saved a bit of money, in that my London trip was paid for by the bank. I only had to pay for the European leg and, of course, Mina's entire trip. I didn't see why it mattered as long as the bank didn't lose money, but Nathan was miffed that I 'had not sought approval'. It left a bad taste in my mouth.

On a far brighter note, Rachel, Andy, Kitch and Galiya had visited Chennai and things had gone remarkably well. So well, in fact, that a priest had already been approached and he had given them a super auspicious date, one that he assured them came one's way only once in several years. 'Don't miss it for the world!' he had told them. The marriage was now just a few days away.

The other thing of note from among Kitch's tidbits was that Rachel's mum and aunt had visited Dubai, and Rach had thrown a party for them where Andy was introduced to them and some of her friends.

'Did it go well?' I asked Kitch eagerly.

'Well, it wasn't a huge success, but it was okay. They didn't try to stop the wedding or anything.'

'*What!* Who? Why?'

'Rachel's mum. You see, there was some confusion. Both Rachel's mum and her sister had decided to wear sarees, to get into the feel of things. Unfortunately, Andy couldn't quite tell them apart.'

'No! What happened? Do they look alike?'

'Not really,' said Kitch, 'that's the weird part. But of course, they are both British, around fifty and were wearing sarees.'

'But what did the idiot *do*? Nothing untoward, I hope?'

'No, no! Nothing like that. Only, he offered dessert to the aunt thrice and not even once to her mum. He thought her aunt was her mum.'

I mulled over this, trying to figure out the logic. 'So, if he thought her aunt was her mum, how does that account for the third time?' I asked. 'It should have been two.'

'What happened was this. He offered dessert – which, by the way, was carrot halwa with vanilla ice-cream – to Rachel's aunt, who was very touched and thanked him profusely. Seeing the opportunity to score a brownie point with his future mother-in-law, he decided to serve *her* as well, only, he offered it to the aunt again by mistake. She was a little taken aback and pointed out to him that she had just finished what he had given her. So Andy backed off and decided to leave it at that. But a little while later, he says he felt absolutely certain that the lady who had just come into the room was Rachel's mum, so he heaped halwa on a plate and gave it to her with a charming smile. But it turned out to be the aunt again. This time she neighed like a frightened horse and ran away. Her mum was a bit pissed off, I believe. But there was no harm done. Rachel told her he didn't mean to ignore her and it was just a joke. She couldn't exactly tell her the truth.'

'But Kitch! We can't just let this be. I mean, the poor fellow may be having a disease... well, not a disease maybe, but some sort of condition. Remember when he mixed up those two sisters?'

'Relax, it's okay, Jai. You get too uptight over these little things. Maybe he has a little problem telling foreign women apart. Most fifty-year-old British women look alike anyway. It's okay!'

'It's *not* okay, Kitch. And it's not a *little* problem not being able to tell foreign women apart,' I told him sternly, 'especially when the bugger is about to marry one.'

16

Till Death Do Us Part

The flight which was to have arrived the previous night finally landed in Chennai at about 8 a.m. on the day of the wedding. There had been a technical snag with the aircraft. The muhurtham was between nine and ten-thirty. We would be just in time, if we were lucky. It would be a shame if we were late because Harry was looking forward to savouring every bit of the ceremony. He had never been east of Dubai and his knowledge of India was limited to the Taj Mahal and stories that his grandfather had told him in his childhood. It was just Harry and me, because the others had taken an earlier flight.

I was fidgety from the moment the flight landed. I didn't want to be late for the most important part of the wedding. You could attend a Gujarati wedding in London or Kenya and still not know the exact moment when the bride and groom got married. In Tamil weddings it's not like that. It's a major event. The close relatives cluster on the stage to demonstrate their standing in the scheme of things; the not-so-close ones also try to clamber on in order to appear in the video. The bride sits in her father's lap, and the groom gets up from his cross-legged position, stands up and braces himself. The head priest swells with importance and signals to a group of musicians; the relatives shout out 'Gettimelam, gettimelam' upon which the nadaswaram players and the drummers go into a frenzy and reach a crescendo, ostensibly to drown out any negative remark or sound that may involuntarily emanate from anyone in the vicinity at the critical moment. At this point, the groom ties the all important 'thaali' – the Tamil word for a sacred chain used in weddings, not to be confused with the Hindi or Gujarati food thaali – around the bride's neck. The parents shed tears of joy, the groom looks bemused, the bride looks coy and then the two are man and wife. A few more customary procedures and there they are, permitted to take a brief break from the proceedings in order to receive blessings and gifts from elders and friends before going through with the rest of the rituals.

Harry, ever since he had received Andy and Rachel's wedding invitation, had been bitten by 'Indianitis'. Suddenly all the interest in India that normally should have been dispersed over two or three decades surfaced in a rush. In the last few weeks, he read whatever books on India he could get his hands on. He read *City of Joy*, he read a book on the history of textiles in India, he read *The God of Small Things*.

From the moment we walked into the airport, he was The Excited Tourist. His eyes darted here and there, taking in everything eagerly. He saw a large wooden statue of Ganesha and rushed towards it. 'That's Lord Ganesha, the elephant god!' he exclaimed, impressing himself with his knowledge even as I rushed to the customs counter, beckoning him to follow. On the way, Harry kept pointing to statues of goddesses that were kept at different points in the airport and asking me who they were.

'I don't know!' I said after a cursory look. 'We have hundreds of goddesses. C'mon, Harry!'

Harry came trotting behind me, reluctantly dragging himself away from a statue. 'I want to understand India in its entirety,' he said, a little petulantly, 'the *quintessential* India.'

'Hang on till the wedding is over, Harry,' I panted, pulling my suitcase behind me. 'We have less than an hour to reach Royapettah. You can understand your quintessential India at leisure after that.'

The customs officer took a fancy to Harry for some reason, and asked him to open his suitcase. It was filled with several jars of Marmite, cans of baked beans and a few dozen toilet-paper rolls. The officer blinked a couple of times. 'What is this?' he asked.

'It's toilet paper,' Harry replied. 'You see, I… umm… er… ah,' he concluded.

The officer stared at the suitcase and then at Harry with a nasty gleam in his eye. 'You may also have been told that we shit in the streets,' he said. 'Why have you not brought bathroom? And what are all these tins?'

'That, well, you see, it's my first visit to India and I wasn't sure about…'

The officer turned to me and spoke in rapid Tamil, which I mostly understood: 'Your white friend must be expecting an elephant outside the airport to take him to the hotel. Tell him to do an Indian rope trick and climb the elephant.' He walked off in a bit of a huff.

'Wow! That bloke was intimidating, Jack. What was all that about? Did he say something about the Indian rope trick? Do I get to see it around here?'

'Harry, stop talking! Run!'

Half an hour later, we were doing reasonably well for time but moving in fits and starts; for a few metres, our driver would race ahead, stop suddenly with a back-jolting jerk just in front of an unmarked speed breaker, pick up speed and then come to a screeching, heart-numbing halt within a millimetre of the car in front. At all times, we were – to Harry's extreme discomfiture – within touching distance of vehicles on both sides.

'Is there a problem, Jack? Or is this regular traffic?'

'Oh, just routine stuff, Harry.' I looked at my watch. We would probably make it with ten minutes to spare. By my reckoning, we were just three kilometres away from the wedding hall. 'We're doing okay now, Harry. We'll get there in time.'

'Phew!' he said. 'This is some ride; it's scarier than a roller coaster.' He looked back nervously. 'Why are they honking at us, Jack?'

'They're not honking at us, they're just honking. It's therapeutic. It releases frustration. Relax, Harry, and take a deep breath. You are in the land that discovered yoga.'

Harry took in a deep breath, filling his lungs with dust and carbon dioxide, and promptly choked. 'I say! Will I... cough... will I have time to wear my Indian costume?'

The phone rang. It was Kitch.

'Jai! Where are you? *Where?* Okay, now listen! There's a problem. We've forgotten the thaali! The wedding can't happen without it. We realized after we came here in the morning and called our maid to bring it, but that mandu idiot girl hasn't come yet. And she's not answering the phone. Do me a favour, da. Rush home and bring the damn thing. Do you know the way from where you are?'

'Sort of, Kitch. I think we are near the end of Chamiers Road now… Tell you what, Kitch, you talk to Harry, I'll guide the driver. *Driver!* Turn right here, right, *right,* mere bhai, *right turn*!' I turned to Harry and explained as best as I could, 'They've left something at home. They can't get married without it. We need to pick it up. Here, talk to Kitch.'

Harry took the phone and I tried to figure out the best way to reach Kitch's place when approaching it from the wrong side; I had only been to his place from my house. Kitch appeared to have asked Harry to describe the scenes outside the window, so he could follow our progress. 'I can see a tree,' Harry was saying. 'More trees… there are some people sitting on the pavement, apartment blocks, lots of people walking on the road, there's a poster of an elderly, bald gentleman wearing dark glasses, more posters of him and even more post… what? Okay, okay, no need to get cross, Kitch! Now I see lots of yellow auto-rickshaws, cycles, bikes… cars, whoa! Blimey! What was that? A pothole? Heavens, Jai, I thought we had fallen into a ditch. I say, Kitch, there doesn't seem to be anything particularly remarkable… we're just going down a road… Oh, there's something that looks like a hotel. I beg your pardon? Yes, it's Sheraton… okay.

Jai! Ask him not to turn left. Straight ahead, Jai! Straight!'

We covered another few hundred metres. 'There's a restaurant on the right,' said Harry, continuing his monologue, 'and there's a huge pit, they're digging up the road.'

'Can you put him on speaker, Harry?' I butted in. 'I think we're pretty close.'

'What, Kitch? A big cow? Yes, yes, I can see it. Left turn here, Jai. I say, Kitch! Listen! There's no road to the left. The cow is crossing the road now… it's going towards…'

'Not a *real* cow, dumbo!' Kitch's exasperated voice boomed over the speaker. 'A picture of a cow on a billboard.'

'There!' I pointed some hundred metres ahead.

'Oh, okay. That's the one then! Left turn here, er… left… What's your name, sir? What-is-your-name?'

'Kulandaivelu, saar,' said the driver.

'Umm… okay,' Harry acknowledged, slightly flummoxed. 'Now, turn left at the signal just ahead, sir!'

'Not allowed, saar. Only going right here. No left, no straight. Right going only.'

'NO!' Kitch bellowed, his voice loud and clear over the speaker. 'I don't care! There's no time to take the diversion. If there's no policeman, turn left. Jai! Harry! Turn left! Driver! Left turn eduppa!'

The cabbie needed no further persuasion. He had heard the voice of authority. He swerved left and then was directed right and left again down Subramaniyan Street, into Abhimarapuram 1st Main Road, stopping at Kitch's bungalow on the left. The familiar sound of screaming schoolkids threatened to burst our eardrums. Bidding the driver to wait, Harry and I leapt out and rang the bell. There was no response.

At the other end of the line, Kitch was joined by his parents. 'Bang on the door,' his father exhorted us. *'Break it down!'*

'Aunty, can't we just buy another thaali?' I suggested.

'No!' his mother shrieked. 'That is the one for which we have done puja this morning in front of the deities. If you can't get that one, there will be no wedding, that is for sure! This may be a bad omen!'

Harry had disappeared behind the house. He resurfaced suddenly.

'Harry!' I said, placing my palm over the phone. 'Kitch's mum says they'll stop the wedding if we don't retrieve the thaali! Rachel will be devastated!' I rang the bell again. 'I think there's no power. I can't hear any ringing.'

'That can't be,' Harry surmised in his typically clinical manner. His initial feelings of apprehension and nervousness seemed to have abated and he was getting into the thick of the action. 'From the backyard, I could see an open door on the balcony of the first floor. There's a fan running.'

'That's another electric phase,' shouted Kitch. 'She *must* be there. Can you go back there and shout for her?'

We rushed behind the house. Standing below the balcony, my lungs ready, I suddenly realized I didn't know what to shout.

'What's her name?' I asked Kitch.

'I don't know!' he replied. 'Can't remember right now.'

'Ask your mother.'

'They are all very busy on the stage with the priests and everything. I can't ask anyone now. Just shout, guys. Shout anything!'

Harry and I exchanged a look.

'Hello!' I shouted. 'Suniye!'

'Excuse me, miss!' shouted Harry. 'Are you there?'

Kitch's voice sounded again. 'I think her name is either Damini or Dhanalakshmi. I have a feeling it starts with D and ends with I.'

'Damini!' I yelled.

'Dammy-nay!' Harry shouted. '*Dammy-nay!*'

'Dhanalakshmi!' I shouted.

'I say!' said Harry. 'I don't think I could do that one very well, Jack! I think I'll stick to the first name. What was it now.... Danny-may! Danny-may!'

'Actually, it's neither of those,' said Kitch, sounding excited. 'I remember now. It's Damayanti!'

'Jesus!' Harry exclaimed. 'How do you spell that, Kitch?'

'Screw the spelling, damn it!' Kitch's agitated voice reverberated on the phone. 'Shout, man! Just shout!'

Harry and I looked at each other wildly and then at the balcony above us.

'Damayanti!' I screamed. 'Damayanti! Damayantee-ee! This is not getting us anywhere, Harry. Harry? Where are you?'

Harry might be in a strange land, full of strange happenings, but he was no poltroon. He had his head screwed on right and he was fit and strong. His grandfather had been in the British Navy and he himself had boxed two years for Oxford. 'I'm up here,' he shouted. Leaving my phone on the grass, he had shinned up a water pipe that led almost up to the balcony.

'Harry, that's fantastic, dude. Way to go!' I cheered.

He showed me a thumbs up sign and braced himself for the final assault. Suddenly something hit the wall. 'Ow!' cried Harry. Something else hit Harry on the ear. I picked it up. It was a sharp pencil. Then there was another, then an eraser, followed by the core of an apple.

'Ow! I say! Stop it, you guys!' Harry shouted, waving at something behind me. I turned around. It was the schoolkids! They had all gathered by the wall and looked mutinous. Angered by the fact that someone was trying to enter their beloved Andy uncle's house by stealth, they had decided to take matters into their own hands. Those little hands were working fast and furiously now. Pencils, erasers, pebbles, tiffin boxes, leftovers, books... anything they could lay their hands on, they were bent on hurling over the wall at Harry.

An intruder at their benefactor's house, and a white man at that! Over sixty years of freedom and now this! With one desperate leap, Harry jumped onto the balcony and disappeared from sight. This gave fresh impetus to the rebellion next door. It spilled over, like the champagne in Mina's milk during our Austria trip. Several kids, some of them armed with rulers, sticks and stones, jumped over the wall and rushed towards me. If they couldn't get the criminal, they would settle for his accomplice. I did the only thing I could. Abandoning all thoughts of Harry, Kitch, Rachel and Andy, I stooped down, grabbed my phone, turned on my heel and fled. Leaping into the cab, I shouted, 'Go!'

'Where, saar?' Kulandaivelu asked.

'Anywhere!' I shouted. 'Just go! Go!'

The driver, meanwhile, spied the pint-sized uniformed revolutionaries and, looking horrified, stepped on the pedal. With a roar and a puff of dust, the car raced down the street.

My phone rang again. I didn't even realize the line had got cut. But it wasn't Kitch calling back as I had expected. It was Harry.

'Jack,' he said, his voice shaking. 'Th-this lady, this... this maid girl... I think she is dead.'

17

Chilling in Chennai

My phone fell by my side. My heart stopped. In fact, every part of my body stopped, except, perhaps, the inside of my head, and even that seemed to have completely lost its bearings. It was spinning madly and meaninglessly like a fluffy ball that has got enmeshed in some kind of vicious machinery.

Why did something like this have to happen? A young couple had got together after such difficulty, and on the morning of their wedding they had to leave the thaali at home and have their maid lying in a pool of blood? What kind of justice was this? I would willingly take on several recessions and liquidity crises if only that could somehow take away this current problem. If only the maid were not dead. If only the thaali were in my hands this minute. Nothing could bring anyone back to life but, foolishly, that's all I could pray for; at that moment, I wanted nothing else.

'Where are you, Jack? Hello? Hello, Jack, are you there?'

Somewhere in the distance I could hear Harry's voice but it didn't register immediately. It took time for the voice and what it said to penetrate the layers of cotton wool that had been substituted for my brain. Once it did, I was filled with guilt. This was Harry's first visit to my country and I had left him alone in a strange house with a dead body, after allowing him to shin up a twenty-foot water pipe. And leaving him there, I, Jai Shantilal Patel, had scampered like a petrified rabbit, at the mere sight of a handful of primary schoolkids armed with pebbles and small wooden rulers. I was disgusted with myself.

'I'll be there in a jiffy, Harry.'

I reached the house. There was no sign of the kids. Harry had kept the door open and was in the living room, walking around in circles, clutching his head and making low moaning noises. His face was pale and his lips were quivering. 'This is terrible, Jack. This is utterly awful. What on earth are we to do?' he asked agitatedly. 'Do they have emergency services in India? We need to call a doctor. Though I think it might be too late. Jack, I've never seen anyone look so... so d-dead.'

He looked so weak and vulnerable that I suddenly found my strength. I needed to take care of two bodies – one dead, one barely alive. The hour had produced the man.

'Stiff upper lip, Harry,' I said bravely before running up the stairs. 'Let me take a look.'

I was strong all the way up, but as soon as I reached the landing of the first floor, my feet stopped by themselves. My upper body tried to continue the impetus that my legs had briefly provided, but my feet just glued themselves to the floor and refused to listen to my brain. I was plain scared.

Nothing in life prepares you for this kind of thing. I had never seen a corpse at close quarters before and definitely not alone in a room. I hesitated, trying to mentally prepare myself. I hoped Harry would go in first. After all, he had seen it before. But the poor simp stuck close to my back. 'Harry,' I said, trying rather unsuccessfully to pivot my body around my stationary feet in such a way that Harry would come between me and the dreaded room. 'But Harry, *why* is she dead? I mean, how do you even know she is?'

'She's sprawled on the floor in a frightfully weird way. There's no sign of life; none whatsoever.'

'B-blood?'

'I don't think so, Jack. I didn't notice any.'

I inched into the room, dragging my reluctant feet behind me. There she was, right in the middle of the room, lying on her stomach, hands outstretched and legs slightly apart. But it wasn't as grotesque a picture as I had imagined. And there was one thing that made hope suddenly surge within me, like a penny stock company that has suddenly struck oil. She was wearing a blouse and a long skirt but, more relevantly, she had used her dupatta to cover herself, as with a blanket.

'Harry!' I exclaimed. 'There's just a chance, isn't there, that she... she might be sleeping. I mean, there's no blood or anything. Besides, she is lying under the fan and has covered herself. Maybe she is asleep – in very deep sleep', I added, trying to sound convincing.

'But she looks so lifeless, Jack. Besides, surely she wouldn't sleep on the *floor*.'

'Why not? She's a maid. She wouldn't sleep on Kitch's parents' bed like Goldilocks.'

'But then, why...'

The phone rang again. 'What's happening, you guys? We have just half an hour to go for the end of the muhurtham.'

'Kitch, we are inside the house. The girl is lying on the floor,' I reported.

'Never mind where the girl is lying! The thaali is lying in front of the gods' pictures on the ground floor. Get it and move.'

'But Kitch, this girl, I'm not sure... she looks rather lifeless, but I'm hoping... I mean, there's a small chance that she might just be asleep.'

'Pull her up and see! Don't waste time. Kick her in the butt! Stop loafing around, Jai, goddammit! Shout, pull her hair, throw some water on her and move your asses, both of you.'

'Damini?' I ventured, a shiver racing through my spine as I suddenly remembered every ghost story I had ever heard in my life. 'D-Damayanti!'

'Jack, I think I will try some mouth-to-mouth resuscitation,' Harry whispered.

I patted him encouragingly and edged closer to the staircase. Harry shot in my direction a look that nicely blended fear and agony, summoned up courage, and then tilted her face up, held her by the chin and shook her head. He thrust his lips out like a goldfish and bent down. Suddenly the girl opened her eyes and let out a piercing scream.

In hindsight, I don't entirely blame her. It couldn't have been easy for her to be shaken awake by a strange, wild-eyed, tousled-haired white man apparently bent on manhandling her. But at that moment, I was paralyzed with fear. The scream was so unexpected that it sounded like the wailing of a banshee. The next second, she was sprinting down the stairs.

Harry looked at me. I looked at him. It was an inexplicably magical moment that we shared. A moment which, I knew immediately, would bond us for life. Once the first terrifying point in time –

at the onset of that scream – had passed, the relief we felt was monumental.

By the time we rushed downstairs, the girl was nowhere in sight. We found the puja room. There was the thaali, glistening on a shiny silver tray, beckoning to us. 'Kitch,' I said, trying hard not to let the phone slip through my sweaty grip, and making no attempt to disguise the note of filmy triumph that had automatically entered my voice, 'we've got it. I'm holding it in my hand. We'll be there in twenty minutes, max.'

We slammed the door shut and ran to the cab. The cabbie fixed a pair of accusing eyes on me. 'Dushta naai,' he snarled. I didn't know what the first word meant. But I knew the second one was Tamil for dog. The man had obviously got all fired up for some reason. Maybe he was just peeved at having been made to wait. But he didn't stop there. He let forth a torrent of Tamil words, many of them words they would never teach you in school.

'No understand Tamil' I said untruthfully, hoping to stump the man.

But he was up to the task. 'Then I talk English,' he barked. 'What you doing that poor running girl, bloody? Huh? What you doing, maira pudingi, son of a what-not?'

He suddenly shifted his savage gaze from me to Harry. 'You come from damn foreign land to chase after our girls? To wipe the virginity of our holy womenfolk, what they are guarding like most precious jewel? I heard shouting that girl! Bloody common rowdy! I will break your legs and give it to your hands or my name is not the Kulandaivelu!' he said.

Harry uttered a wordless cry of horror and staggered back.

'No! I didn't… I wasn't… You misunderstand me, sir! I was just trying some mouth-to-mouth resusci…'

'Mouth to mouth! Muruga! What bloody you think? You think you coming like white God for kissing and destroying the innocence of our girls? I call police and ask them hitting you with chappal and sending you jail! Wretched dog!'

'I say, no! No, Mr Colin-day-way-loo! I-I didn't do a thing. Jack! Tell him! Don't just stand there, man! Talk to him!'

'No, sir,' I said, looking at the driver desperately. 'Please understand, brother. We are friends of the owner of this house. His brother is getting married. They forgot the thaali. We came to get it… Look.' I thrust the shiny tray at him. 'That girl was sleeping. She just got scared when she saw us. My friend is having his muhurtham now. If we are late, the wedding will be stopped. He will have love failure, heart failure! Only twenty minutes for the muhurtham! Help us… sir, saar, anna!'

The man looked at me, then at Harry and finally at the tray. He lowered his eyelids. His eyes were not visible, but I sensed they had lost their fire. Bending forward, he briefly rested the bridge of his nose on his thumb and his index finger.

'Feelings, saar!' he said in a voice choked with emotion. 'Total feelings! Too much, I'm feeling it!' A pearly tear escaped his downcast eyes. Or it may have dropped from the beads of sweat that bathed his forehead. In Chennai, one can never tell. Tapping his chest with the index finger of his right hand, he continued, 'Emotional is touching the heart, saar!'

Then he looked up. His eyes were moist but determined. He had the air of a man who had taken a decision and intended to stick to it. He stuck out his lower lip in a gesture of defiance and raised his finger. 'Do or die, let us to try!' he pledged, jutting his chin out.

We had won him over. Turning into a rugged man of action, he leapt into his car, shouting, 'Come on, gentlemans, let us to go! I am the Kulandaivelu, I never say no!'

Poetry, I realized, was no more the privilege of noble princes or hungry philosophers. In the twenty-first century, it had descended to the level of the masses. And they had embraced it. Mina could take a lesson or two from this man. 'It is never too late,' he assured us, 'come whatever the fate!'

For the next twelve minutes, we zipped, zapped and zoomed; we swerved, skidded and screeched. Once we crashed and twice we flew as Kulandaivelu set out to conquer kismet. Harry, in complete contrast, was huddled in one corner of the backseat, unable to share the driver's enthusiasm. After his brief flirtation with bravado in Kitch's house, he seemed to have resigned himself to being a puppet in the hands of destiny. His eyes were shut. Little murmurs emanated from his mouth – he seemed to be praying. For Kulandaivelu, however, it was clearly a case of the end justifying the means. He was a man with a frenzied mission. 'My motto never to slow,' he raged. 'Today, even red means go!' At the end of those twelve minutes, we were at our destination.

'I'll settle the fare, Harry,' I said. 'You take this thing and run inside.'

Harry hesitated. For a homegrown British gentleman of regular habit, it was not easy to thrust himself in the limelight in a foreign country, that too in a wedding hall packed with strangers.

'B-but, I say! There are hundreds of people in there. How do I find Kitch?'

'He'll find you. Just hold the tray aloft and run. Go!'

For about four seconds, he stood there. He may have been praying or just frozen. He could have been savouring the moment or summoning the spirits of his ancestors. Whatever it was, it worked. The plucky lad was suddenly filled with renewed vigour. This was the India his ancestors had ruled for some three hundred years. He could not fear the country or her people. He picked up the tray, licked his lips and strode purposefully into the hall.

Meanwhile, Kulandaivelu, after starting off by saying he was loath to charge for such a noble cause, was now bargaining for a rather substantial sum. Having forgotten to bring any rupees with me, I persuaded him to accept dirhams and then rushed inside.

Inside the hall, there was drama aplenty. This, after all, was Chennai. Subtlety was not the city's forte. A small crowd, whooping and rejoicing, had lifted Harry on their shoulders and was waving him around like a banner. He had been relieved of the precious thaali, which had found its way to the stage. Seconds later, the nadaswarams and drums took over, people crowded around the stage and the rest of the audience craned its necks to catch a glimpse of the defining moment. Tradition, after playing hard to get, had embraced young love and blessed it. Photographers clicked away, Harry their clear favourite, followed by Andy and Rachel.

Later that evening, the reception was held at the same venue. The highlight was a dance programme by twenty-odd students from the school behind Kitch's house. Harry and I stood at the back of the hall, trying to remain inconspicuous. The tumultuous events of the morning were fresh in our memory. The teachers, helped by Kitty, had worked on a medley of two or three Tamil songs and combined it with two theme songs of the Chennai Super Kings. The kids wore yellow t-shirts, the boys with Rachel's picture on them and the girls with Andy's.

At the end of this programme, Kitch's dad made an announcement that a very special family friend had agreed to be the guest of honour and had also consented to sing a song. Then he beckoned to me and took me to a room adjoining the hall. 'I know you are very fond of music. Let me introduce you to our friends Sangeetha and her husband Shankar Mahadevan.'

Shankar Mahadevan! Here I was, once again, face-to-face with the man. One look at each other and I knew immediately that he remembered.

'Y-you!' he spluttered.

'I can explain!' I cried and proceeded to do so hastily. He looked at me for a moment and then threw his head back and guffawed.

'He is not the first north Indian to have got confused between the two names. Don't mind me, but I really thought you were a nutcase,' he said, and his wife immediately jabbed him in the ribs.

Then he went onstage and rendered a Tamil hit number to thunderous applause. One by one, the schoolkids clambered up on stage and started performing an impromptu dance. It was the most heartwarming thing I'd seen in a long time. As the singer raised the tempo, the kids worked up such a frenzy that they were just a blur. Down below, the audience clapped madly. The song ended with a bang and another impromptu act. The kids bodily lifted the singer and carried him off the stage, cheering madly. One of the smaller kids left the group, went back to the mike and announced in a squeaky voice, 'Shankar Mahadevanku o podu!' It brought the house down.

The next morning, we discovered that, thanks to the musician's presence, the wedding ceremony had been covered by two Tamil dailies and one English paper. The English paper carried a small two-column news item under the heading 'Brit's timely entry unites hearts'. The Tamil papers devoted a lot more space to the wedding. One of them had a half-page article with a title that read 'Tsunami hero gets married in dramatic style'. It included pictures of Andy, Rachel, the schoolkids and Shankar Mahadevan. The other one, a tabloid, screamed in bold print across two pages: 'White man ensures no delay in Chennai boy's first night with white woman'.

That night, Peggy, Harry, Rachel, Kitch, Ravi, Andy, Mina, Galiya and I were relaxing by a hotel pool and sipping cold long drinks. I could see that Rachel was still recovering from the rigours of a full-blown Tamil wedding.

'Mrs Rachel Anand Iyer!' I teased. 'Aren't you looking a little too sexy for a newlywed Tam-Bram bride? Is your husband refusing to buy you clothes?'

'My young horse will refuse me nothing, Mr Patel!' she replied. 'But I spent three hours in front of the wedding fire. I feel more like a piece of meat than anything human. I don't think I will wear regular clothes again for a long time. Just lotions and some bare essentials.'

I looked at Harry, who was glugging down pint after pint with single-minded focus. 'Speaking of essentials, Harry,' I said, grinning at him, 'now that all this is over, you are free to go about understanding the quintessential India.'

He looked me straight in the eye and twitched his lip, in an action that passes off for a smile among Brits. 'I have a suspicion that I already have, Jack,' he said drily.

'I have some good news,' announced Kitch's cousin Ravi, who had just finished answering a phone call. 'Mary is back home.'

'Who's Mary?' Kitch asked.

'The maid. The one who disappeared. It seems

she had just wanted to rest for a few minutes and fell asleep. When she woke up she got so scared she ran away to a relative's house. She came back today, full of apologies.'

Distracting Harry from his drink is not easy. But it happened now.

'Did you say her name was Mary?' asked Harry. 'Not something starting with D?'

'No, I'm quite sure it's Mary.'

Harry looked at me and then at Kitch. Kitch grinned sheepishly. He shrugged his shoulders and spread out his hands helplessly. 'I don't know why I felt so certain it started with D. Maybe that was the previous maid,' he said with a laugh.

Harry glared at him. He had suffered much. He did not seem to think his newfound newspaper celebrity status compensated for what he had gone through. 'Asshole!' he growled.

After the wedding celebrations, we split ways. The newlyweds went to Bhutan for reasons best known to them. Perhaps they wanted spirituality or maybe they wanted to ferret out the secret to the country's high level of 'Gross Domestic Happiness'. A rather worried Peggy returned to Dubai. The new management had apparently not been very receptive to her suggestions for the business. Kitch's cousin Ravi was spearheading some sort of social movement in India. He had even got offers to join a political party. Harry went off to see the Taj Mahal.

Peggy had told Kitch and me to remain in India, take a few days off and then go straight to Udaipur for the off-site.

'Peggy, surely we are not that strapped for cash!' I had said, rather surprised. After all, AdAb was still a strong and widely respected bank.

'No, it's not just that, Jack. There is something brewing... something I'm working on. I will be back in Chennai in three days. I want to meet you and Kitch here and then we can go to Udaipur together.'

It was rather odd, but I was happy to leave it to her to sort things out. We took advantage of it by pushing off to a 'green' resort near Bangalore – Kitch, Galiya, Mina and I. Mina is a sucker for anything green. We had met this chap who had started an eco-friendly place just outside Bangalore. He told Mina about his earth-saving project and Mina promptly arranged for us to be cut off from civilization for a couple of days. During this time, we would detox – probably by being fed wheat grass and aloe vera – before heading to Udaipur and Dubai and retoxing. The plan suited Kitch because he had an appointment with his godman prospect client near Agumbe in Karnataka. He would probably be able to drive there from Bangalore.

Anyway, there we were in a clean, bright but rather sparse room. It had nice French windows on which an earthworm was slowly making its way up. I wondered if this was part of the deal. I am not a reptile-friendly person. Outside, there were patches of brown and green; trees, bushes and grass punctuated by mounds of earth or bare sand. It was obvious from our drive up that we were at least ten miles away from civilization.

I went to have a wash, but couldn't find the bathroom. A minute later I found it, outside the room. It was one of those open bathrooms, with a stone floor and a shower in the middle, covered by foliage on all sides and the open skies above. You could shower and smile cheerily at the birds flying above you... that kind of stuff. Again, not my thing.

'How divine!' Mina gushed. She is one of those nature freaks. Her idea of fun and relaxation is to watch a bird dip its beak into her cucumber juice or have a worm climb up her leg while she is sipping her tea.

I maintained a silence as stony as the bathroom floor as I surveyed the place. Unable to find any towels or soap, I called reception and discovered that these had to be bought separately – dull-looking, rather expensive towels made of organic cotton and other indigenous material, and some rock-like soap certified to be handmade in an eco-friendly manner by residents of the nearby village. They had no shampoo.

Mina had managed to infect Galiya with her enthusiasm and the two of them prepared to leave almost immediately on a trek to Hasiru Gudi to watch tribals weave mats from coconut tree leaves, but Kitch wormed his way out of it. I had a genuine reason for not joining them: I was nursing a bad sprain. While showering, in a bid to take my mind off the slightly disconcerting fact that I was practically out in the open in the nude, I had chosen to sing. I was singing Shankar Mahadevan's 'Rind posh maal' from *Mission Kashmir*, an old favourite, and had just reached the high-pitched finale which needed every ounce of concentration, when a smallish winged creature decided to join me both in song and shower. Hurtling itself in my direction with a buzzing sound, it latched itself uninvited to my chest.

For a moment I did nothing. I could have been a sculpture in stone. Then I half-yelled half-screamed and went through a series of motions – some intended, some not – calculated to scare, shake or push the creature off me. One of the unintended actions – and the only one that actually succeeded – was to slip on a slightly mossy piece of stone and crash to the floor, wrenching my knee painfully in the process. Stopping both song and shower that instant, I limped back to

the room, leaving behind the winged devil and my peace of mind.

The girls were back in time for lunch, armed with handwoven mats and baskets. At the restaurant, we were given a choice between liquid, raw and mixed food. We chose the mixed. It wasn't too bad. There was a sprout-and-bean salad and a salad with lettuce and tomatoes. There was soup, boiled potatoes, chapattis made of soyabean and whole wheat, some vegetables from their garden and a dessert made with coconut milk.

Over the course of the meal, a lady came around with a notepad, asking if we would like to 'sleep under the stars'. Mina promptly signed up for all four of us. So, that night, we were put up at a camp nearby, where someone gave us a short astronomy class, mostly with reference to stars that should have been there rather than stars that were there – it was a cloudy night.

We lay down, talking of this and that. I gave my knee a good rub with some oil that the hotel manager had produced, made no doubt from organic seeds. The hotel had provided sleeping bags which had been spread on the grass. It was a quiet night, bereft of breeze. Leaves on trees in the distance moved very slightly. Closer to us, the clumpy bushes were still, like they were carved out of rock.

'This is it,' said Mina blissfully, looking at the starless sky. 'Just the way nature intended it to be.'

The rest of us remained quiet.

'What was that?' asked Galiya after a while.

'What?' I asked, alert at once.

'Something just rushed past me.'

'It must be a leaf or something,' said Mina.

'I-it was not a leaf. It went near Jack's head. It had eyes.'

I sprang up like a horizontal jack-in-the-box. 'W-w-wazizard?'

'What?' Galiya asked.

'W-was it a lizard?'

'Of course not,' said Mina quickly. 'Jai, it was probably just some baby insect. It won't harm us.'

'I'm scared too, like Jack,' Galiya mumbled.

'I'm not *scared*,' I protested. 'I just don't like creepy-crawlies. Most people don't. What's wrong with that? And I'm not so sure about this idea of sleeping under the stars,' I went on. 'There are no stars in the first place.'

'Jai, please try not to make a fuss. You're behaving like your cousin Dolly. This is all part of nature. It is one big system – plants, animals, birds, insects and us. We have to...'

Something went plop on Kitch's bed and hopped away. I leapt up, painfully wrenching my knee all over again.

'I'm going to the room,' I said in a voice filled with self-pity and pain. 'Sleeping under the stars is one thing. But sleeping with lizards and frogs is quite another.' I hobbled away purposefully, not even turning to look behind me. I could hear them getting up and scrambling, one by one.

The next day, we returned to Bangalore and stayed there while Kitch drove off for his tryst with the godman.

'You don't have to take any forms with you,' I told him. 'He can just snap his fingers and make his account appear in Geneva.'

'Along with a few million dollars,' Kitch said optimistically. 'Still, I'll take a few forms along. I might meet some rich disciples; guys with money that now means nothing to them. They might open an account, or even better, just give it all to me.'

So while I went to see a doctor, Kitch went to meet Putla Baba.

While I was at the doctor's clinic, Kitch called. 'Jai, this is some place. This is real nature. It's raining like crazy and there is greenery everywhere. It's almost bursting with vegetation. I have stopped for lunch now. The ashram is an hour away from here, in the middle of a jungle!'

'Enjoy!' I said. 'Ask the guy to drive carefully. The ghat roads can get slippery when it rains.'

'So what is the problem?' the doctor asked me.

'I have sprained my right knee,' I told him. 'It hurts a lot if I turn it left.'

He grabbed my right knee and promptly turned it left, making me cry out. He smiled and nodded his head. He seemed satisfied.

'Yes,' he said. 'It seems to be a sprain. Let us take an x-ray anyway.'

'Jai!' Kitch called again. 'It's a weird place, this. They have statues all over the place – putlas. That's why they call him Putla Baba. They have kept me waiting in a large room. The guy who left me here said, once Baba decides to meet someone he leaves them in this room, and they have to stay here even if it takes days or weeks for Baba to meet them. I'm feeling a little uncomfortable about all this. Also, there are some devotees in the next room doing a weird slow dance followed by a frenzied shimmy. I saw them through a gap in the window. They are wearing nothing on top.'

'That's not so uncommon with these devotees, Kitch, you should know.'

'These are women.'

'Oh, wow!'

'Not so wow in a place like this, Jai. It just adds to the weirdness. I can't quite explain it. Shhh! Someone's just come. Call you later.'

I went to the radiologist. It was a long wait. There was a sign outside that said 'Suspicious pregnant women please tell doctor about x-ray'.

I had a vision of a room filled with women, their bellies protruding, eyes darting here and there, casting suspicion on each other and furtively whispering to the doctor.

'Stand very still and turn your right knee to the left,' the x-ray chap advised me when my turn came.

'I can't do that,' I told him. 'If I could, I wouldn't be here.'

'If you don't do it, the x-ray will not serve the purpose,' he said sternly.

I finally consented and went through the painful process of twisting a twisted knee and standing in that position for several seconds as I waited for the chap to click. When I went back to the doctor, he placed the x-ray against a bright light and declared that it was a sprain.

'Take these tablets for a few days and apply this ointment. Lots of rest.'

When I came out of the doctor's office, I realized that Kitch had called me thrice. Hurriedly, I rang him.

'I've escaped!' he gasped. 'Thank god! The guy who came in was the tea boy. I asked him about all those statues of strange people and he told me they were statues of people whom Baba doesn't like. He said Baba has the power to turn anyone into a putla! I just ran for my life. I'm in the car now. Hogi, ree!' I heard him telling the driver. 'Bayga bayga hogi!'

I turned to the cute receptionist at the clinic. 'What is "bayga bayga hogi" in Kannada?' I asked.

She thought for a moment. 'It means "Drive like crazy".'

18

The Damocles Sword Dangles

We had a day to spare in Bangalore after Kitch got back. Meanwhile, Peggy, after stopping in Mumbai for a day, was already in Chennai. She called to ask if she could meet up with our parents, so Kitch and I arranged it. I was a little surprised, though. I would have thought she'd wait for us to return. It made me all the more certain that something was cooking. We were on the verge of completing one full year at the bank. Just a year, though it felt longer. I think we had managed to pack quite a bit into it.

While we were in Bangalore, Kitch and I had the idea of starting a restaurant there. I came up with a concept that Kitch and Mina just loved. We'd call it K2K: Kashmir to Kanyakumari. We would serve one or two delicacies from each Indian state, rather than just focus on one type of cuisine. They thought it was a unique idea.

'Frankly, Jai,' Kitch said, 'I wouldn't be terribly

upset if something was up at AdAb. I kind of miss the restaurant business. On the other hand, it's so much fun being together and working together. If we could find a way to handle the restaurant business together, I'd love it.'

We spent that evening checking out a few pubs and a restaurant or two. Bangalore has many pubs catering to – in complete contrast to Chennai – a thriving pub culture. 'In Chennai, people seem to drink either at restaurants in five-stars or in the streets or slums. There's not much in between,' said Kitch. 'If only we could get a licence to start a pub or two in Chennai, I'm sure we could make a roaring success of it. Can you think of some sexy name, Jai?'

'You can call it Sam Bar,' Mina laughed. 'You know, like *sambar*! You might attract both the drinkers and the idli eaters.'

Kitch was delighted. 'It is the perfect name for a Chennai pub!' he exclaimed. 'Sam Bar! Wow!'

'I want to start a non-vegetarian place, guys,' said Galiya. 'We need to cater to all tastes, right, Jack?'

'Right, Gal. We need to make both ends *meat*. Hey, how about this for a name: *Meating Point*. M-e-a-ting Point. Isn't that cool?'

'Meating Point! Good one, Jack.'

'And we can do the e-a-t part of the name in a different colour! So we sort of cover everything.

Eat, meat and a place to meet!' I said, feeling rather pleased with myself.

'The youth market is where the big margins are made,' Kitch said. 'Either they have money to throw or they behave as if they do. Either way, it's good for us. What attracts the youth, the late teens and early twenties? What do they want? What sells?'

'Well, we can't put that there,' said Mina. 'Sex and violence in a restaurant would be illegal!'

'I know!' I shouted. 'We can have music like we had at Armani!'

The others looked at me sceptically. 'And you think that's what our young people are screaming for?'

'No, don't you remember?' I said excitedly. 'That client party at Armani! There was a lady on the violin and a guy on the saxophone. We can get two musicians like that and name the restaurant "Sax and Violins"! That will bring in the youth in the thousands!'

'Idiot!' said Mina with a laugh.

'And when the youth find out what the restaurant is really about, they'll have it burned down in two minutes,' said Kitch.

By the time we got to Chennai, Peggy was already there. She had already met with both our families and had a long chat both with my dad and Kitch's.

Kitty told us Peggy took her and Shree out for dinner and seemed most interested in her dance school and other plans.

That night Kitch and I met Peggy in her hotel room. Over the next hour, things became clear. A lot had been happening in the background. How little we knew about it, so immersed were we in our own worlds. We had been so focussed on Pedro, godmen, Sunny and all the rest of them that we had completely missed the bigger picture. Peggy filled us in on a lot of murky details and summed it up, saying, 'Is our future bright? I think so. Is our future here? I don't think so. As far as AdAb goes, things ain't looking good.'

Kitch and I looked at each other. He shook his head and smiled wryly. What an institution! Or was this what most large corporations were like? Where ego ruled the roost, loyalties meant more than competence and manipulation superseded strategy. Where long-term benefits were sacrificed at the altar of short-term fixes and clients were mere pawns in the scheme of things.

'When you go to Udaipur, Jai beta,' my mum said, 'make sure you visit Nathdwara and Virpur. You need the Lord's blessings always, not just when you are in trouble.' Little did she know trouble was already brewing.

Twenty-four hours later, we were warmly

welcomed by the uniformed and turbaned hotel staff and escorted to a boat that would take us to the hotel in the middle of a lake. The hotel itself was a splendid structure in the style of palaces of yore. The pristine lake, the sprawling green lawns, the atmosphere... it is difficult to describe in a few words, but it was, in short, quite magnificent. I made it a mental note to bring Mina here some day.

We stopped at the reception and then I headed to my room; a delightful one – big, done up in pretty colours, beautiful in all respects, except one. Ahmed. Damn! I had forgotten about this business of sharing rooms.

'Oye tiger! Kya haal hai? I was waiting for you,' he said.

I eyed him warily.

'I don't know how much you know about this, Jai, but finally things are taking shape in this bank. My contribution and experience are being recognized. You must have heard of my 200 million dollar account. Bank ko hila diya hai. I have shaken up the place. Now they want to make me head of the entire business. Your Peggy will have to find some other job soon, bhaisaab. She has personally brought in ten accounts for just 150 million. And I have a single account for more than that. See the difference in class, yaar. I have been told to build the team. I hope you will act sensibly and stay on my side. You're a good guy.'

I looked at him.

He smirked. 'And that finance fellow, Nathan, kambakht! We have taught him a lesson. He used to take a cut from hotels to put them on our approved list. We have caught him red-handed, Jan, Peter and I. Benaqaab kar diya usko, hamne. Bloody thief! Now that bastard will realize that he should not have played around with me.' He struck a flamboyant pose, swaggered and blew a kiss, slowly and deliberately, with his index finger. 'Nallavanukku nallavan,' he said.

I started. That sounded like Tamil.

'Kettavanukku kettavan,' he continued with a toss of his head and a nonchalant wave of his hand. Then he contorted his mouth, rolled his eyes upward, waggled his finger at me and snarled, 'Dushta nai ku yaman!'

For a moment I forgot all about AdAb. 'W-wha...?' I gasped. 'Who taught you that!'

He grinned. 'Your friend Kitch,' he said. 'We saw a Tamil movie together once. The hero keeps repeating these lines and shoots a villain each time he says it. I learnt it from there!'

'Any idea what "dushta" means?' I asked, a little hesitantly. It felt weird asking a Pakistani the meaning of a Tamil word. But I was curious. That scene outside Kitch's house with Kulandaivelu was still fresh in my mind.

'Evil,' he responded promptly. '"Dushta nai"

means "evil dog". The whole thing means, I am good with good guys and bad with bad guys. And with evil dogs, I'm the God of Death. Tit for tat. Nathan was an evil dog. I screwed him.'

Evil dog! That driver Kulandaivelu had called me an evil dog! I remained silent, pondering over it and the scenes that followed.

'Listen, hero,' said Ahmed. 'I'm telling you now. You come over to my side. Your Peggy has no role in this bank. Khel badal gaya hai, janaab. Peter and Jan are very strong with the new chairman. It's a different ball game. Peggy will be finished, take it from me. You and Kitch work under me and I will give you a grade jump. Kya khayal hai?'

'Thanks, but no, Ahmed. I'm comfortable with Peggy. She's been a good boss. I think I'll stay where I am.'

'Ey, hero, don't talk like a fool. I'm telling you that woman is history. There is going to be a major change. Most of the Brits and Americans will be thrown out. I'm giving you a chance. If you don't take it, there is no future for you. If you mess with me, you will be finished, I'm telling you.'

I shook my head.

'That American bitch will let you down,' he shouted. 'Americans are like that. I know them! They are nobody's friend. First they will screw you, then they will help you and make you pay for their help.'

'No, Ahmed, we're a team. I'm not going anywhere.'

He glared at me. 'You're a *coward*!' he said, with all the emphasis at his disposal. 'That's why you are not standing up for yourself like a man. We are from the same subcontinent. Instead of sticking together, you're just running behind that bitch! Why are you doing this? You want long legs, I can arrange. Any nationality, just tell me.'

'Maybe I *am* a dushta nai,' I told him. 'That's why I'm running behind a bitch.'

'Fuck you, yaar,' he said, more resigned than angry. 'I had promised Peter I would get your support. But if you won't come…' He shrugged his shoulders. Suddenly he got up. 'I'm going to try and find some night spots in this place,' he said. 'Do you know where to go?'

I shook my head again.

'Yaar, what kind of a man are you? ' he asked me. 'You don't know the hot spots in your own country. Useless!'

I decided to spend my evening visiting the Srinathji temple at Nathdwara. When I got back at night, there was no sign of Ahmed. I must have dozed off the moment my head touched the pillow. It had been several days since I had slept my full quota of seven-to-eight hours.

I woke up late the next day to the sound of vigorous splashing and the tune (or rather, the

lack of it) of a recent Bollywood hit. Turning on my side, I saw Ahmed in the nude, in the shower. In my dazed state, I stared and blinked for a few seconds, trying to make sense of this weird dream. Then I realized, to my horror, that the bathroom had only a glass partition from the room. Quickly, I turned to the other side and pretended to be asleep, still reeling from this early morning shock. Perhaps this was some kind of honeymoon suite, I told myself. When it was my turn to shower, half an hour later, I hesitated outside the bathroom.

'Arre yaar, don't worry. I may be a pathan but I am only interested in women. So carry on guru, ho ja shuru.'

19

Sir Santa Claus

The hotel lunch looked delicious but we didn't do justice to it. It was a crazy day. Peter and Jan spent a good portion of the morning's proceedings in the meeting room spewing venom on Peggy (whenever she was not in the room) and ignoring her (when she was). They spoke about their plan. It was long on lofty goals, though short on details. As Kitch put it, their strategy seemed exactly the same as their objective, rather than a plan on getting there. They also issued a lightly veiled threat to anyone who did not 'cooperate' with them, along the lines of George Bush's 'you're either with us or against us' ultimatum. Ahmed made a presentation too, which was quite funny, unintentionally though. He spoke well, but the slides he had made were school-boyish (including the rather outdated SWOT analysis) and even had a few spelling mistakes. It ended with a slide (italics mine, spelling his) that read 'Whatever *hapen's*, we shall *RAISE* and SHINE!'

Less than a year ago, Kitch and I had joined what we thought was a staid British bank on the verge of further glory by merging with a European biggie – a far cry from the excesses of American greed and capitalism. And look what we had plunged into. One football tournament, a few changes at the top, one manipulative coterie and there we were – a regional office on the verge of turning topsy-turvy against the backdrop of a crumbling Europe.

There was no doubt about it. Peggy was clearly being pushed aside and Ahmed was being anointed the new high priest of private banking. Jan was being made the deputy regional manager while Peter's wider role would make him the monarch of the middle east. All senior employees who had been part of the Abbott empire were being toppled and replaced by loyalists to the Dutch. It was clearly the dawn of a brash new world. An aggressive, if amateurish army ready to *raise* and shine, whatever *hapen's*.

That evening, Peggy called all her team members to her room. We made ourselves comfortable while she finished a rather long phone call. We overheard snippets of the conversation where our names figured, but couldn't make out very much.

'I'm really sorry to have kept you guys waiting. Man! This is one heck of a mess we've got out here! I take full responsibility for it and I really do apologize. I can only hope to make up for this by plunging you into an even bigger mess!'

We looked at each other quizzically.

'Rachel honey, Jack, Kitch, Gavas, Omar, Harry, listen up. I have a proposition to make and I need you to make a decision by tomorrow. I have no idea what the right decision for you is, that's something you have to figure out. I'm leaving, guys. And that's putting it respectably. You've seen how it is. I'm not wanted here. I've seen it coming for a couple of months actually, ever since I was in London attending those mancom presentations. So I've made alternate plans. Whether those plans fly or not depends on what you decide. I've had a chance to discuss this individually with some of you, but I haven't had full information about the deal before this. So listen! You guys have a well-wisher. In fact, an admirer, who wants to put up 10 to 15 million pounds to help start up a private equity fund that will focus on small businesses, especially enterprises that work with art and culture, environment-friendly businesses and professionally run charitable organizations. And he wants us to run it.'

'Us?' Rach squeaked. 'Peggy! What the hell do we know about running a venture of this kind?'

Peggy smiled. 'What we don't know, Rach, we'll learn. Did Kitch know anything about running restaurants until two years ago? Did Jack know farming?'

'But Jack still doesn't know much farming!' Rachel protested.

I grinned sheepishly. 'But who is this admirer of ours, who is willing to risk 15 million pounds? It's a massive responsibility. Almost scary!'

'You'll never guess, sweetie! It's Sir Sidney.'

A howl of surprise nearly brought the roof down.

'What!'

'Good lord!'

'B-but h-how on earth? Where did he spring from?'

'Peggy, this is crazy! But fantastic. Is it going to be like running our own business? How sweet of him!'

'Shhh! Guys, shut up a bit, will you? I've been in touch with Sir Sidney right from the time we met in Dubai. We met almost every day when I was in London and have been in regular contact since. As you know, he is an India lover and was bowled over by Kitty and the rest of you that day in Dubai. He's been thinking of planning his retirement along these lines. He thought it would come next year, but the World Cup results effectively advanced it by several months. He is encashing his share options and that is fetching him some 25 million pounds at current levels. The recent run-up in share prices has been good for him. Whatever our perception of this bank has been, the market sees it as a fast-growing and profitable bank.

'Sir Sidney's grand-daughter is joining Kitty's dance school in Chennai next month. I spoke to Kitty about it in Chennai. He wants her dance school to branch out. He wants more restaurants from Kitch and Galiya serving healthy organic food. He wants Jack's father to get into agriculture big time – hopefully with help from Mina and Jack. Kitch's dad is on the verge of setting up a new plant for herbal medicines. Sir Sidney wants to be in on that. Tim's alternative energy idea might also find backing. Sir Sidney is fascinated by Bollywood as well. He is crazy about… what's her name, Jack? Shelp… Shapely Shedy?'

'It's Shilpa Shetty, but Shapely wouldn't have been a bad name for her, either.'

'It seems Sir Sidney met Amitabh Bayshan in London at some function attended by the Prime Minister and the Queen. He asked him if he had starred opposite Shilpah and apparently he hadn't. So Sir Sidney wants to make a Bollywood love triangle featuring Bayshan, Shilpah and Sharook Khan. He wants lots of songs and lots of villains.'

Kitch shut his eyes tight and moaned. 'Peggy,' he begged. 'The first thing the old man needs to be told is that his job is to finance the venture. If he's going to start thrusting his ideas on us, we'll

get nowhere. The guy seems to be senile. If he made a love triangle with these three and lots of songs, even *I* wouldn't watch it.'

'Oh, don't worry, Kitch. We'll run it as professionally as we can. He's just terribly enthusiastic about the whole thing, that's all.'

'Maybe I could be the villain in the film,' Omar said. 'The hero can get Shilpa in the last scene, but I wouldn't mind following and tormenting her until then.'

'Oh, that reminds me! Sir Sidney wants Shane Warne to be the lead villain.'

'Ah! Now we're talking!' Kitch enthused.

'I can be his henchman,' Harry said. 'Even a small role in a Bollywood film might help impress Ya-sho-dha-ra.' During his recent visit to Agra, Harry had fallen in love with a travel agent called Yashodhara Chattopadhyay. He liked everything about the girl, except her name. But she insisted on his calling her by her full name, so he had been practising gamely. Mina tried to help him out by suggesting a pnemonic 'Yeah, show the RA (Royal Air Force)', but on the very same day he goofed up twice, once writing her name in a text message as 'Yashothern', confusing the Royal Air Force with the Royal Navy, and then calling her 'Ya-sho-me-dha-ra'.

'I will be the comedian,' Gavas piped up. 'In fact, I can appear as myself, with my own name.

That itself will make people laugh. Please go on, Peggy.'

'Well, thank god I'm being allowed to continue. Now, where was I? Oh, yeah. So, that was the chairman. But there's more where the dough is coming from. Three of my clients want to put up about 20 million dollars. One of Jack's clients, Sunny Singh, wants to invest five. I think a couple of Rachel's clients will be keen too and maybe one of Omar's. Of course, I have spoken to very few people about this, just a casual mention to some guys I happened to meet in Dubai last week. But I think we have close to 50 million dollars in the kitty already. I've already started working on the licence and I think we will have it in about two weeks. I'm looking at a team in Dubai to handle the central coordination work and teams in India to manage the businesses. I would like all of us to be in it. We might be able to rope in Kapoor as well, Jack, don't you think?

'This is going to be tremendously exciting. But it's not a surefire winner. It'll be as successful as we can make it. I'm willing to give it all I've got. Sir Sidney wants to start everyone off with a 10,000 pound bonus as a token of goodwill. He wants to pay this from his personal wealth, not from the business pool. I think we can afford to fix our salaries at our current levels, but after a year, we might have to take a pay cut and draw a percentage of earnings instead. I'll let you all decide how you want to play that one. I was on the phone with Sir Sid just now and he has just sent in the first installment of three million pounds which will cover the guarantee amount required by the licensing authority for our business, plus my estimated expenses for the first year. So, guys, what do you think? Are we good to go?'

For a moment, we stood transfixed, trying to absorb everything that had been said. Then, like a bunch of alcohol-fuelled monkeys, we jumped, howled, chattered and finally put our arms around each others' shoulders and did a jumping huddle.

We had a celebratory party that night. As I was walking to Peggy's room armed with some weapons of mass celebration, I bumped into Jan and Peter. They must have got wind of what was happening and Peter was livid. His face was as red as a baboon's bum.

'If you guys dare leave,' he hissed, 'I swear I will not take it lying down. I will screw all of you.'

'Enjoy!' I replied and went on my way.

20

The End? Or the Beginning?

Having taken the decision to quit, we made our individual plans for the next one month. Gavas advanced his annual vacation by several weeks and took off for the US and Canada. Omar was away in Australia and New Zealand, exploring barrier reefs and doing bungee jumps. Kitch and Galiya left on a gastronomic tour of eight Indian states to sample their most authentic delicacies, as part of the preliminary work for the launch of K2K.

Suddenly, what had been a pipe dream a week ago, almost a joke, now seemed imminent. The idea of being funded with millions to open new restaurants and expand his existing ones had set Kitch on fire. The man spoke about nothing but food.

Andy and Ravi threw up several ideas that Peggy was assiduously poring into. The one she liked the most was setting up the 'RSPCAA' – Rescue Students from Political Constraints on Academic

Aspirations – a fund that would support students whom the government's 'reservation' policy had kept from securing seats in top educational institutions despite high marks. Harry was back in Dubai, working away at the formalities for setting up the company. Mina was busy trying to acquire land near ours and enjoying the financial muscle power that was coming her way. I spent two days with her and then returned to Chennai to discuss a few ideas with my father as well as Kitch's.

I was at Kitch's house the following evening, waiting for his dad to return home, when my phone rang. Harry was on the line. The licence had come through and potential office locations had been shortlisted. He wanted me to come over and help him choose one.

'I say, Jack, there's so much to do, and it's awfully exciting. And do you know what, Yashodhara is coming to Dubai tomorrow, how about that! I wish she would let me call her Yash like all her friends do. But she insists I call her by her full name, and I just can't! And she giggles every time I try. These Indian names are so confusing. What's that disgusting chomping noise on the line? Are you eating something?'

'Yes,' I said, 'Mary has just given me bhajiyas and tea.'

'Well, give my regards to her. She gave me

an initiation into India that I shall never forget. Besides, I rather think it was when I was narrating her story to Yasho-dhara that she started liking me. So Mary figures highly in my list of friends I owe a debt to. And hers is the only Indian name I can remember without straining my brain.'

When I conveyed this to the girl, she said, 'My name Dhanashree, sir. Mary, no.'

I blinked. This girl was really complicating my life. 'Your name is not Mary?'

'No, sir. Dhanashree, name. Dhanam calling for short.'

'But…'

'First Dhanashree only name, sir. My father-mother keeping Dhanashree name. Then become Salma. Last year become Mary. Now again Dhanashree. You tell your friend, if he giving money then again I am keeping name Mary. Money getting, name changing, no problem.'

Back in Dubai, I met Kapoor. We had discussed the new development with him and he loved the idea of working with us. It had already been decided that he, along with Harry, would be permanently based in Dubai with Peggy. Kapoor had just returned from a holiday in Egypt, which his wife had pushed him into.

'Did you enjoy it?' I asked them.

'Beautiful!' his wife rhapsodized.

'It was okay,' Kapoor answered, non-committal, with a guarded look in the direction of his wife. As soon as she left the room, he took off like an angry aerated drink can that has been opened after a good shake. 'That whole place is like one big museum! Kya fayda? What is the bloody use? I am interested in *today*, not in history. I don't care if someone scratched a stone four thousand years ago! We kept climbing up steps and looking at dead bodies. How many dead bodies can you look at? And so many tourists! Just like Africa. This world has no time for family and friends. But people travel miles to look at animals and dead bodies. Jai, tell me, would you go miles just to look at a potato? No! Because you have already *seen* a potato. It should be the same with animals! They have no names, they can't talk, they all look the same. Once you know what a lion looks like, why should you go across continents to see more? Anyway, most of these animals are just hiding in the bushes. They are not interested in us. Why are *we* so interested in *them*? Have we no self-respect? Holidays should be for spending time with parents, grandparents, children, grandchildren, uncles, aunts and cousins. Not for rushing around to take pictures of a buffalo's backside. Or go to Egypt and stare at dead bodies. I don't know what this world is coming to. Paagal hai, sab ke sab.' He lowered his voice. 'And now she wants me to send an email to everyone telling them all about the holiday. I may have been foolish enough to have gone there to see dead bodies but I am not so completely mad that I will waste time writing about them.'

A day or two later, I was in office, cleaning out my desk, when someone called me. 'Sir, there is someone to meet Gavaskar or Peggy ma'am. Neither of them is here.'

'I'll meet them,' I said, pulling my head out of the clutter.

A small-built man in a tight black suit was waiting in the meeting room. He had a blank sort of face; small, round and vacant, with ears that stuck out. He stretched out his hand.

'Myself, Madhusudan S. Pikle,' he said.

I shook his hand, trying to remember where I had come across that name.

'I have come for the party,' he said.

'Party?'

'Yes, the big party that I have been invited to,' he said with a hint of pride.

I scratched my head. Pikle… I knew that name. 'I'm sorry, I'm afraid I'm not quite clear. You are…'

He stepped back and drew himself to his full height, such as it was. His face took on a serious, dignified expression and a familiar, deep baritone came out from somewhere deep inside his throat.

'Rishte mein tumhare baap lagte hain, naam hai shahenshah!'

I collapsed onto the sofa. This was *that* chap, the mimicry fellow, Gavas's cousin! Gavas must have told him about it and, in the light of everything that happened since, no one gave the programme a second thought. And everyone had forgotten about the invitation sent to this guy.

I stared at him helplessly. 'Oh, god!' I said.

He simpered, his face lighting up. 'Yes, my god act is the most popular one in Mumbai. And each time, I change the act slightly, so nobody gets bored of it. But I do a lot of celebrity mimicry as well. I can do Shahrukh, Aamir, Akshay, Saif, Dharmendra, Kamal Haasan, Amitabh, Rajinikant, Govinda, Nana Patekar...'

'Mr Pikle, I'm terribly sorry. You see, there have been a lot of changes within the bank in the last few days and the upshot of the whole thing is that the programme got cancelled. I really do apologize. Gavas is in the US now. He must have forgotten to inform you. It completely slipped my mind as well.'

He looked at me dispassionately. 'So, no party?'

'I'm afraid not. I'm so sorry. We will try and make up for this somehow.'

'I can do Hollywood stars also,' he said, unperturbed. 'Watch!'

He closed his eyes and sniffed a couple of times. When he opened his eyes, almost as if by magic, his eyes had a hard, steely glint in them, his nose seemed to have sharpened and his lips had shifted slightly to one side. When he spoke, it was from the corner of his mouth, as if there was a rosogolla in it. There was no mistaking the character. 'Let me tell you somethin' you already know,' he drawled. 'The world ain't all sunshine and rainbows.'

I stared, fascinated. It was weird, even eerie, to hear Rocky Balboa's voice and dialogues come out from the mouth of a small Indian body.

'... it ain't about how hard you hit; but about how hard you can get hit and keep moving forward. That's how winning is done.' Then his mouth shifted and formed a straight line. The rosogolla seemed to melt. His nose bulged out, his eyes became docile and lifeless, and his face reverted to its former bland appearance.

'Sylvester Stallone,' he said unnecessarily.

I stood up and clapped.

Except for Omar, who was probably still walking around in a t-shirt with 'Thunder Down Under' printed on it, the rest of us were in Dubai. The big question was what to name our new company. We had to hand in the name to the licencing authorities the next day.

Peggy made a game out of it. She gave us half an hour to come up with a suggestion each. 'The one whose suggestion is accepted gets this iPad,' she said, flashing one around. 'Remember, this is a business with a difference. It is essentially like a private equity firm, but smaller. We will focus on small, simple businesses. We will create value, but profit will not just be measured in terms of money. Some of what we do will also have a social angle to it. Our businesses will be environment-friendly, we will promote art and culture wherever possible, and raise awareness of our core values. Now go put your grey cells to work. I've used up all of mine talking to Sir Sidney the last few days.'

Almost an hour later, Peggy was seated on a mat on the floor like a queen holding court with her subjects. The new furniture was yet to come.

'Okay, let's start. Andy,' she announced.

'It's not a nice one, I'm not very good at these things,' he started defensively.

Rachel giggled.

'Go, Andy, go!' Harry yelled encouragingly.

'It's Sex, short for Securities Express!'

Peggy stared at him blankly while the rest of us laughed and rolled on the floor, adding to his discomfiture.

'It's about investments, y'know, so I put in the word "securities", and I just sort of added "express". Then I thought of a short, attractive word that everyone likes... I told you I wasn't good at this!' he ended tamely.

'I couldn't agree with you more, honey!' Peggy replied, trying to keep a straight face. 'Rach?'

Rachel cleared her throat. 'My suggestion is Lace!' she said.

'*Lace!* What's up with the young couple? Marriage seems to have done something to you. This is a boutique investment firm, sweethearts, not a sleaze shop!'

'No, but Peggy, listen! It's an acronym. L-A-C-E. It stands for Laboratory for Art, Culture and Enterprise.'

'Hmm... well, okay! That gives it a whole new twist, doesn't it?'

'So I get the iPad?'

'Not so fast, darling. Anyone else? Kitch? *Kitch!*'

Kitch was busy with the iPad, watching pictures of Pamela Anderson during her India visit. 'Oh, sorry!' he said, a little shamefacedly. 'I was surfing the net for inspiration and got a bit distracted.'

'I am not surprised,' said Galiya coldly. 'What else did you expect, looking at pictures of Pamela Anderson in a clingy saree and a tiny strappy blouse?'

'The blouse is not tiny,' replied Kitch the perfectionist, peering at the picture. 'It's normal sized. It only *seems* small! Everything is relative.

And look! This iPad rocks. I can make Pamela Anderson bigger by just moving my fingers like this. See?'

Peggy threw a cushion at him and Galiya took the iPad away from him.

'Mina, Jack?'

'We've got two between us,' I announced. 'The first is P4. It stands for Platform for Private Placement, Profitably. The second is Baobab Investments. Baobab is an African tree that appears to be growing upside down because its branches resemble roots. It's got multiple uses and it is known as the tree of life. It finds a place in myth and legend and is even worshipped. So it's kind of symbolic. We have a few taglines to go with the name. "Uniquely different" is one. Another is "Baobab Investments. *Where's the herd*?", to signify that we stand alone.'

I looked around expectantly, but no one burst into applause.

'Okay! Nice ones, Jack and Mina. I think I prefer P4. The Baobab may need too many explanations, though it does seem an interesting idea. Next?'

Harry had two suggestions. One was PPod: Producing Profits and Opportunities with Discretion. The other was B squared or B^2 – Bespoke Businesses.

'I like PPod,' Peggy said. 'But Bespoke… well, it's too British, isn't it? Sir Sid would understand, but I doubt anyone else would. This is another Baobab, though slightly worse.'

Galiya came up with Power – Profits, Opportunities, Wealth, Ethics and Responsiblities.

Gavas suggested Footprintz. 'I put a z at the end instead of s,' he said proudly, 'to give it a cool touch. I also have a tag line. "Footprintz – Profits, responsibly".'

'Rather neat that, Gavas. Though I think I prefer the uncool spelling, the one with the s at the end. The name does have a rather nice connotation, doesn't it, I mean, one of being a bit of a pioneer. Listen guys, all this is pretty good stuff. It's actually more than I had hoped for. There's no Indian touch in any of these but that's okay. However, I don't think I can decide right now, so I think I'll just sleep over it… sorry, *sorry*!' she said as a howl of protest erupted. 'We'll decide tomorrow for sure. And if my brain is still numb, we'll just put it to vote.'

'Okay,' said Kitch. 'So, umm, what about lunch?'

'I have an idea. Does everyone know Andy has just landed a major Tamil film role? Let's get some food delivered. Meanwhile, we can ask Andy to give us a preview of his best scenes.'

'Hey, wait. Before that, I have a second suggestion for the name,' said Andy, never one to be subdued. 'Rachel tells me this is called venture capital and you said you wanted an Indian touch. So how about India Adventure? You know, like India Ad-venture?' There was no response. Andy grinned. 'Okay, here goes! I hope you like my acting more than my suggestions for the name.'

'I can't wait to see this movie,' Peggy gushed after watching Andy enact a scene. 'It'll probably be my first Indian film. I'm sure it will come out before anything Sir Sidney makes! Is it a love story?'

'Yes, it's based on a tsunami where I fall in love with one of the fishergirls.'

'Oh, wow! How exciting! What's it called, Andy?'

'It's a Tamil film and was initially titled *A Fishy Tale*, but I am told the state government penalizes producers financially if they use non-Tamil titles, so it has been changed to *Ei, Meenkaari! Unnai Katti Pidikka*, which loosely translates as "Oh, fishergirl! If I could hug you".'

I visited Sunny Singh the following afternoon. Sunny Singh was delighted with this move of ours. He tossed me a can of beer and opened one for himself.

'Thank god you are leaving that bank. I don't know how you managed for a year, even *I* was feeling suffocated.'

His father joined us soon and Sunny told him

how this group of youngsters had started a private equity firm. 'I am putting five million dollars in it. They will do well, these boys. They just need encouragement and some freedom to think and work. That bank was like a jail. Bunch of losers.'

'Oh, jolly good, jolly good,' roared the father through his bountiful grey beard. 'It is good to be your own master. When you control your destiny, if you are hard-working, you will be a winner, not a loser. And the winner should have champion!'

I raised my eyebrows enquiringly.

'Champion!' he repeated. He left the room and returned moments later with a bottle with 'Champagne Pol Roger' written on it. He was smiling triumphantly.

'Enough of this silly beer,' he thundered. '*Champion* for the winner!'

Later, Sunny's driver took me home. I left my car at Sunny's place because his dad had made me drink so much 'champion' that I was fizzing and frothing and popping just like that ghost in Kitch's room.

On my way home, the phone began vibrating in my pocket. It was Lalwani. 'Seventeenth December,' he said. 'Mark your calendar. You have to be there. We are inaugurating factory. Set up in record time, just like that. Early January, my first zalzalah will hit the market. But this one, I have made easier to blow. The one you brought, too difficult. My son is blowing it, but I'm not able to do it. Almost my lungs were bursting off.'

The next day, Mina called me at work and asked me if I could join her for lunch at her favourite restaurant. Galiya was taking her somewhere and she wanted to meet me after that. She sounded a little breathless on the phone.

'Can you come right away, please? It's a little important. Can you come now, Jai?'

So I went. Galiya was there too. When they saw me they whispered something to each other and started giggling like schoolgirls. They looked flushed and happy.

'You two look like teenagers about to go on your first date. What's up?' I asked them.

They continued acting silly.

'Tell him,' said Galiya.

'*You* tell him!' Mina said.

I was getting quite irritated. I opened my mouth to issue a firm rebuke. I didn't leave my work halfway and rush here for all this.

'We're both pregnant!'

I started violently. 'W-what, really?! P-p…!' I opened my mouth, then closed it and swallowed a couple of times. 'B-both of you?'

They nodded, then held each other's hands and giggled some more.

I hugged both of them. I didn't know what

to say. I was excited and happy, yes. But I was also apprehensive, a little incredulous and even a shade embarrassed. Then, like an idiot, I giggled too.

That night, we celebrated at Kitch's place. For some reason, we kept meeting at Kitch's apartment; partly, I guess, because of Olga. But somehow it always seemed more fun here than anywhere else. The living room was nice and cozy and we all had our favourite spots to sit in. Kitch had kept his word and managed to get the 'LOVE' photograph back into the bedroom.

With her plate piled with rice and vegetables, Peggy looked around for Galiya. 'Any VK?' she asked.

'Oh, by the way, I know what VK stands for. I think I have mastered the word,' said Harry. 'After Yashodhara, everything seems simple.'

“Let's hear it, Harry,' I said, feeling rather tense. If a Brit could pronounce Tamil words, what skills would I, a mere Gujarati, be left with?

'*Wotto columbay*!' he said.

I heaved a sigh of relief, even as Kitch covered his face with his palms and groaned.

'Thank god we may never have to hear you say that word again,' he told Harry. 'Galiya is off VK completely. I think she had an overdose of it. She has switched to onion thokku.'

'Oh, darn it!' Harry exclaimed. 'Just as I had mastered the previous one.'

I finished writing my diary for the day and kept it aside. Mina was asleep beside me. I looked at her. A strand of hair was falling over her face stubbornly, making her nose twitch. I watched it twitch a couple of times, then smiled, pushed the hair back and switched off the light. Lying in bed, I took stock of things. They looked good to me.

Family, check.

Friends, check.

Health, check – though that six pack remained a pipe dream.

Wealth – hmm… would be nice to have some more, but check.

Colleagues, check.

Baby, bless the little thing, check.

There was a little issue about Jan threatening to get immigration to put a temporary entry ban on our passports, but I rather thought we had the UAE law on our side. We were professionals and we would be completing the mandatory one year of employment in a week's time. In any case, I was sure we could face a small thing like that. As Rocky Balboa and Madhusudan Pikle would say, 'It ain't about how hard you hit but about how hard you can get hit and keep moving forward. That's how winning is done.'

I turned over and looked at Mina. She was sleeping peacefully. The straying hair was now firmly in its place. Gently, I touched her stomach. My baby was in there.

Acknowledgements

Mukul Deva for putting me on to HarperCollins.

Neelini Sarkar, my incredibly talented editor.

Roshan Bhaskar, my youngest reader and so far my biggest fan. May his tribe increase. This is possibly the only book he has read that is about human beings. The rest seem to be about wizards, dragons, Greek, Roman and Egyptian gods.

My sister Shobhana, the only one who takes my writing as seriously as I do.

My wife Anandhi for putting up with my frequent silences and, in her own crisp words, 'letting me write'.

Every noble soul who bought my first book and liked it; it encouraged me to write this one. So they have no choice but to read it.

My heartfelt thanks to these members of the august but rapidly dwindling group of bibliophiles: Nagendra, Raman, Francesca, Sarabjit, Ashwin, Monisha, Mansi, Mathangi, Satya and H.E. Sanjay Verma, Consul General, CGI Dubai.

Everyone who took the trouble to criticize my first book, thank you for taking time and voicing your opinion. After giving your comments a great deal of thought, I have decided to continue writing in the same vein.